(H)

© 2010

3/18/20 X

"very good"

CODE BLUE

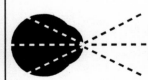

This Large Print Book carries the
Seal of Approval of N.A.V.H.

PRESCRIPTION FOR TROUBLE SERIES

CODE BLUE

MEDICAL SUSPENSE WITH HEART

RICHARD L. MABRY, M.D.

THORNDIKE PRESS
A part of Gale, Cengage Learning

GALE
CENGAGE Learning

Detroit • New York • San Francisco • New Haven, Conn • Waterville, Maine • London

GALE
CENGAGE Learning™

LIBRARY OF CONGRESS CATALOGING-IN-PUBLICATION DATA

Mabry, Richard L.
   Code blue : medical suspense with heart / by Richard L. Mabry. — Large print ed.
    p. cm. — (Thorndike Press large print Christian mystery) (Prescription for trouble series)
   ISBN-13: 978-1-4104-3110-3
   ISBN-10: 1-4104-3110-X
   1. Women physicians—Fiction. 2. Large type books. I. Title.
PS3613.A2C63 2010b
813'.6—dc22   2010033216

Published in 2010 by arrangement with Abingdon Press.

Printed in Mexico
1 2 3 4 5 6 7 14 13 12 11 10

ACKNOWLEDGMENTS

Once upon a time, I thought writing a book was a simple process done by one person. I've since learned differently. This book has been made possible by the contributions of dozens of people, all of whom deserve my thanks.

First I want to express my appreciation to my wonderful agent, Rachelle Gardner, as well as my great editor, Barbara Scott. This couldn't have happened without you. You not only believed in me but you did a wonderful job of smoothing the rough places in my work. To the good people at Abingdon Press, thanks for letting me be on your team.

I've been the recipient of invaluable education, mentoring, and encouragement from some fantastic writers, and I want them to know how much I appreciate it. My thanks go to James Scott Bell, Alton Gansky, Gayle Roper, Karen Ball, Randy

Ingermanson, DiAnn Mills, and many others who gave so unselfishly to help me along my road to writing.

To my children — Allen, Brian, Ann — who never lost faith that their dad could do anything he put his mind to, thanks for believing in me. I love you, and I'm proud of you.

The untimely death of my first wife, Cynthia, was the impetus for my starting to write. During our forty years of marriage, she was a wonderful companion who influenced every aspect of my life. I hope that influence shines through in my writing.

I'm immeasurably indebted to my wife, Kay, whose love has made life worth living once more. In my writing endeavors, she is my biggest fan. She functions as my first reader, helping and encouraging me to do my best work. I'm eternally grateful.

No sooner had I retired from medicine than God opened another door and pointed me in the direction of writing. I have no idea what comes next, but I can hardly wait to find out. To Him be the glory.

— Richard L. Mabry, M.D.

1

The black SUV barreled out of nowhere, its oversized tires straddling the centerline. Cathy jerked the steering wheel to the right and jammed the brake pedal to the floor. Her little Toyota rocked as though flicked by a giant hand before it spun off the narrow country road and hurtled toward the ditch and the peach orchard beyond it.

For a moment Cathy felt the fearful thrill of weightlessness. Then the world turned upside down, and everything went into freeze-frame slow motion.

The floating sensation ended with a jolt. The screech of ripping metal swallowed Cathy's scream. The deploying airbag struck her face like a fist. The pressure of the shoulder harness took her breath away. The lap belt pressed into her abdomen, and she tasted bile and acid. As her head cleared, she found herself hanging head-down, swaying slightly as the car rocked to a standstill.

In the silence that followed, her pulse hammered in her ears like distant, rhythmic thunder.

Cathy realized she was holding her breath. She let out a shuddering sigh, inhaled, and immediately choked on the dust that hung thick in the air. She released her death grip on the steering wheel and tried to lift her arms. It hurt — it hurt a lot — but they seemed to work. She tilted her head and felt something warm trickle down her face. She tried to wipe it away, but not before a red haze clouded her vision.

She felt a burning sensation, first in her nostrils, then in the back of her throat. Gasoline! Cathy recalled all the crash victims she'd seen in the emergency room — victims who'd survived a car accident only to be engulfed in flames afterward. She had to get out of the car. Now. Her fingers probed for the seatbelt buckle. She found it and pressed the release button. *Slowly. Be careful. Don't fall out of the seat and make matters worse.* The belt gave way, and she eased her weight onto her shoulders. She bit her lip from the pain, rolled onto her side, and looked around.

How could she escape? She tried the front doors. Jammed — both of them. She'd been driving with her window partially open, enjoying the brisk autumn air and the parade of orange and yellow trees rolling by in the Texas landscape. There was no way she could wriggle through that small opening. Cathy drew back both feet and kicked hard at the exposed glass. Nothing. She kicked harder. On the third try, the window gave way.

Where was her purse? Never mind. No time. She had to get out. Cathy inched her way through the window, flinching as tiny shards of glass stung her palms and knees. Once free from the car, she lay back on the grass and looked around at what remained of the orchard, blessing the trees that had sacrificed themselves to cushion her car's landing.

She rose unsteadily to her feet. It seemed as though every bone in her body cried out at the effort. The moment she stood upright the world faded into a gray haze. She slumped to the ground and took a few deep breaths. Her head hurt, her eyes burned, her throat seemed to be closing up. The smell of gasoline cut through her lethargy. She had to get farther away from the car. How could she do that, when she couldn't even stand without passing out?

Cathy saw a peach sapling a few feet away, a tiny survivor amid the ruins. She crawled to the tree, grabbed it, and walked her hands up the trunk until she was almost upright. She clung there, drained by the exertion, until the world stopped spinning.

Something dripped into her eyes and the world turned red. Cathy risked turning loose with one hand and wiped it across her face. Her vision cleared a bit. She regarded the crimson stain on her palm. Good thing she was no stranger to the sight of blood.

Now she was upright, but could she walk? Maybe, if she could stand the pain. She wasn't sure she could make it more than a step or two, though. A stout limb lying in the debris at her feet caught her eye. It was about four feet long, two inches thick — just the right size. Cathy eased her way down to a crouch, using the sapling for support. She grabbed the limb and, holding it like a staff, managed to stand up. She rested for a moment, then inched her way along the bottom of the ditch, away from the car. When she could no longer smell gasoline and when her aching limbs would carry her no farther, she leaned on her improvised crutch to rest.

Cathy stared at the road above her. The embankment sloped upward in a gentle rise of about six feet. Ordinarily, climbing it would be child's play for her. But right now she felt like a baby — weak, uncoordinated, and fearful.

Maybe if she rested for a moment on that big rock. She hobbled to it and lowered herself, wincing with each movement. There was no way she could get comfortable — even breathing was painful — but she needed time to think.

Had the SUV really tried to run her off the road? She wanted to believe it was simply an accident, that someone had lost control of the vehicle. Just like she'd wanted to believe that the problems she'd had since she came back home were nothing more than a run of bad luck. Now she had to accept the possibility that someone was making an effort to drive her out of town.

She'd never thought much about the name of her hometown: Dainger, Texas. She vaguely recalled it was named for some settler, long ago forgotten. Now she was thinking the name seemed significant. Danger. Had the problems she'd left behind in Dallas followed her? Or did the roots lie here in Dainger? Possibly. After all, small towns have long memories. Of course, there could be another explanation. . . . No, she couldn't accept that. Not yet.

Cathy turned to survey the wreckage of her poor little car. She saw wheels silhouetted against the sky, heard the ticking of the cooling motor. Then she picked up new sounds: the roar of a car's engine, followed by the screech of tires and the chatter of gravel. It could be someone stopping to help. On the other hand, it could be the driver of the SUV coming back to finish the job. She thought of hiding. But where? How?

She watched a white pickup skid to a stop on the shoulder of the road above the wreckage. A car door slammed. A man's voice called, "Is anyone down there? Are you hurt?"

No chance to get away now. She'd have to take her chances and pray that he was really here to help. Pray? That was a laugh. Cathy had prayed before, prayed hard, all without effect. Why should she expect anything different this time?

"Is someone there? Are you hurt?"

How should she react? Answer or stay quiet? Neither choice seemed good. She tried to clear the dust from her throat, but when she opened her mouth to yell, she could only manage a strangled whisper. "Yes."

Footsteps crunched on the gravel shoulder above her, and an urgent voice shouted, "Is someone down there? Do you need help?"

"Yes," she croaked a bit stronger.

"I'm coming down," he said. "Hang on."

A head peered over the edge of the embankment, but pulled back before she could get more than a glimpse of him.

In a few seconds, he scrambled down the embankment, skidding in the red clay before he could dig in the heels of his cowboy boots. At the bottom he looked around until he spotted her. He half-ran the last few feet to where she stood swaying on her makeshift crutch.

"Here, let me help you. Can you walk?"

Blood trickled into her eyes again, and even after she wiped it away, it was like looking through crimson gauze. Cathy could make out the man's outline but not his features. He sounded harmless enough. But she supposed even mass murderers could sound harmless.

She gripped her makeshift staff harder; it might work as a weapon. "I don't think anything's broken." Her voice cracked, and she coughed. "I'm just stunned. If you help me, I think I can move okay."

He leaned down, and Cathy put her left arm on his shoulder. He encircled her waist with his right arm, supporting her so her feet barely touched the ground as they shuffled toward the slope. At the bottom, he turned and swept her into his arms. The move took her by surprise, and she gasped. She felt him stagger a bit on the climb, but in a moment they made it to the top.

Her rescuer freed one hand and thumbed the latch on the passenger side door of his pickup. He turned to bump the door open with his hip, then deposited her gently onto the seat. "Rest there. I'll call 911."

Cathy leaned back and tried to calm down. His voice sounded familiar. Was he one of her patients? She swiped the back of her hand across her eyes, but the image remained cloudy.

The man pulled a flip-phone from his pocket and punched in three digits. "There's been a one-car accident."

She listened as he described the accident location in detail — a mile south of the Freeman farm, just before the Sandy Creek Bridge. This wasn't some passerby. He knew the area.

"I need an ambulance, a fire truck, and someone from the sheriff's office. Oh, and send a flatbed wrecker. The car looks like it's totaled."

"I don't need an ambulance," Cathy protested.

He held up a hand and shushed her, something she hadn't encountered since third grade. "Yes, she seems okay, but I still think they need to hurry."

Cathy heard a few answering squawks from the phone before the man spoke again. "It's Will Kennedy. Yes, thanks."

Will Kennedy? If she hadn't been sitting down, Cathy might have fallen over. She scrubbed at her eyes and squinted. Will? Yes, it was Will. Now even the shape of his body looked familiar: lean and muscular, just the way he'd been — *No. Don't go there.*

Will ended his call and leaned in through the open pickup door. "They'll be here in a minute. Hang on."

He took a clean handkerchief from the hip pocket of his pressed jeans and gently cleaned her face. The white cotton rapidly turned red, and Cathy realized that the blood had not only clouded her vision. It had masked her features.

"Will, don't you recognize me?"

He stopped, looked at her, and frowned. "Cathy?"

"Yes." There were so many things to say. She drew in a ragged breath. "Thanks. I appreciate your stopping."

He gave her the wry grin she remembered so well, and her heart did a flip-flop. "I'd heard you were back in town, and I wondered when you'd get around to talking to

15

me. I just didn't know it would be like this."
He paused. "And forget about telling me
not to have them send an ambulance. I
don't care if you are a doctor now, Cathy
Sewell. I won't turn you loose until another
medic checks you."

Cathy opened her mouth to speak, but
Will's cell phone rang. He answered it and
walked away as he talked, while she sat and
wondered what would have happened if
they'd never turned each other loose in the
first place.

As the ambulance sped toward Summers
County General Hospital, Cathy wondered
what kind of reception she would get there.
Who would be on duty? Would they ac-
knowledge her as a colleague, even though
she hadn't been given privileges yet? When
her thoughts turned to recent events, she
forced herself to shut down the synapses
and put her mind into neutral.

The ambulance rocked to a halt outside
the emergency room doors. Despite Cathy's
protestations, the emergency medical tech-
nicians kept her strapped securely on the
stretcher while they offloaded it. Inside the
ER, Cathy finally convinced her guardians
to let her transfer to a wheelchair held by a
waiting orderly.

"Thanks so much, guys. I'll be fine. Really."

At the admitting desk, the clerk looked up from her computer and frowned.

"Cathy?" She flushed. "I . . . I mean, Dr. Sewell?"

"It's okay, Judy. I was Cathy through twelve years of school. No reason to change." Cathy looked around. "Who's the ER doctor on duty?"

"Dr. Patel. He just called in Dr. Bell to see a patient. Dr. Patel thought it might be a possible appendix." She lowered her voice. "Dr. Bell took one look and made the diagnosis of stomach flu. I couldn't see the need to call in another doctor for a consultation, but Dr. Patel is so afraid he'll make a wrong diagnosis." She pursed her lips as she realized her mistake of complaining about one doctor to another.

"Just be sure Dr. Patel doesn't hear you say that." Cathy tried to take the sting out of the words with a wink, but the blood dried around her eyes made it impossible. "Can you call him? I've been threatened with dire punishment if I don't get checked out."

Judy reached for the phone.

"Don't bother, Judy. I'll take care of Dr. Sewell myself."

17

Cathy eased her head around to see Marcus Bell standing behind her. He wore khakis and a chocolate-brown golf shirt, covered by an immaculate white coat with his name embroidered over the pocket.

This was a trade Cathy would gladly make — finicky Dr. Patel for superdoc Marcus Bell. In the three years he'd been here, Marcus had built a reputation as an excellent clinician. He was also undoubtedly the best-looking doctor in town.

"Let's get you into Treatment Room One." Marcus steered Cathy's wheelchair away from the desk. "Judy, you can bring me the paperwork when you have it ready. Please ask Marianne to step in and help me for a minute. And page Jerry for me, would you? Thanks."

Cathy had been in treatment rooms like this many times in several hospitals. Now she noticed how different everything looked when viewed from this perspective. As if the accident and the adrenaline rush that followed hadn't made her shaky enough, sitting there in a wheelchair emphasized her feeling of helplessness. "I feel so silly," she said. "Usually I'm on the other end of all this."

"Well, today you're not." Marcus gestured toward the nurse who stood in the doorway.

"Let's get you into a gown. Then we'll check the extent of the damages."

Marcus stepped discreetly from the room.

"I'm Marianne," the nurse said. Then, as though reading Cathy's mind, she added, "I know it's hard for a doctor to be a patient. But try to relax. We'll take good care of you."

Marianne helped Cathy out of her clothes and into a hospital gown. If Cathy had felt vulnerable before this, the added factor of being in a garment that had so many openings closed only by drawstrings tripled the feeling. The nurse eased Cathy onto the examining table, covered her with a clean sheet, and called Marcus back into the room.

"Now, Cathy, the first thing I want to do is have a closer look at that cut on your head." Marcus slipped on a pair of latex gloves and probed the wound.

Cathy flinched. "How does it look?"

"Not too bad. One laceration about three or four centimeters long in the frontal area. Not too deep. The bleeding's almost stopped now. We'll get some skull films, then I'll suture it." He wound a soft gauze bandage around her head and taped it.

Marcus flipped off his gloves and picked up the clipboard that Cathy knew held the beginnings of her chart. "Why don't you tell me what happened?"

At first, Cathy laid out the details of the accident and her injuries in terse clinical language, as though presenting a case to an attending physician at Grand Rounds. She did fine until she realized how close she'd come to being killed, apparently by someone who meant to do just that. There were a couple of strangled hiccups, then a few muffled sobs before the calm physician turned into a blubbering girl. "I'm . . . I'm sorry." She reached for a tissue from the box Marcus held out.

"No problem. If you weren't upset by all that, you wouldn't be normal." Marcus took an ophthalmoscope from the wall rack and shined its light into her eyes. "How's your vision?"

"Still a little fuzzy — some halos around lights. I figured it was from the blood running into my eyes."

He put down the instrument and rummaged in the drug cabinet. "Let's wash out your eyes. I don't want you to get a chemical keratitis from the powder on the air bag. I'll give you some eye drops, but if your vision gets worse or doesn't clear in a day or so, I want you to see an ophthalmologist."

"Oh, right." The fact that she hadn't thought of that underscored to Cathy how shaken she still was.

"Now, let's see what else might be injured." Marcus took her left wrist and gently probed with his fingers. Apparently satisfied, he proceeded up along the bones of the arm. His touch was gentle, yet firm, and Cathy found it somehow reassuring. "We'll need some X-rays. I want you to help me figure out the right parts."

"I can't help you much. I'm hurting pretty much everywhere," Cathy said. "But I haven't felt any bones grating. I think I'm just banged up."

Marcus turned his attention to her right arm. He paused in his prodding long enough to touch her chin and raise her head until their eyes met. "You're like all of us. You think that because you're a doctor you can't be hurt or sick."

"That's not true. I don't — Ow!" His hand on the point of her right shoulder sent a flash of pain along her collarbone.

"That's more like it. We'll get an X-ray of that shoulder and your clavicle. Seatbelt injuries do that sometimes. Now see if you can finish telling me what happened."

This time she got through the story without tearing up, although Marcus's efforts to find something broken or dislocated brought forth a number of additional flinches and

21

exclamations.

"I really do think I'm fine except for some bruises," she concluded.

"Really?"

"Okay, I'm also scared. And a little bit mad."

A tinny voice over the intercom interrupted her. "Dr. Bell, is Marianne still in there?"

"I'm here," the nurse replied.

"Can you help us out? There's a pedi patient in Treatment Room Two with suspected meningitis. They're about to do a spinal tap."

"Go ahead," Marcus said. "We can take it from here."

No sooner had the nurse closed the door than there was a firm tap on it.

"Jerry?" Marcus called.

"Yes, sir."

"Come in."

The door creaked open, and Cathy turned. The pain that coursed through her neck made her regret the decision. A man in starched, immaculate whites strode into the room and stopped at an easy parade rest. A smattering of gray at the temples softened the red in his buzz-cut hair.

Marcus did the honors. "Dr. Sewell, this is Jerry O'Neal. Jerry retired after twenty years as a Marine corpsman, and he's now the senior radiology technician at Summers County General. He probably knows as much medicine as you and I put together, but he's too polite to let it show."

"Pleasure to meet you, Doctor," Jerry said.

Marcus handed the clipboard chart to Jerry. "Dr. Sewell's been in an auto accident. She has a scalp laceration I'll need to suture, but first, would you get a skull series, films of the right shoulder and clavicle?" He thought a bit. "Right knee. Right lower leg. While we're at it, better do a C-spine too."

"Yes, sir," Jerry said. "Is that all?"

Marcus looked back at Cathy. "If you catch her rubbing anything else, shoot it. Call me when you've got the films ready."

Cathy half expected Jerry to salute Marcus. Instead, he nodded silently before helping her off the exam table and into a wheelchair.

"Don't worry, Dr. Sewell. You're in good hands."

She tried to relax and take Jerry at his word. "Why haven't I seen you around before this?"

Jerry fiddled with some dials. "I work weekdays as a trouble-shooter for an X-ray equipment company in Dallas. I'm only here on weekends. It fills the empty hours."

That's why I was taking a drive on Saturday afternoon. Filling the empty hours. That started a chain of thought Cathy didn't want to pursue. Instead, she concentrated on getting through the next few minutes.

The X-rays took less time and caused less discomfort than Cathy expected. She could see why Marcus thought so highly of Jerry. Soon she was back in the treatment room, lying on the examination table. Jerry put up two of the X-rays on the wall view box and stacked the others neatly on the metal table beneath it.

"I'll get Dr. Bell now. Will you be okay here for a minute?"

Cathy assured Jerry that she was fine, although she finally realized how many bumps and bruises she'd accumulated in the crash. Every movement seemed to make something else hurt.

When she thought about what came next, her anxiety kicked into high gear. Would Marcus have to shave her scalp before placing the stitches? She recalled her own experiences suturing scalp lacerations in the Parkland Hospital Emergency Room. Maybe it was a woman thing, but she'd felt sorry for those patients, walking out with a shaved spot on their head, a bald patch that was sometimes the size of a drink coaster. She hated the prospect of facing her patients on Monday in that condition. Truthfully, she even hated the prospect of looking at herself in the mirror. She was thinking about wigs when Marcus reentered the room.

"Let's see what we've got." He stepped to the view box and ran through the X-rays. "Skull series looks fine. . . . Neck is good. . . . Shoulder looks okay. . . . The clavicle isn't fractured. . . . You are one lucky woman. Looks like all I have to do is suture that scalp laceration."

Cathy was surprised when Marcus didn't call for help but rather assembled the necessary instruments and equipment himself. When he slipped his gloves on, she closed her eyes and gritted her teeth. The fact that she'd been on the other end of this procedure hundreds of times just made her dread it more.

Marcus's touch was gentle as he cleaned the wound. Soon she felt the sting of a local anesthetic injection. After that, there was nothing except an occasional tug as he sutured.

Cathy processed what she'd just felt. "You didn't shave my scalp."

"Now why would I want to mar that

25

natural beauty of yours? I didn't paint the wound orange with Betadine, either. I used a clear antiseptic to prep the area and KY jelly to plaster the hair down out of my way. The sutures are clear nylon that won't be noticeable in your blonde hair. When I'm finished, I'll paint some collodion over the wound to protect it. In the morning, clean the area with a damp cloth, brush your hair over it, and no one will know the difference."

Cathy couldn't believe what she'd heard. "Natural beauty?" This was certainly at odds with what she'd been told about Marcus Bell. Since the death of his wife, Marcus apparently wanted nothing to do with women. Rumor had it he'd turned aside the advances of most of the single women in Dainger. Was he flirting with her now? Or was this simply his bedside manner?

Marcus snapped off his gloves and tossed them in the bucket at the end of the table. "See me in a week to remove the stitches — unless you want to stand on a box and look down on the top of your own head to remove them yourself."

"Okay, I get it. I'll stop being my own doctor," she said.

"How about something for the pain?"

"I think I'll be okay."

"Tetanus shot?"

"I'm current."

"Then how about dinner with me next Thursday?"

Once more, Cathy felt her head spin, but this time it had nothing to do with tumbling about in a runaway car.

Cathy had always dreaded Monday mornings, but none so much as this one. Today it was time to show her face to the world.

She took one last look in the mirror. Cathy had figured that her fair complexion would make her bruises show up like tire tracks on fresh snow, but the judicious application of some Covermark had done its job well. The redness she'd noticed in her eyes two days ago had responded well to the eye drops Marcus prescribed. And, true to his prediction, she'd been able to style her hair so that the blonde strands almost hid the stitches in her scalp. A little more lipstick and blusher than usual, drawing attention to her face instead of her hair, and maybe she could fake her way through the day.

No matter how successful she'd been in covering the outward signs of the accident, it was still impossible for her to move without aches and pains. She popped a couple of Extra Strength Tylenol, washed

27

them down with the remnants of her second cup of coffee, and headed out the door to face another week. If the medication kicked in soon, maybe Jane wouldn't notice that Cathy moved like an old woman. Maybe Jane hadn't heard the news about the accident. Yeah, and maybe the President would call today and invite Cathy to dinner at the White House.

Cathy tried to sneak in the back door, but Jane's hearing was awfully good for a woman her age. She met Cathy at the door to her office, clucking like a mother hen and shaking her head. "Dr. Sewell, what happened to you?"

What a break it had been for her when Jane — a trim, silver-haired grandmother with a sassy twinkle in her eye — answered her ad for a combination office nurse and secretary. She'd helped Cathy set up the office, given her advice on business, and provided a sympathetic ear on more occasions than she could count.

Cathy recognized Jane's question as rhetorical. Having grown up in Dainger, Cathy knew how quickly news spread in her hometown. She'd bet that Jane had known about the accident before Cathy had cleared the emergency room doors on Saturday. By now, probably everyone in town knew.

"I was out for a ride in the country. I needed to relax and clear my mind. Then someone ran me off the road out near Big Sandy Creek. My car went out of control, flipped, and took out a row of Seth Johnson's peach trees." Cathy winced as she dropped her purse into the bottom drawer of her desk. "Dr. Bell sutured a laceration on my scalp."

"Any other injuries? Do we need to cancel today's patients?"

Cathy shook her head, aggravating a headache that the Tylenol had only dulled. "Other than the fact that I feel like I've just finished a week of two-a-day practices with the Dallas Cowboys, I'm okay."

"It's good that you have a nice light schedule today. You can take it easy."

Cathy frowned. A "nice light schedule" for a doctor just getting started as a family practitioner wasn't exactly the stuff she dreamed about. She needed patients. The money from the bank loan was about gone, and her income stream was anything but impressive. But she'd do the best she could. Anything had to beat living in Dallas, knowing she might run into Robert.

Speak of the devil. Cathy actually shuddered when she saw the return address on the envelope sitting in the middle of her desk: Robert Edward Newell, M.D.

She clamped her jaws shut, snatched up a brass letter opener, and ripped open the envelope. Inside were two newspaper clippings and a few words scribbled on a piece of white notepaper with an ad for a hypertension drug at the top of the page. The first clipping announced the engagement of Miss Laura Lynn Hunt, daughter of Dr. Earl and Mrs. Betty Hunt, to Dr. Robert Edward Newell. The second featured a photo of Laura Lynn and Robert, she in a high couture evening gown, he in a perfectly fitting tux, arriving at the Terpsichorean Ball. The note was brief and to the point: "See what you've missed?" No signature. Just a reminder, one that made her grit her teeth until her jaws ached. Leave it to Robert to rub salt in her wounds.

She forced herself to sit quietly and breathe deeply until the knot in her throat loosened. Then she wadded the clippings and note into a tight ball, which she consigned to the wastebasket with as much force as she could muster.

No use rethinking the past. Time to get on with her life. "Jane," she called, "may I have the charts for today's patients? I want to go over them."

Jane returned and deposited a pitifully

small stack of thin charts on Cathy's desk. The look in Jane's eyes said it all. *Sorry there aren't more. Sorry you're hurting. Sorry.*

Cathy picked up the top chart but didn't open it. "Do you think I made a mistake coming here to practice?"

Jane eased into one of the patient chairs across the desk from Cathy. "Why would you ask that?"

"I applied at three banks before I got a loan. When I mention to other doctors that I'm taking new patients, they get this embarrassed look and mumble something about keeping that in mind, but they never make any referrals. Several of my patients tell me they've heard stories around town that make them wonder about my capabilities. And my privileges at the hospital have been stuck in committee for over a month now." Cathy pointed to the stitches in her scalp. "Now the situation seems to be escalating."

"You mean the accident on Saturday?"

"It was no accident. I'm convinced that someone ran me off the road and intended to kill me."

"Did you report it?" Jane asked.

"Yes, but fat lot of good it did. If Will Kennedy hadn't insisted, I think the deputy who came out to investigate the accident would have written the whole thing off as careless driving on my part." Cathy grimaced. "Of course, he may do that anyway."

"What was Will Kennedy doing there?"

"He came along right after the wreck. When I couldn't manage under my own power, Will carried me up the embankment. Then he insisted I go to the emergency room, and when they were loading me into the ambulance he slipped his card into my hand and whispered, 'Please call me. I want to make sure you're okay.' " Cathy pulled a business card from the pocket of her skirt, smoothed the wrinkles from it, and put it under the corner of her blotter.

"Did you phone him?"

Cathy shook her head. "I started to, but I couldn't. I'm not ready to get close to any man. Not Will Kennedy. Not Marcus Bell. Not Robert Newell." She took in a deep breath through her nose and let it out through pursed lips. "Especially not Robert Newell."

"Who is — ?"

Before Jane could finish, Cathy spun around in her chair and pulled a book at random from the shelf behind her. "Not now. Please. I need to look up something before I see my first patient." She paged the book, but none of the words registered.

Jane's voice from behind her made Cathy close the book. "Dr. Sewell, you asked me a question. Let me answer it before I go. I don't know if someone's really making an effort to run you off. I've heard some of those rumors. They're always anonymous, like 'Somebody told me that Dr. Sewell's not a good doctor.' Or 'I heard Dr. Sewell came back to Dainger because she couldn't make it in Dallas.' You have to ignore the gossip and rumors. They're part of living here."

Cathy swiveled back to face Jane. "I thought it would be easier to get my practice started in my hometown."

"It might be, except that people here will compare you to your daddy, who was the best surgeon Dainger ever saw. In that situation a young, female doctor will come up short, no matter how qualified she is."

Cathy tossed the book on her desk and held her hands up, palms forward. "If someone wants to get rid of me, they're close to succeeding. I don't know how much longer I can go on."

"You're a fighter, and I'm right here with you. Just stick with it." Jane turned and walked toward the doorway.

"Thanks. I appreciate it."

Jane stopped and faced Cathy once more.

"Have you been out to visit your folks?"

"It won't do any good. There's nothing for me there. I don't have anything to say."

Jane shook her head. "Sometimes you don't have to say anything. Sometimes you simply have to make the effort and go. It's the only way you'll ever put all that behind you."

2

"Mr. Nix, how can I help you?" Cathy squirmed a bit, hoping to achieve a more comfortable position. When she purchased equipment for her examination rooms, she hadn't figured she'd ever be this sore. Next time, she'd think about a rolling stool with a bit more padding.

Cathy thought the man sitting on the edge of the treatment table might have shown the briefest of smiles. Or was it a smirk?

"My family doctor's retiring, Dr. Sewell, and I need my heart medicines renewed. Since my bank has a vested interest in your making a go of it here, I thought maybe I'd try to help you out a little by giving you some of my business."

Cathy bristled at the word "business" and the condescending attitude that went with it, but she did her best not to show her displeasure. She couldn't afford to alienate this man over something as minor as his choice of words. Besides, each day she saw medicine changing from a profession to a business. What used to be "patients" were now called "consumers" and "physicians" had become "providers."

Let it go. She plastered a smile on her face. "Let me look at the records Dr. Gladstone's office sent. Then I'll check you over. After that, we can talk about continuing your medications. I'm sure Dr. Gladstone did a good job, although I may suggest we tweak your medications a little bit."

She read through the chart, blessing Dr. Gladstone's old-fashioned, copperplate penmanship. Milton Nix, age fifty, occupation banker. *You have to give him high marks for modesty,* she thought. Most people would have put down "President of the First State Bank of Dainger."

"How've you been feeling, Mr. Nix? Any problems?" She glanced up and decided the man looked pretty much the same as when she sat across from him three months ago and virtually begged him for a loan to start her practice. At that time, the other banks in town had already turned her down, using a variety of excuses — no room in town for another family doctor; she had too much debt already in student loans; a woman doctor would never be successful in this town.

Nix, unlike his counterparts at the First National and the Continental Banks, had finally decided to take a chance on her.

"I'm feeling fine, Dr. Sewell," Nix said. "But I've got a busy day. Can we get this thing moving?"

Okay, enough small talk. Back to the chart. Nix was five feet ten, one hundred fifty pounds. On the thin side, but his weight had been stable for years, so put aside thoughts of a cancer somewhere. Usual visits for coughs and colds. A couple of prostate infections. Congestive heart failure, controlled with Lanoxin and a beta-blocker.

"Mr. Nix, I don't find any electrocardiograms in here," Cathy said. "When was your last one?"

"Any what?"

Cathy regretted her error. Never drop into doctor-speak. She'd been taught that early in her training. "Did Dr. Gladstone do any heart tracings?"

Nix shook his head. "Don't remember. I think Doc probably did one or two at first, but on my last few visits he took my blood pressure, listened to my chest, poked and prodded a little, and wrote me a prescription. Can't you do the same thing?"

"Since this is your first visit here, I think

37

it's best to get a little more information. Let me listen to your heart and lungs, and check your blood pressure. Then I'll have my nurse run a cardiogram. She'll draw some blood for a few lab tests. Nothing to worry about, but I think it's safer that way."

Mr. Nix grumbled his way out of the exam room and down the hall after Jane, who was already at work charming him. Cathy finished reading through the chart and decided that "Doc" Gladstone hadn't really done a bad job with Mr. Nix. She did see one minor change she wanted to make, though.

Cathy left the exam room and found Karen Pearson sitting in her office. She recalled Karen's first visit a month ago when the office still smelled of fresh paint.

"Dr. Sewell, I'm pregnant," Karen had said. "I've been seeing Dr. Harshman, but I've changed my mind. This is my first baby, and I want you to do the delivery."

Cathy had tried to be circumspect. The ethics of the matter aside, even to give the appearance of stealing the patient of an established physician was guaranteed to cause friction with the other doctors in the community. And she had a hard enough time in that area already.

Karen was insistent, though. She said that her current obstetrician lacked the bare

38

minimum of consideration. "Every woman that Dr. Harshman's taken care of says they'd go to a veterinarian before they'd go back to him," was how she'd put it.

Finally, Cathy had put in a call to the administrator's office at Summers County General Hospital to ask if her request for obstetric privileges had been approved.

"Sorry, Doctor," the secretary said. "It's still in committee."

After that, Cathy's repeated calls were always met with an excuse. The paperwork got misplaced. One of the board members was out of town. They were checking precedents. Cathy knew why Karen was in her office today, and she dreaded giving her the answer.

"Karen, how are you doing?"

"I'm less than a month from my due date," Karen said. "Dr. Sewell, I'm still hoping you can take over my care. Do you have obstetrics privileges yet?"

Cathy felt her heart drop. She was sure Karen would know the answer just from the look on her face. "I'm sorry, Karen. I'm still trying. You know, we've been through this already. Why can't you stay with Dr. Harshman?"

"Oh, please, Dr. Sewell. You know very well what that man's reputation is. And now, he says I might need a Caesarean section. I was worried enough about him doing a regular delivery. I can't stand the thought of him doing a C-section. Can you do it, Dr. Sewell? Please?"

"I'm sorry, Karen. I wish I could help. But I'm having trouble getting privileges to do normal deliveries, and there's no way they'll let me do a C-section. Have you considered switching to Dr. Gaines?" Cathy said, naming the other obstetrician in Dainger.

"His practice is full. His nurse told me that I have a perfectly competent doctor and suggested I stick with him."

Cathy extended her hand to Karen, partly to help her from the chair and partly as a gesture of compassion. "I'll keep trying. Don't give up."

"I won't. I've been praying that you'd be the one to deliver my baby. God will take care of this."

Cathy bit off the reply that was on the tip of her tongue. With words of assurance that sounded hollow in her ears, she left Karen and turned her attention to Milton Nix.

Jane met her in the hall and held out an EKG tracing. "Mr. Nix is in exam room one."

Nix looked up when Cathy walked in.

"Did that fancy test help you find anything that Doc Gladstone didn't figure out with his stethoscope?"

Cathy studied the tracing, looked at the chart once more, and made a decision. "I'll want to see what the blood chemistries show us, but at this point I think you're doing well. Your beta-blocker is okay, but I want to make a slight change in your other heart medicine. I see that your prescription has been for the brand-name drug, Lanoxin. I suspect that Dr. Gladstone wrote it that way years ago and just never changed it. If I write the prescription a bit differently, the pharmacist can give you a generic form and save you a little money."

Cathy could see Nix's lips open, then shut. If he had any complaints, he kept them to himself. He probably wasn't anxious to have anything changed in the regimen he'd been following for years, but this wasn't really much of a change. Besides, she figured the "saving money" part would win him over.

She reached for her prescription pad and dug into the pocket of her white coat. Where did that pen go? "Excuse me. I can't find my pen. I'll be right back."

Nix reached into his shirt pocket and pulled out two ballpoints. "Here. They've

41

got the bank's name on them. When you're through, leave 'em in the waiting room. Maybe I'll get some return on my investment for this trip after all." She might have been mistaken, but there seemed to be the ghost of a grin on his thin-lipped face as he handed the pens to her. Two in one day. That must be some kind of a record for Milton Nix.

She wrote the prescriptions exactly the way she'd been taught: carefully, with attention to legibility, calculating the number of pills that should be dispensed, double-checking the directions. She added refill instructions and signed the prescriptions before tearing them off the pad and handing them to Nix.

"Just follow the directions on both of these, and call me if you have any questions."

As she passed the prescriptions to Nix, she noticed that the ink in the pen she'd been using was blue. She'd need to make sure she didn't use Milton's pens in the office anymore. That was another thing her mentors had emphasized. Use black ink. It photocopies better and gives a neater appearance. She could hear the voice of Dr. Seldin, the chief of internal medicine, saying, "If you're sloppy in little things, you'll be sloppy in the big ones too. Take the time to do it right."

Cathy sat staring into space, the phone receiver in her hand. When a strident stutter tone shattered the silence of her office, she replaced the handset. Idly, she noted that her hand was steady when she did so. Her surgery instructors had always said she had good hands, even under pressure. She wished her mind were as steady right now.

Two phone message slips. Two calls. And, just when she thought the situation couldn't get worse, she sank further into the pit of anxiety and depression that had held her for these past several months. Josh would have a field day with this.

"What's wrong?" Jane paused in the door, a chart in her hand. Cathy shook her head. Uninvited, Jane eased into the chair across the desk. "You want to talk about it?"

Cathy reached for the soft drink sitting on her desk. "Those message slips you gave me? The first was from a sheriff's deputy. About my accident." She lifted the can to her lips, found it empty, and tossed it into the wastebasket under her desk.

"Did he find the other driver?"

"He said that since there's no evidence of a collision and no witnesses, he's writing it off as driver error on my part." Cathy sighed. "Actually, he reached that conclusion right after he arrived on the scene, but Will pointed out the skid marks and pressured the deputy to at least look into it."

Jane leaned forward. "Will that affect how your insurance company handles the claim?"

"No longer an issue. If my insurance had been in force, this might have raised my rates. But the second call was from my agent. The company just notified him that my last premium check bounced, so apparently, my policy wasn't in force at the time of the accident." Cathy squeezed her eyes closed for a moment. She wouldn't allow herself to cry in front of Jane. "The agent was nice. He said he'll make calls to some people higher up in the company. He'll try to get them to reinstate the policy. He even said he'd talk with the owner of the dealership that's renting me a car and see if he'll discount the bill since I may be paying it out of my own pocket."

"So you're driving without liability coverage?" Jane's voice was calm, but Cathy saw the concern in her eyes.

"The agent's given me temporary coverage. But this is something else I've got to straighten out." Cathy shrugged. "I need to make one more call."

Jane took the hint and tiptoed out, closing the door softly behind her.

Cathy fanned out the three message slips like a bridge player studying a critical hand. Sheriff. Insurance Agent. The last call from Dr. Marcus Bell was marked "Urgent." She punched in his number.

"Thanks for calling back," Dr. Bell said.

"I hope it's good news, Marcus. I could use some."

"Actually, it is," he said. "The credentials committee will consider your request for hospital privileges tomorrow night."

"Finally." Cathy saw a glimmer of hope through the gloom that had surrounded her for so long. If she could expand her practice, the extra income might help solve her rapidly multiplying financial worries.

"Would you like to attend the meeting? If you want me to, I'll arrange it."

Cathy turned that thought over for a few seconds. Would her presence improve her chances of a positive response? It couldn't hurt. "Yes, please."

"Great. They meet at six in the conference room," Marcus said. "Would you like to have dinner with me afterward?"

Cathy experienced a return of the guilt she'd felt after turning down Marcus's previous dinner invitation. He'd tried not to show it, but she'd seen the hurt in his eyes. And he seemed like a nice guy, one who might turn out to be a friend — maybe more than a friend. Her lips formed a "Yes," before she stopped herself. Hard on the heels of the tiny flutter she'd felt at the prospect of dating Marcus came memories of her past relationships. No, she wasn't ready to take a chance.

"I'm sorry, Marcus. I want to meet with the committee, but can I take a raincheck on dinner?"

Jane took the chart Cathy handed her, filed it with a flourish, and said, "That's it. You're through for the day."

Automatically, Cathy looked at her watch. Three o'clock. Another light day spent doing insurance physicals, caring for emergencies other doctors couldn't see, refilling the prescriptions of some of Dr. Gladstone's patients who'd decided to give Dr. Sewell's daughter a chance since their faithful old GP was retiring. She knew her bank balance — knew it to the penny — and if her practice didn't pick up soon, Milton Nix's bank would bring in an auctioneer and sell off the office furniture and equipment she'd gone so deeply in debt to buy.

Not only that, today another patient had told her, "Dr. Sewell, I don't believe those rumors I've been hearing. You're a good doctor." There was no longer any question in Cathy's mind. Someone in town wanted her gone.

Should she make the call? See if the job offer at the medical school in Dallas was still open? No, she couldn't. Going back to Dallas would mean leaving the refuge she hoped to find here in her hometown. Going back to Dallas would mean taking a chance on seeing Robert, having to interact with him. Going back to Dallas would mean returning to the scene of her greatest humiliation. No, Dallas held too many memories. She'd stay here.

A chilling thought struck her. Could Robert be behind all this? His father had both wealth and influence, and Robert was already on his way to achieving that status. It wouldn't be beyond either of them to call in some favors, spread a little cash around, and make her life miserable.

She tried to be logical about it. Why would Robert try to force her out of Dainger? Out of spite? Maybe. He didn't want her back. The newspaper clipping was proof enough of that. But if she returned to Dallas, he could "arrange" to bump into her from time to time, just to rub it in. But surely even Robert wouldn't go that far. Would he?

She shucked off her white coat and tossed it into the laundry hamper, grabbed her purse and briefcase, and headed for the door. She paused at Jane's desk. "I'll be on my cell phone if you need me. See you tomorrow."

"Are you going . . . ?" Jane left the question dangling.

Cathy chose to ignore it. "Remember, I have an appointment in Fort Worth tomorrow morning. I'll be in about ten."

She'd have to make arrangements about a car, but for now the rental was still hers. Cathy sat in it with the motor idling, uncertain about her next step. Emotions and thoughts tumbled about in her head. She didn't want to think about her folks. Didn't want to relive those events. But Josh kept telling her that she had to face it. She had an appointment with him tomorrow, and she knew he'd probably mention it again. Maybe today was the day.

Cathy backed out of her parking spot and set a course that she knew she could never forget, no matter how long she was gone from Dainger. Away from the professional building that Jacob Collins had built to house his pharmacy and a few doctors' offices. Jacob, her high school classmate, now her landlord. She wondered how he'd react if she was unable to pay the rent this month or next.

She drove carefully — her mind consumed with thoughts of the past — up the short hill to the Y intersection, where a right turn would take her to Fort Worth. She turned left, then right, then left again. Soon she was on the edge of town, passing the homes of Dainger's more affluent families.

Milton Nix lived there. The open doors of the double garage revealed a midsize gray sedan and a dark SUV. Cathy replayed Nix's visit in her mind. Had she missed anything? She wanted all her patients to do well, but she especially needed the goodwill of the banker.

That rambling ranch house belonged to Judge Sam Lawton. The garage doors were closed. A Ford pickup, its original dark blue faded in spots, stood in the drive. In the yard, two young Hispanics wielded a leaf-blower and string trimmer. Given Sam's age, she guessed he'd stopped doing his own lawn work. Apparently, he could afford it. Cathy had heard rumors that Sam put away a good bit of money before the voters turned him out of office, money that didn't come from his salary as a county judge. Apparently, small towns had their share of under-the-table deals and influence peddling.

The next house stood out from its plainer neighbors, its magnificent architecture set off by a striking landscape. A small red Cadillac stood in the driveway in front of the closed doors of a three-car garage. Whoever lived there certainly had money. When she saw "Collins" on the mailbox, Cathy decided that either Jacob was more successful than she thought, or his wife had pressured him into that expensive showplace. Cathy wondered idly who Jacob had married. She'd have to ask around.

The sunny day and mild temperatures combined to relax the muscles in Cathy's shoulders as she rolled slowly along the narrow road. She let her mind wander, putting faces with most of the homes, remembering happier times growing up here. She'd wanted for nothing. Ran with a clique of girls from upper-class families. She grimaced when she realized what a spoiled brat she must have been.

There it was around the next corner: a modest one-story house built of white Austin stone, surrounded by two acres of green grass and spreading oaks, bordered by a white-rail fence. There had been a time when she knew every inch of the property, knew the best trees to climb and the hiding places where no one could find her. She couldn't read the faded letters on the mailbox, but Cathy remembered when it said "Sewell" in shiny black letters. There was no sign of activity at the end of the gravel driveway. The doors to a detached, two-car garage were closed.

Cathy stopped at the entrance to the drive, her car's right wheels on the gravel shoulder of the road. She sat in silence for several minutes, her mind flitting back and forth like a hummingbird. Then, movement in the rearview mirror caught her eye as a black SUV raced over the hill. Cathy watched in horror. The vehicle veered to the right on a collision course with the rear of her little rental. She rammed the car into gear and screeched into the driveway, scattering crushed gravel in her wake. The SUV sped by with no signs of slowing, and she felt her car rock with the force of its passing. Was this the same SUV that had driven her off the road once already? Was it more evidence of a plot against her, or was this another sign of paranoia?

Cathy shivered. It took her a moment to gather her thoughts. Finally, she looked up the driveway at the house. This was no longer home. She knew where she had to go. It was time. Her decision made, she took a deep breath and eased her car out onto the road.

A half-mile later, Cathy pulled in under a metal arch and navigated down a patched and pothole-scarred narrow lane. She let the car creep along as she searched for familiar landmarks. The names were hard to read, but finally she saw it ahead. Cathy parked, locked the car, and followed a dirt path, beaten down by the tread of many generations of feet.

When she found the large granite slab, she dropped to her knees on the green grass in front of it. Despite the sun she felt on her back, the stone felt cold as she let her fingers trace the letters carved deep into it: SEWELL. Her shoulders shook. Finally, she sobbed, "Daddy, I miss you so much. And I'm so very sorry."

Cathy's expectations had stemmed from cartoons she'd seen in *The New Yorker*. She'd lie on a couch, pouring out her soul as she sniffled softly. The psychiatrist would stroke his pointed beard and murmur, "I see. Very interesting."

But there were no couches in this office. Instead, she sat in a padded leather armchair. A small, round coffee table holding a box of tissues separated her from Dr. Josh Samuels, who occupied a similar chair to her left, angled slightly so that they might have been host and guest on some TV talk show. Only the framed diplomas and certificates on the wall behind the littered desk gave any hint of what went on in this room, that and the faint aura of dread and apprehension that lingered in the air.

Josh — he'd corrected her the first time she called him Dr. Samuels — did have a beard, but not the pointed Van Dyke variety. Instead, his neatly trimmed full beard, black with a smattering of gray, stretched from ear to ear, forming a marked contrast to his shaved head. Cathy had never seen him wear a suit and doubted that he owned one. He wore a white dress shirt, its button-down collar open at the neck, with the sleeves folded back two neat turns. His khakis were starched and creased.

Halfway through today's session, during one of the pauses that Josh never seemed to find awkward, Cathy leaned forward and blurted out, "I went to the cemetery yesterday."

"And?"

"I cried. I talked with my folks. I told Daddy how sorry I was."

"About what?"

She wanted to tell Josh that if she knew the answers to all his questions she wouldn't be sitting here with the clock ticking away another fifty-minute hour. She wanted the psychiatrist to unlock the twisted dreams that made her wake up in a cold sweat. Most of all, she wanted to ask him if he thought she was crazy.

"I don't know. I suppose that, in some way, I feel responsible for their deaths."

Josh crossed one leg over the other, displaying worn white Reeboks and a hairy calf above tan crew socks. He laced his hands together over his knee and leaned forward. His expression invited comment.

"I've told you some of this," she said.

"Tell me the rest."

Several sips of water from the glass in front of her didn't ease the dryness in Cathy's throat.

"I was in my final year of medical school, home for Christmas vacation. They tried to hide it, but it was obvious that my folks weren't getting along. My mother dropped some hints that she thought my dad was unfaithful. I saw she'd become extremely distrustful. She was suspicious of him, of his time away from home, his contact with female patients. All my life, I'd thought that my father could do no wrong. But I loved and trusted my mother. I didn't know what to think. Finally, I couldn't take it any more. I told them I was going back to Dallas, and I didn't want to talk to them again until they worked it out."

"And?"

"Daddy called me in May, the day before I was scheduled to graduate from Southwestern Med School. I hadn't even sent them an invitation, but he had friends at the school, and he found out the details. He said Mom had been having some . . . he called them emotional issues, but he thought they were under control. They wanted to see me graduate."

The therapist focused his unblinking gaze like a laser beam.

Cathy felt as though there wasn't enough oxygen in the room. She took several deep breaths. "I was thrilled. Daddy said they'd see me after the ceremony."

Josh made a faint motion with his hand that Cathy knew meant, "Go on."

"The rain started after they left Dainger. The Highway Patrol said it came down in sheets, a typical Texas spring storm. Daddy had been delayed with a patient. He was afraid they'd miss the graduation, so he was driving too fast. He came around a curve, lost control, and the car skidded into a bridge abutment. He and Mom were killed instantly."

"And you're angry?"

"Yes!" she exploded. "At God, for letting it happen. At my parents for not having the perfect marriage I thought they should have. At Daddy, for putting his practice before his daughter so he had to hurry to make up lost time. And . . . and at myself, for making it such a big deal that he drove like that to keep his promise."

"And you feel guilty?"

She reached for a tissue. "Yes. The guilt of their deaths has been like a fifty-pound weight on my shoulders ever since."

"Do you really think the accident was your fault?"

Cathy wanted to bolt. How should she know? Wasn't that what she paid this frustrating man to help her find out?

"Think about it." Josh leaned forward, and his posture spoke encouragement. "Think it through."

Cathy closed her eyes for a moment. She dredged up scenes she'd imagined from that horrible night, pictures she'd visualized so many times she could no longer tell fantasy from reality. The images ran through her head like a late-night, black-and-white

56

movie. She swallowed hard. "Maybe not."

"Are you sure?"

"No. I'm not sure of anything. And why are we talking about my parents, anyway?"

Josh's expression told her to figure it out for herself. But nothing made sense to her right now. The last several months had been a downward spiral. Unable to sleep. Hard to concentrate. Now someone had tried to kill her. Or at least, she thought they had. Was someone out to get her? Or was she following her mother into — ? No, she wouldn't think about that. Couldn't Josh help her? He had to.

As though reading her thoughts, Josh said, "Cathy, we'll get you through this. It will take some time and some effort on your part. It won't be easy. But we'll get there. For right now, believe me when I say that you're not the first person to experience these emotions. They're not pleasant, but I don't think they're pathologic."

Cathy started to speak but he stopped her with an upraised hand. She had decided after a couple of sessions that Josh must have an internal clock in his head. He wore no watch, and there were no clocks in the room, but he'd never been wrong when he said it before, and a glance at her wrist

57

confirmed that he was correct now.

"Our time is up. I'll see you next week."

3

Cathy left Josh's office and navigated through Fort Worth's downtown traffic. By the time she reached the highway, she was more than ready to trade the relative hustle and bustle of the city for the slower pace of life in Dainger. That is, if only someone there weren't out to drive her out of town or kill her. Or were they?

She'd barely cleared the city limits when a sudden, driving rain hit her windshield like bullets. Texas rain. Cathy had seen it every spring and fall since she was a child. It was the kind of rain that had killed her parents. She eased her foot off the accelerator.

On the drive back from Josh's office, Cathy finally let down her guard long enough to think about what she'd dismissed during her session. She was sure she wasn't imagining her problems. The rumors circulating around town. Her request for hospital privileges that encountered a roadblock at every turn. The black SUV intent on her destruction.

But did they represent some kind of plot? Or could they be unconnected, random events? Was what she felt a simple case of paranoia? Was she sliding into the same mental illness that had consumed her mother and threatened to tear her parents' marriage apart? Paranoid schizophrenia. She remembered a line that had made her laugh during medical school. It didn't seem so funny now. *Just because you're paranoid doesn't mean they aren't out to get you.*

If this wasn't paranoia, was there a single driving force behind everything that was happening? If so, who or what was it? Could it be Robert? Was it all some sort of sick joke? Cathy figured that calling off the engagement had caused more damage to Robert's pride than his heart. But would he go this far to get even? And how would he do it? Maybe he hired someone. That would be his style, all right. Pay to have his dirty work done.

Might it be one of the local doctors? Sure, they weren't anxious to share their patients with a newcomer — certainly not with a woman doctor. And especially not with a female family practice specialist who had the nerve to ask for privileges far beyond what these men had always doled out to the general practitioners in town. But would one of them go this far? Maybe she'd get a clue at the credentials committee meeting tonight. Meanwhile, it did no good to worry about it. That's the advice she always gave her patients.

Cathy squinted past the flashing wipers and gripped the wheel a bit tighter. Josh said she'd be okay, and she had to trust him. Meanwhile, she determined to put her mental state out of her mind. She chuckled at the irony of that statement. *Snap out of it. Think productively; don't worry aimlessly.* There was certainly enough to occupy her thoughts. Her practice. Hospital privileges. Finances.

She squared her shoulders and sat up straighter in the cramped driver's seat of the little rental car. She'd handle these problems. She'd handle them the way she'd been taught to approach any diagnostic problem: examine the possible causes, make the right diagnosis, call up the proper treatment from her memory bank, implement it, and move on to the next. It had always worked in her medical practice. Unfortunately, it wasn't so simple when it was her life she struggled to put back together.

Cathy decided to start with finances. Her

floundering practice barely made enough to pay her monthly bills. If she expected to remedy that, her patient base had to grow, and this required hospital privileges. She'd asked for extended privileges, but so far the credentials committee hadn't even granted her the standard ones given to family practitioners. For years the doctors who controlled the hospital had made it an article of faith that general practice meant taking care of sniffles and bellyaches. But Cathy's training in family practice was excellent. She proudly displayed her certification by the American Board of Family Physicians on her office wall. She could do so much more if only they'd let her.

Why did her request for privileges keep hitting snags? Was this part of the plot against her? Was a doctor behind all this? It would be easy enough for a member of the credentials committee to arrange for repeated delays in considering her request. For that matter, any physician on the hospital staff could put in a word here and there, encouraging the committee to drag out the process.

Then Cathy had another thought. Were the two bankers who turned down her loan request under pressure from one of the doctors in town — maybe their own physician?

Or could one of those bankers have something against her and be taking his dislike of Cathy a step further than simply cutting off her access to finances?

The driver behind her tapped his horn. She glanced in the rearview mirror and saw a string of five or six cars behind her. The double yellow line stretched ahead of her down the two-lane highway and out of sight. She waved her apology and clicked her right blinker, then carefully steered the car onto the shoulder and rolled along until the caravan behind her had passed. Texas friendly. Sometimes it was good to be back home in a smaller town. Sometimes. Not always.

The rain had stopped and the sun peeked out of a cloud-bank in the east. She lowered her window and took a deep breath of the rain-washed air. *Let your mind go blank,* she thought. *Try to relax.* She'd be at the office in another five minutes. There would be plenty of time to worry then.

Jane dropped a message slip on the desk in front of Cathy. "Your insurance agent called. He said it was important."

Cathy pulled the phone toward her and dialed. She felt certain this was more bad news. It took only a few moments to determine that she was right.

"I'm sorry, Dr. Sewell. I'm not getting anywhere with the company about paying for the damage to your car. I got all the way up to a senior manager in claims adjustment, but I can't get him to budge. It's that NSF check. They ran it through twice and by the time it bounced the second time, the grace period had expired. There's a letter somewhere in the system informing you that the policy has lapsed."

"I can't believe this," Cathy said.

"I know how you must feel. I'll call a friend of mine in the business and see if there are any stones I've left unturned."

She took a deep breath, but it didn't change the sinking feeling in her stomach. "I've had that policy since I left home for college over ten years ago. Never missed a quarterly payment."

"That's what I told them. But there's no doubt that the company refused the last check you sent because of insufficient funds."

"After I got the loan for my practice I transferred my account to Mr. Nix's bank. I don't know how they managed to bounce the check. I'm sure there were funds in my account to cover it. There must have been a mix-up at the bank."

"Then you might see if the bank will contact the company," Steve said. "I'll do what I can, but — and I hate to say this about one of the companies I represent — you may wind up having to sue them before they'll pay for the damages to your car."

Okay, if that was what it took, so be it. Cathy hung up and pulled the wrinkled card from the edge of her desk blotter. She stared at it for a moment. *Don't think; just do it.* She punched in the numbers and felt a slight quickening of her pulse as she waited for the call to be answered.

"Yes, this is Dr. Cathy Sewell. Is Will Kennedy available?"

"Will he know what it's about?" his secretary asked.

"Just tell him who it is. He'll know."

The strains of a soft-rock song filled the silence, then Cathy heard a click and Will's voice. "I thought you'd never call. Have you recovered from your cuts and bruises? Can we schedule that dinner now?"

Cathy's gut tightened. "I'm sorry I haven't called. I apologize. I appreciate the dinner invitation, but I'm too overwhelmed to think about a social life. But physically, I'm doing okay. Thanks for asking. The reason I called is that I've got some legal issues. Are you available?"

The silence on the other end of the line gave Cathy serious second thoughts. Had she hurt his feelings because she called him for professional help, not dinner? Or did the hurt run deeper? Was it about their past? She was about to tell him to forget she'd asked when he said, "I'll help you in any way I can. When would you like to sit down and tell me about the problem? I'd suggest we do it over dinner, but I get the sense you're not ready for that."

Cathy's heart urged, *Yes. Let's have dinner out. Let's pick up where we left off.* But her head intervened. "No, I'm not ready for that. I'm sorry."

"Tell you what. I'm in court most of the day. Can you come by my office at five this afternoon?"

"That sounds fine." She hung up, still wondering when — if ever — she could let herself care for a man again. With a sigh, she pulled a yellow pad toward her and made a list of all the questions she wanted to ask Will. By the time Jane called to tell her the day's first patient had been shown to the treatment room, the list filled half the page.

The man perched on the edge of Cathy's examining table was dressed for success.

The label of an exclusive tailor peeked from inside the suit coat hanging on the back of the exam room door. Gold links closed the cuffs of a crisp dress shirt as white as a first snowfall.

The effect was spoiled by the gaps between the shirt's buttons and the roll of fat spilling over the edge of the man's collar. His florid complexion screamed high blood pressure. The network of fine blood vessels tracing across his nose told Cathy more about his drinking habits than the history sheet clipped to the chart in her hand.

"Doc, I don't want to hurry you," he said, "but I've got to get back to work. My wife made me come. Says she's tired of me chewing Tums and gulping Mylanta all day. But I know it's just heartburn."

"Why do you say that?" Cathy asked.

"Hey, my schedule would give anybody heartburn. Out of the house in the morning with a can of Red Bull to get me as far as the Starbucks for my double espresso. Grab a burger and fries for lunch, unless I'm taking a client out. The only real meal I get in a day is dinner with the wife, assuming I get home in time. It's a dog-eat-dog world out there. I made the Million Dollar Roundtable the last three years, but insurance doesn't sell itself. I've got to keep pushing if

I want to send Junior to college."

"Mr. Phillips, why don't you slip off your shirt? I need to check you over."

Instead of complying, Phillips gave her a hard look. "I don't have time for that." He pulled back his cuff and consulted a watch that looked to Cathy like a Rolex. "Got an appointment in fifteen minutes. Just give me some of that stuff like I see advertised on TV, would you?"

Cathy looked at the vital signs Jane had recorded on Phillips's chart. She tried to keep the urgency she felt out of her voice.

"Mr. Phillips, your blood pressure is through the roof. The pains you've described are probably angina — signs of an impending heart attack. If you'll excuse an overused expression, you're a ticking time bomb. I want to get an electrocardiogram, have Jane draw some blood for studies, including your cholesterol and lipids. You'd better cancel that appointment."

The man eased his ample bottom off the table and reached the door in two strides, snagging his coat on the way. "You doctors are all alike. Do some tests. Run up a big bill. Well, I don't have time for this. I thought I'd throw some business your way. Maybe get you to buy some insurance from me in return. But I'll just call my regular doctor. He won't ask for a bunch of tests. I won't even have to go to his office. No sir, he'll call in a prescription for me." The last words trailed down the hall as the man made his exit.

Jane stuck her head in the door. "Mr. Phillips didn't stop at the desk on the way out. What are the charges? Does he need a follow-up appointment?"

Cathy shrugged her shoulders before returning them to the slumped position they'd assumed. "No charge. And follow-up? I suspect the next time I or any doctor sees him will be in the emergency room or the morgue."

The first thing that struck Cathy was the comfortable feel of Will's office. The framed diplomas and certificates on the wall were balanced by paintings with a Western theme, one of which she recognized as a reproduction Remington. Stacks of files and a jumble of law books, most with yellow Post-it notes, fluttering from the pages like the plumage of some rare bird, covered the surface of a round table in the corner. Will's desk, made of an oak door sanded and varnished to a glowing patina, held a phone, a computer, a handheld cassette recorder, and a leather-bound Bible. The only picture on the desk was of Will with his parents. She hadn't seen Pastor and Mrs. Kennedy for years, but they didn't appear to have changed. A little frisson of pleasure — a faint, warm shiver — ran through Cathy as she noticed the absence of any woman's picture in the room.

Will waved Cathy to a couch and pulled over a client chair so he faced her, their feet almost touching. He balanced a yellow legal pad on his knee, pulled a fountain pen from his shirt pocket and uncapped it, and gave a gesture that he was ready to hear her story.

"I guess I should start by apologizing for not calling you earlier," she said. "I . . . I don't have a good excuse. My life's been sort of topsy-turvy since I came back here, and I suppose I didn't want to add another complication."

Will waved away both the apology and the excuse. His expression stayed neutral.

Cathy opened her purse and pulled out her list. "I think I need to engage your professional services. Can we talk about your rates? I can probably handle them, but I want to be sure. Finances are sort of tight right now, until my practice takes hold."

"Tell you what," Will said. "Let's put any discussion of fees aside for the time being. If necessary, we can engage in some good, old-fashioned bartering. You need legal

70

services. I'll probably need medical attention sometime. Why don't you tell me what's troubling you?"

She'd rehearsed it a dozen times on the way over, but somehow the words of her ordered presentation eluded her. Hesitantly at first, then speaking faster and with more force as she thought about the injustice of it all, she described her problems with the insurance company.

When she finally ran out of steam, Will asked his first question. Soon, with no recollection of how the segue occurred, she found herself venting about her frustration with the hospital credentials committee. She confessed her worries about running through the money she'd borrowed from the bank to get her practice started, without being able to repay it. She admitted she was afraid someone wanted to drive her out of town. When it was over, Cathy felt as though she'd just completed a three-hour emergency operation.

"Would you like a glass of water . . . a soft drink?" he asked.

"Water, please." She gulped greedily from the bottle Will handed her. "Wow, I'd hate to have you cross-examine me. I usually don't even open up this much to my — I mean, I think you did a great job of getting the information you need and a lot more. I hope you'll forgive me for dumping like that."

He ignored her comment and scanned his notes. Cathy counted the pages as he flipped through them: twenty-four. She wondered why she'd been so comfortable confiding in Will. She'd felt secure, the way she'd felt in his arms back when — Never mind. Bad idea to even think about the past.

"So, what would you advise?"

"About the insurance company? Since that was where you started, I presume that's the situation where you need my help. Right?"

She nodded.

He took in a deep breath through his nose and let it out through pursed lips. "Did you receive any kind of notice from the insurance company that your policy was about to lapse for nonpayment?"

"It went to my old address. It eventually got forwarded, but I didn't get it until after the accident."

"Had you notified the insurance company of your address change?"

"Yes. I know I did. I still have the list of all my notifications."

He closed his eyes, steepled his fingers, and leaned back in his chair. "We might

72

eventually get the insurance company to pay, but there may be a better way. This whole thing started with the bank's error. Let me try there first."

"What can we expect from them?"

"If the bank contacts the insurance company and admits it was at fault in failing to honor the check, maybe we can get the company to reinstate the policy. Of course, since that would result in their being liable for several thousand dollars in damage to your car, there likely would be something of a fight. If the insurance company refuses to pay, we could always sue the bank."

Cathy made a conscious effort to unclench her teeth. "No. You can't imagine how hard it was for me to get Nix and the bank to loan me enough to start my practice."

"How much?" Will asked.

It made her a little sick at her stomach to say the words. "Seventy thousand dollars. Due in a year — actually, nine months from now. I don't want to do anything to put that in jeopardy."

"So —"

"Look," Cathy said, "I can't call up Nix and say, 'Oh, by the way, it's your fault my car insurance wasn't in effect when I ran off the road, so if you don't pony up five or six thousand dollars for the damages, I'll sue you.' I just can't do that."

"What's so special about Nix? So he loaned you money. That's his business. But how do you know he's not the one who made sure the check bounced? There might be a reason he'd want to hurt you."

Cathy couldn't believe she hadn't thought of this before. Wasn't Robert's father on the board of a bank in Dallas? Could there be a connection between him and Nix? What if Nix took steps to assure that Cathy's insurance lapsed, then arranged an accident that totaled her car? So what if she defaulted on her loan? In a bank that size, the loss would be almost insignificant. Still, she couldn't imagine Milton Nix doing something so underhanded. In her mind, she'd always considered bankers to be trustworthy. Anyone responsible for such large sums of money had to be honest and dependable. Maybe she had been naïve.

She shook her head. "All I know is that he loaned me money when no one else would, and now he's a patient of mine. If there's anyway to avoid it, I don't want to involve him in this mess."

Will leaned forward and gently touched her hand. "And that's why I'll help."

"I'm still worried about paying for all this."

"Do you have a dollar?"

Automatically, Cathy pulled her wallet from her purse. Then she looked up and frowned. "Why?"

"Just give it to me."

She handed it over.

Will stowed the bill in his wallet. "Okay, that was mostly symbolic, but it makes most people feel better. Now you've officially engaged my services. We've established an attorney-client relationship. I can act on your behalf in legal matters, and the first thing I intend to do is talk with Ella Mae Mercer."

"Who?"

"You probably don't remember her. Her maiden name was Ella Mae Becker. Married Ken Mercer right out of high school. Eventually, she figured the wife of a mechanic wasn't about to climb very high in the social ladder in Dainger, especially when he spent most of his nights working on cars in his backyard and all his weekends drinking beer."

"And what does — ?"

Will held up his hand. "Patience. It gets better. Ella Mae divorced Ken, got a job at the bank as a teller, and worked her way up to Vice President. Nix may be the President of the bank, but Ella Mae Mercer carries a lot of weight. Let me have a talk with her. We'll see if she'll contact the insurance company and talk sweet reason with them."

"Will Mr. Nix go along with her?"

"If you believe the rumors around town, she's either the one who runs the bank or the one who runs Nix. Opinions are divided." Will's grin carried as much information as his words.

Cathy's cheeks warmed. "Oh." She cleared her throat. "I hope you can get her to help."

"I'll let you know." He scanned his notes. "Now, what about getting your privileges approved at the hospital?"

"Sorry that came out. Guess I needed to vent." She squared her shoulders. "I'm a big girl. I need to fight my own fights, but I don't have any leverage with the insurance company. I'm glad to hear that you may be able to help there." She pulled out her checkbook. "You wouldn't tell me your fee schedule, but I'm sure you want more than a dollar for a retainer. How much?"

"If you don't want to barter — a thousand dollars."

Cathy's heart jumped into her throat. "I . . . I can't . . . I mean . . ."

"Or we can make a trade. Have lunch with

me on Sunday."

A dozen responses rushed through her head, but the one that won the day came from her heart. "I guess this is why you always were the best debater in school. I hope you're this good when you talk with Ella Mae. What time and where?"

"I'll pick you up at ten-thirty."

"Why so early?"

"We don't want to be late for church. We'll be going there first." He grinned. "But it will be worth it. Mom's fried chicken is the best you've ever tasted. She and Dad will be so glad to see you. You've been gone too long."

4

Cathy hesitated in the doorway of the hospital conference room until she caught Marcus Bell's eye. He pointed to the far corner, away from the table where the committee members were seated. She eased into the chair and looked around, wondering if one of the physicians assembled here tonight was responsible for the harassment. Maybe after the meeting she'd have a better idea.

Marcus tapped his water glass with a spoon. Conversation died down, coffee cups were pushed away, and six men looked expectantly toward the head of the table. Marcus took a sip of water. "I guess we'd better get this meeting underway."

Cathy let her eyes roam around the long table, putting names with faces. At the head of the table, Marcus, as Chief of Staff, was the chair of the Credentials and Privileges Committee of Summers County General Hospital. There were six other members, but Cathy had already been told that votes were generally swayed by the opinions of two men: Dr. John Steel and Dr. Arthur Harshman. They were seated opposite each other. Somehow, the positioning seemed right to Cathy.

Steel was middle-aged, a bit portly, and casually dressed. He had an easy air and seemed to smile freely. Cathy had referred several cases to Steel and considered him a competent surgeon who cared about his patients. He, in turn, had recommended her to some of his patients who were looking for a family practitioner. Their relationship had been good to this point. She hoped it wouldn't change because her request included privileges for appendectomies and a few other surgical procedures.

Harshman was a different kettle of fish — a cold fish, actually. He looked to be about sixty, with a touch of gray at the temples of his coal-black hair. Whereas Steel wore a sport shirt and slacks, Harshman was dressed in a dark blue suit that fitted his spare frame as though custom-tailored. When he removed his steel-rimmed glasses to clean them with a spotless handkerchief, Cathy thought his eyes looked like ice before the spring thaw.

Despite trying not to let Karen Pearson's

tales about Harshman influence her opinion of the man, Cathy found herself vacillating between fear and dislike. There seemed to be no question among his colleagues about Harshman's professional capabilities, but the way he dealt with patients was the subject of constant gossip around the hospital. Cathy's dealings with him had been limited to a few words exchanged in the doctors' lounge. She had no idea what to expect from him in response to her request for privileges to perform deliveries.

The other men around the table represented a cross-section of the physicians in the community: an internist, a pediatrician, a radiologist. The last member of the committee was Dr. Ernest Gladstone, the family practitioner whose impending retirement had sent a trickle of new patients to Cathy. He'd been mildly cordial in their limited dealings so far. Cathy hoped he wouldn't be put off by her desire to go beyond what he'd done in his own practice.

Marcus opened the meeting with the usual boilerplate: acceptance of the minutes of the last meeting, voting to renew privileges of various staff members, accepting the resignation of several doctors who were retiring. Cathy was surprised that Gladstone's name wasn't on that list. Maybe he wanted to leave the door open in case he got bored with retirement.

"Now we come to the application of Dr. Cathy Sewell for staff membership and privileges. You've all received a copy of the relevant forms. In addition to the usual privileges granted to family practice specialists, Dr. Sewell has requested additional privileges in surgery and OB. You'll note that, in support of her request, she's provided letters from the heads of those departments at the University of Texas Southwestern Medical Center, where she did her residency training." Marcus uncapped a fresh bottle of water and drank before continuing. "What is the pleasure of the committee?"

So that was it? No introduction of her to the group? No chance for her to speak? She started to open her mouth, but a glance from Marcus and an expression that said, "Trust me," made her lean back in her chair and remain silent.

"I think we're extraordinarily lucky to have someone with these qualifications practicing in Dainger." John Steel squared the stack of papers before him. "I'd suggest that we grant all the privileges requested, with the stipulation that Dr. Sewell allow one of our surgeons to scrub as an unpaid

81

observer on her first three cases and one of our obstetricians to observe her first three deliveries."

Cathy took a deep breath. One hurdle down. If the surgeon supported her, that could only help.

"I'm totally opposed to granting obstetric privileges of any kind to someone other than a board-certified specialist." Harshman's nasal voice cut through the room, and Cathy's heart skipped a beat. He turned to look directly at her. "Doctor, I'm sure you did a fine job on the uncomplicated deliveries they let you do under supervision during your training, but obstetrics can be like flying — boredom interspersed at times with moments of stark terror. You never know when you'll be dealing with a placenta praevia or an abruptio placenta."

"Ease up, Arthur." Dr. Gladstone's rich baritone carried a note of authority that Cathy found surprising. "You've gotten too used to old coots like me doing family practice. The world is changing. In case you haven't noticed, the 'kindly old GP' has been replaced by the board-certified family practitioner. These men — and women — have been trained to do a great deal more than I ever did. Why don't you follow John's example? Give her the privileges, observe her first three deliveries?"

"Never." Harshman's visage was like pink marble, cold and unmoving.

The discussion continued for another fifteen minutes. Each time Cathy started to defend herself, Marcus silenced her with a look or a gesture. Finally, Dr. Gladstone called the question, and the matter was put to a vote.

"The motion is for Dr. Cathy Sewell to be granted staff membership, with privileges for all the procedures she has requested, but with the following stipulations: a member of the surgical staff is to observe her first three operations and a member of the obstetrics staff will observe her first three deliveries. All in favor, raise your hand."

Three hands went up: Gladstone, Steel, and the pediatrician.

"Opposed?"

Three other hands went up: Harshman, the internist, and the radiologist.

"The chair declines to break the tie. Let's table this request and re-vote on granting standard family practice privileges."

The motion was quickly made and seconded. It passed five to one, with Harshman still dissenting.

"Dr. Sewell, welcome to the staff." Marcus extended his hand, and there was a mild smattering of applause.

Cathy shook the hands that were offered, nodded coldly to Marcus, and left the room, still smarting. Why hadn't he broken the tie? And why hadn't he let her defend herself? She had depended on him, and he'd let her down. Just like Robert. Just like Carter. Just like Daddy.

Cathy sat at the table in her landlady's kitchen and cut into a steaming biscuit.

"Well, look at you. Pretty as a picture." Bess Elam stood in the doorway, drying her hands on her apron. "Going to church today?"

Cathy lowered the two biscuit halves onto the plate in front of her, looked at her landlady, and calculated what she could tell her without starting rumors that would spread through Dainger like a measles epidemic. She decided on a partial truth. "That's right. I'll be attending the First Community Church."

"Glad to hear it. Pastor Kennedy is a wonderful preacher. Sometimes we sneak over to hear him when our own pastor's out of town."

Cathy picked up the biscuit again and buttered it. "I hope you don't mind. You told me yesterday to come over this morning and

84

help myself. They smelled so good I couldn't resist."

"Not at all. You shouldn't have to eat Sunday breakfast by yourself over in that garage apartment. Let me pour you some coffee to go with it."

Soon the two women were seated at the kitchen table with coffee in front of them. Cathy applied a dab of Bess's homemade boysenberry jam and popped the last bit of biscuit into her mouth. The sweet flavor of fresh berries lingered on her tongue until she washed it away with a sip of coffee.

"Do you remember how to get to the church?" Bess asked.

"Yes, but someone's giving me a ride."

"Oh? Who would — ?"

The sound of the doorbell stopped Bess in mid-sentence. Cathy felt her pulse quicken. Could she manage to slip out before Bess saw Will? Cathy pushed back her chair, but Bess was already at the door, opening it.

"Will Kennedy? You come in this house and have some coffee and a biscuit." She buried him in a hug before turning back to Cathy. "Is this your ride to church?"

Judging by the burning in her cheeks, Cathy had wasted the blusher she applied that morning. "Yes, he is."

Will smiled at Cathy. "I knocked on your door, but there was no answer, so I thought I'd check Bess's kitchen. Glad I did. I'll take a rain check on that biscuit, Bess. You and Joe doing okay?"

"Fine and dandy. Now you take good care of Dr. Cathy. She's my star renter, and she'll be my doctor if I ever need anything. Now that Joe and I have a good doctor, a good lawyer, and a good preacher, I guess we don't need anything else."

Will had parked his pickup at the curb. He held the door for Cathy, a gesture she thought died with the advent of the women's movement.

"Thank you," she murmured.

Since almost every place in Dainger was no more than twenty minutes from any other place, the ride to the church was short. Will filled the time with comments like, "That's the old Henderson place. They're both in a rest home now, and their kids are selling it."

Cathy glanced at the Bible on the front seat between them. "I'm sorry I didn't bring my Bible this morning. I'm afraid there are still some boxes I haven't unpacked, and it must be in one of them. I keep hoping that my practice will take off and I'll be able to get a house instead of renting the apartment

86

over the Elam's garage."

"I can understand your not unpacking everything, but I hope you'll dig out your Bible soon. I think you'll find it helpful in dealing with the stress you're under right now."

Cathy flinched. *Here we go. Pressure me into church, then give me the lecture about how terrible it is that I haven't been on great terms with God since my parents died. God let me down then, and so far as I'm concerned, it's up to Him to make the first move.*

To Cathy's surprise, Will switched the topic back to local gossip. After a few minutes, she relaxed.

Will guided her gently through the parking lot, stopping to shake hands and exchange hugs with what seemed like half the folks there. Once through the doors, she started toward the church sanctuary, but Will stopped her with a hand on her arm. "No, let's go here first."

She followed him down a hall to an open door marked Pastor's Study. He tapped at the door and then motioned Cathy in.

Looking at Matthew Kennedy standing next to his son, Cathy could imagine what Will would look like someday. Both men stood a shade over six feet and were slim but muscular. The primary difference, aside from the few wrinkles Pastor Kennedy had developed since Cathy last saw him, was that the elder Kennedy's thick head of hair had turned silver-white, while Will's was jet black. Other than that, the men might have been brothers.

The pastor took Cathy's hand in both of his. "It's so good to see you again. I was so sorry about your father and mother. I'd hoped to speak with you after their service but never had the chance." His blue eyes reflected the sincerity behind the words.

"Thank you. That was a tough time. I guess I wanted to put Dainger behind me as quickly as I could after the funeral."

"No matter. You're back now, and we're so glad you're here this morning. I hope you find the service helpful. And Dora and I are thrilled that you and Will are having lunch with us today. Once you've had her fried chicken, you'll never want any of that stuff The Colonel serves."

Cathy tried not to compare the handful of patients she'd seen this morning to what she'd ordinarily see in the family practice clinic at the medical school on a typical Monday. She guessed some doctors would probably be happy to carry such a light caseload. But those doctors didn't have bills stacking up and the bank breathing down their necks.

Jane looked up as Cathy passed the front desk. "How was your weekend?"

"Not bad."

"Heard you attended First Community Church with Will Kennedy. How did you like the service?"

Cathy shook her head. "Between you and my landlady, is there anything that happens in Dainger that you don't know about?"

Jane shrugged. "How did your lunch with the Kennedys go? What did you think of Dora's fried chicken?"

What was it with the chicken? "Lunch was fine. The chicken was probably the best I've ever tasted, and can we please get on with the day?"

"Sure. Your phone messages are on your desk." Jane paused long enough for Cathy to reach the doorway to her office before asking, "Do you plan to see Will again?"

Cathy ignored the question. She closed the office door firmly, slumped behind the desk, and tried to turn her attention to the three pink message slips.

The first call was from a patient exhibiting typical symptoms of the flu. He wanted to "come by for a shot of penicillin." Cathy finally convinced him to come into the office that morning and let her check him over. She knew that if her phone diagnosis turned out to be correct, antibiotics would have no effect on the disease. However, one of the new antivirals might shorten the course of the illness. She made a mental note to recommend flu vaccine to her patients. The season appeared to be starting early.

The second call came from a mother who was worried about her child's diarrhea. There had been numerous cases of rotavirus in the community, and Cathy figured this was probably another one. However, after giving the mother detailed instructions, she encouraged her to call back if the symptoms continued or worsened. She hated to give phone advice, but the mother convinced her there was no way she could bring the child to the office. Besides, Cathy knew the expense would represent a real hardship for the struggling family.

She made notes on the two pink slips and put them in her out box so Jane could file them in the patient charts. Then she saw the name on the third slip: Will Kennedy. Was this about yesterday?

She'd expected a hard sell from Will's parents. Come back to church. Get right with God. Instead, Pastor and Mrs. Kennedy had seemed genuinely glad to see her, making no mention of the way she'd pulled away from the church. Will had confined his remarks to reminiscences of the good times they'd had in high school. He steered clear of any mention of how they drifted apart after they went off to different colleges. She'd started medical school, he'd begun law school, and their lives had diverged even further.

She should return his call. There was an unfamiliar fluttering in her stomach as she pulled the phone toward her, lifted the receiver, and punched in the number. To her surprise, the next voice she heard was Will's.

"Will Kennedy."

"Will, this is Cathy. I expected to get your secretary."

"This is my private line. I hope you'll write it down and use it in the future. After hours, I forward it to my cell phone. I don't want to miss a call from you. Let's not lose touch again."

She felt the same shiver she'd experienced the first time Will had asked her to a high school dance. No doubt about it. Once he'd recognized her, Will's attention at the crash site went beyond being a Good Samaritan. Maybe he'd gotten over the way she'd hurt him in the past. A part of her was thrilled at the prospect of rekindling their relationship. But then the little voice in her head whispered, *You can't trust a man. You can't trust anyone.*

Will's voice cut into her thoughts. "Cathy, did you hear me?"

Cathy pulled Will's business card from beneath the edge of her blotter. She turned it over and transcribed the number from the pink slip to the back of the card. "Thanks. I'm writing it down right now."

"Good."

"Now what's up?" Cathy asked.

"First of all, I had a wonderful time with you yesterday. My folks told me to invite you for Sunday lunch anytime you're free."

"I enjoyed it too."

"But let me get to the business at hand. After you were in my office last week, I went down to the bank and talked with Ella Mae. She called me first thing this morning to report. I don't know how she did it, and I wasn't about to ask, but she talked with one of the higher-ups in your insurance company. Apparently, she was pretty convincing. The deal she worked out is that the insurance company and the bank's liability insurer will split the payment for the damages to your car. You'll be getting both checks within a couple of weeks."

"Will, that's wonderful."

"There's more. I'm a full-service attorney, after all."

Cathy struggled to process the news. "You're amazing. What else have you done?"

"I called James Wood Motors and talked with James. If you'll go by the dealership sometime this week and pick out a car, he'll apply the total of the two checks you're getting against the price. That'll be a pretty hefty down payment on your new one. And he'll forgive the charges on the rental car."

"Better and better. Thanks so much."

"James promised me he'd give you a great deal, but be sure to let me see the papers before you sign anything. He kind of owes me a favor or two and I'm not above asking him to sweeten the deal even more."

It was as though someone had piped pure oxygen into the room. Cathy's head was clearer. The tension in her neck and shoulders eased. Maybe things were looking up. She had a fleeting thought that apparently everyone in Dainger owed Will a favor. She'd have to keep that in mind.

"Thanks," she said. "I believe you mentioned that my having lunch with you would cover your retainer. How much do I really owe you for this?"

"For talking with Ella Mae, you couldn't afford my services. But I'll settle for another lunch next Sunday."

Cathy didn't hesitate. And it wasn't merely the thought of Dora Kennedy's fried chicken that made the decision easy. "Of course." Then Will's comment about Ella Mae registered. "But why was it such a chore to talk with this woman?"

"Because she feels it's her duty to make a play for every man she sees. I think it's sort of a reflex. But maybe you already know that."

Cathy wondered what she'd missed. "I have no idea what you're talking about. Why would I know?"

"Oh." That single syllable from Will brought a picture into Cathy's mind: Will, his cheeks reddening and his hands moving to cover his mouth after saying something he shouldn't. She'd seen it dozens of times when they were teenagers.

"Will, what did you mean?"

"Nothing. Nothing at all. Hey, I'm due in court in fifteen minutes. Got to run. I'll call you later."

Cathy hung up the phone just as Jane stuck her head through the door. "Your first patient is here."

Outside the exam room, Cathy looked at

94

the name neatly lettered in heavy black letters on the tab of the thin manila folder:
Ella Mae Mercer. What were the odds?

5

When Cathy opened the door to the exam room, she thought the woman sitting there would be what one might get after a call to central casting to order up a bank executive. Model-thin, perfectly done makeup, straight black hair cut short and expertly styled. The woman wore a tailored Gucci suit. Glasses with frames by a name designer did little to hide calculating green eyes. No doubt about it. Ella Mae Mercer's presence was intimidating.

"Ms. Mercer? I'm Dr. Cathy Sewell. How can I help you?"

The woman rose gracefully from the straight chair in the corner of the examining room, unfolding her thin frame like a carpenter's rule and extending a hand with rings on three fingers. "Please, it's Ella Mae. I feel as though I've known you for ages, after hearing all about you from your father."

"That's nice to know. And let me thank you for what you've arranged about paying for the damage to my car."

Ella Mae waved off the thanks as though it were a fly. "Don't make me out to be altruistic. Will made it plain to me that if I couldn't make this work, he was prepared to file suit against both the bank and the insurance company. And, unfortunately, I could see that we were at fault."

"I still appreciate what you did. How did you make it work out?"

Ella Mae ticked off the points on her manicured fingers. "I was able to convince your insurance company that, if Will filed suit against them, they might end up being liable for the whole amount. After all, they'd failed to notify you in a timely fashion that you were into the grace period. Of course, I conveniently neglected to remind them that the initial error was ours."

"But that's —"

"It's called business, dear. Anyway, we carry liability coverage, and I was able to negotiate a settlement where our insurance carrier would share the burden. Long story short, you'll get two checks that will cover the damages. You'll sign a waiver, and everyone's happy." She shrugged. "Besides, I owed Will a favor."

Cathy's first impulse was to follow up on that remark. Had Will dated this woman? Was he still seeing her? And why should Cathy care, anyway? But she found that she did. Nevertheless, she moved on with her questions.

The new patient history form showed a chief complaint of "prescription refill." Cathy's eyes strayed over the rest of the form. Medications? Just a few: vitamins, hormones, and a commonly prescribed tranquilizer. One guess which of those Ella Mae wanted refilled.

"So how can I help you?" Cathy asked.

"I'm looking for a family doctor, and I believe I'd be more comfortable with a female, especially one who seems young enough to be knowledgeable about modern techniques."

"Fair enough. Can we ask your previous doctor for copies of your medical records? That way, I won't repeat tests needlessly, and it will help me get a better feel for your general health."

The temperature in the room seemed to drop. "No, let's start fresh."

"Why?"

Ella Mae ignored the question, and Cathy decided this woman was an old hand at the maneuver. "Why don't we do this? I'll make an appointment to come back for a full physical examination, including all the tests you might want, but it will have to be in a couple of weeks. This is a hectic time at the bank right now. That's one reason I'm here today. I need a new prescription for this." She held out an empty amber pill bottle bearing a label from a pharmacy in a neighboring town. "I haven't taken them in some time, but in the past they've helped me through some stressful periods, and I need them right now."

Cathy turned the bottle slowly in her hands, recognizing the name of the tranquilizer Ella Mae had listed among her medications. "I'm hesitant to prescribe these without any knowledge of your medical status, Ms. Mercer."

"Oh, don't give me the doctor-speak." Ella Mae's smile was obviously meant to take any sting out of the words. "I know that these are commonly prescribed, there are few if any contraindications to their proper use, they don't interact with the hormones and vitamins I take, and they're metabolized by the liver." She gestured at her spare frame. "I don't drink. I don't do drugs. And do I look like someone in liver failure? See any bulging belly? Are the whites of my eyes jaundiced?"

Cathy resisted the urge to argue. The woman was probably right. There really wasn't any medical contraindication to giving her a reasonable number of the pills, contingent on her return for a full physical within a couple of weeks. And Ella Mae had been more than helpful in resolving Cathy's problem with the insurance company. Cathy's mentor during her family practice residency had been clear about what to do at a time like this — a time when it wasn't prudent to put up a large fight to win a small battle.

Without further argument, Cathy reached for a prescription pad and carefully wrote out the prescription. "I'm giving you two weeks' worth. That's enough to allow you time to schedule a full physical examination. And please call if you experience any untoward side effects."

"May I have that bottle back? I use the empty ones to hold buttons."

After Ella Mae left, Cathy stood leaning against the examining table for a long moment. The woman didn't strike her as the type who saved buttons. No, she wanted that bottle back because she didn't want anyone else to see the information on it. But what had startled Cathy wasn't the name of the medication, nor the fact that

Ella Mae had driven to the next town to have the prescription filled. What got Cathy's attention was the name of the prescribing doctor: Nolan Sewell.

Josh leaned forward in his chair and said, "Let's talk about what brought you back to Dainger."

Cathy squirmed, not because her own chair was uncomfortable, but because Josh's question brought back unpleasant memories. It was as though someone had given an extra tug at the shroud of depression that had been wrapped about her for the past several months. She reached for the carafe and tumbler on the end table, poured half a glass, and drank.

"Take your time." Josh appeared in no hurry, but apparently this was the direction their session would take today, and no amount of stalling would change that. "Tell me about Bob."

"Robert," Cathy corrected automatically. "Robert Edward Newell. Never Bob. Bob would be common, and Robert would rather die than be common." She swallowed. "Robert's a year older than me. We met when he was in the last year of an ophthalmology residency. I was completing my family practice training. We were at

Parkland Hospital at the same time. I fell for him immediately. He was absolutely charming. His family had money, and the way he dressed and acted showed it. He was sophisticated and self-assured. I felt . . . I don't know. I guess I felt secure with him."

"And you became engaged."

"Yes. It seemed like love at first sight. We decided to get married in July, after we finished our residencies. He planned to set up a practice in Dallas and draw from the upper crust in Highland Park. I was slated to join a multispecialty group in North Dallas, but then I got an invitation to stay on at the medical school as Assistant Professor in the Family Practice Department."

"How did Robert feel about that?"

"He was thrilled. A wife on the med school faculty. A society practice. It was perfect for him."

"So what changed your mind?"

Cathy thought back to that day, and she felt her stomach clench like a fist. "Robert wanted me to move in with him. At first I was naïve enough to think he just wanted me to save money on rent, but he had more in mind than that. I said no."

"Why?"

"Guilt? Fear? I'm not sure. My parents made sure I attended church as a child, and

I guess a lot of it rubbed off on me. It didn't seem right. But more than that, I didn't want sex to be the only reason we were together. I couldn't let our marriage start out that way."

"How did he react?" Josh asked.

"I thought he accepted it. In retrospect, maybe he just made other plans."

Josh displayed a perfect poker face. No judgment, no taking sides. His expression invited her to continue.

"One night I dropped by Robert's apartment unannounced. I'd had a wonderful day and wanted to share the stories with him. I rang the doorbell, but there was no answer. His car was outside, so I knew he was home. I rang again. Then I knocked . . . knocked again . . . and again. Finally the door opened." She squeezed her eyes shut, but the film continued to run in the projector of her mind. "But it wasn't Robert. It was Carrie, one of the nurses in the Parkland operating room. She had on the robe I'd given Robert for Christmas. Her hair was a mess, her lipstick smeared. I barged past her and saw Robert coming out of the bedroom, buttoning his shirt."

"And?"

Cathy opened her eyes and looked at Josh. "He said, 'This isn't what you think.' But it was. I knew exactly what it was."

Josh nodded a fraction of an inch.

Cathy finished the water in her glass. "I pulled off my engagement ring and threw it on the floor. Then I went back to my apartment and cried all night. The next morning I went to the head of the family practice department and told him I couldn't stay in Dallas."

"Did you hear from Robert?"

"He called, but I wouldn't answer. He sent me flowers, and I threw them in the garbage. He wrote letters, but I wrote 'Return to Sender' on the envelopes and dropped them back in the mail."

Cathy leaned back, exhausted. Why did Josh insist on dragging out all these hurtful memories? Her father, Carter, Robert. She tried to make her mind go blank. She wanted to escape, but instead the synapses clicked to make the awful connection. Self-assured, larger than life, someone she could depend on. And they'd let her down. Every one of them.

She looked up at Josh, and it was as though he could read her mind — see the way she'd connected the dots.

He uncrossed his legs and stood. "Think about that. I'll see you next week."

Cathy was surprised at the name on the chart of the next patient. Could this be Dr. Gladstone's wife? Cathy always got a bit antsy when treating the family of another doctor. There was a saying in medicine: complications only happen to nice patients and doctors' families. She hoped it wouldn't hold true here. She took a deep breath and opened the door to the treatment room. "Mrs. Gladstone, it's a pleasure to meet you. How may I help you?"

The older woman sitting in the patient chair beside the examination table was plainly but neatly dressed. Her silver hair was perfectly styled. The lenses of her rimless glasses had a slight pink tint, but that didn't hide the worry in her eyes.

"I've been having some female problems. Dr. Baker has been my doctor for years, but he doesn't do any gynecology. Besides that . . ." She managed to look both demure and embarrassed. "Besides that, I've always thought I'd be more comfortable with a woman doctor."

Cathy was a bit unsettled that her gender apparently had figured into the decision more than her professional abilities. Nevertheless, she simply nodded and began taking Mrs. Gladstone's history. "Why don't you tell me specifically what symptoms you've been having and when they started?"

Just then, Jane tapped on the open door. "Excuse me, Doctor, but you have an emergency call."

Cathy excused herself and hurried to her office. She punched the blinking button on her phone. "Dr. Sewell."

"Doctor, this is Glenna Dunn in the ER. Your patient, Milton Nix, is here. He's complaining of weakness and nausea. His pulse is irregular, and his blood pressure is all over the place."

Cathy's mind kicked into full diagnostic mode. This could represent any one of several things, some of them extremely serious. "Draw blood for electrolytes, sugar, BUN. And get a digitalis level. Do an EKG. I'm on my way."

On her way back to the exam room, Cathy asked Jane to get Milton Nix's chart for her. "Mrs. Gladstone, I'm terribly sorry. I have an emergency. Would you like to wait, or can we reschedule your visit?"

"It's all right. I quite understand about emergencies. You'll never know how many dinners I've eaten alone because of them. It will be fine to —"

"Jane," Cathy called. "Would you schedule Mrs. Gladstone back as soon as possible? Tomorrow if it works for her. A new patient exam including a pelvic. I have to go."

In less than five minutes, Cathy strode into the ER of Summers County General Hospital. A nurse intercepted her and introduced herself as Glenna Dunn. "He's in here," she said, directing Cathy into Treatment Room One. Cathy hesitated at the door, recalling the last time she'd been in this room. But this time she was in charge.

Milton Nix lay sweating on a gurney, his shirt off. An IV ran in his right arm, and a blood pressure cuff encircled his left. A cardiac monitor above his head showed a green line of complexes racing across the screen.

A buxom bottle-blonde, presumably Nix's wife, leaned over him, fanning him with a magazine. She was younger than her husband, but makeup and expensive clothes made it difficult for Cathy to tell just how much. She guessed there'd been a number of nips and tucks in the woman's past.

"Mr. Nix, tell me about it." Cathy took the clipboard from Glenna and scanned the scant information. "When did you get sick? What are you feeling?"

Mrs. Nix opened her mouth, but Nix silenced her with a look. "I've been off my feed for a week or so," he said. "No appetite. Food didn't taste good. Today I vomited several times. And I seem to be getting weaker all the time."

"Anything else?"

"It's sort of funny, but my eyes have been acting up. Everything looks sort of yellow. And lights have halos around them. I sort of figured I might be getting cataracts."

Cathy turned to Glenna. "Is that digitalis level back?"

"No, that takes a while to run. We do have the chemistries, though." She pulled a sheaf of lab slips from her pocket and handed them to Cathy.

One value jumped out at Cathy immediately. Nix's potassium was high. That went along with her presumptive diagnosis — digitalis intoxication. Cathy remembered Nix's medications included a beta-blocker, which would increase his digitalis blood level a bit. But to get symptoms like this he'd have to be taking much larger doses than she'd prescribed.

"Mr. Nix, have you been taking your digitalis the way I prescribed?" she asked.

"Of course. I'm not fool enough to pay a doctor for advice and then ignore it. I did just what you said, even when you had me taking twice as many as Doc Gladstone did."

That couldn't be right. She was certain she'd written for one tablet a day, a direct switch from Lanoxin to generic digoxin. But there would be time to look into that later. Right now, she had to lower Nix's digitalis level. "Glenna, see if the pharmacy has any Digibind."

"Digi- what?"

"Digibind. It's an IV preparation. Lowers digitalis levels. It may take five or ten vials. Get as much as they have. Stat, please!"

Glenna hurried away, and Cathy turned to Mrs. Nix. "I need your husband's prescription bottles. Would you get them for me?"

"Me? Now?" The woman seemed shocked. Undoubtedly, she'd long ago become accustomed to being waited on.

"Yes, now," Cathy said. "And hurry."

Mrs. Nix opened her mouth, but before she could say a word her husband snapped out, "Gail, do it!" She snatched up her purse and scurried from the room without a word.

Glenna almost bumped into Mrs. Nix in the doorway. She held up three small boxes. "The hospital pharmacy only had three vials. And they said it's really, really expensive. Are you sure you want to give it?"

Cathy hesitated. She didn't have a digitalis level to prove her diagnosis. On the other hand, the longer she waited, the more chance that Nix would get into real trouble, probably a rhythm disturbance of the heart. She had to act.

"Yes, give the first vial IV now. There's a special filter you have to use. It should be in the box."

Glenna set to work preparing the infusion.

"Who's the internist on call?" Cathy asked.

Glenna didn't look up from her work. "Dr. Baker. Shall I call him?"

Evan Baker, one of the doctors who had voted with Harshman against her. Cathy didn't want to give him a chance to see her possibly make a mistake, but protocol dictated that she call him in. She hoped her diagnosis was right — not only for Nix's sake, but for her own.

"Yes, please call Dr. Baker, but get the Digibind running first. It should go in over about half an hour. Follow it with another unless I tell you otherwise. I hope we'll have the digitalis levels back by then."

Cathy turned back to her patient. "Mr. Nix, you've got too much digitalis in your system. I need to reverse it before it causes problems with —"

Her eyes were drawn to the cardiac monitor as the pattern became more erratic, then the complexes settled into a rapid rate of almost two hundred beats per minute. Ventricular tachycardia. At that rate, there wasn't time enough for the heart to fill and empty efficiently. The coronary arteries would be starved for blood. If she didn't reverse it quickly, Nix would die.

Cathy opened the cabinet behind her and snatched out the material to start another IV, this one in Nix's left arm. As soon as it was in and running wide open, she snapped the top off a glass vial of Lidocaine and drew the contents into a large syringe. "I'm giving you something in your vein to slow your heart rate." Slowly, carefully, she injected the contents of the vial. No change in the heart tracing. Should she give amiodarone? No, not yet. Too toxic to risk it right now.

Glenna hurried back into the room. "The ward clerk's paging Dr. Baker."

"Good. Now I need your help. Mr. Nix has gone into V-tach. Get ready for a cardioversion."

"Doctor, I don't think you have privileges for that."

Cathy didn't have time to argue medical niceties. Seconds were precious. Still, she was pleased at how even her voice was. "Until Dr. Baker gets here, it's up to me to handle this. Set up the defibrillator."

Glenna quickly moved the crash cart to Nix's side. She whipped off the yellow plastic cover and prepared the defibrillator.

Once Cathy was sure the defib apparatus was ready, she bent over Nix, who lay on the gurney, sweating and pale. She tried to sound reassuring. "Mr. Nix, your heart rate is dangerously high. The way to slow it down is by delivering a shock. You'll feel a jolt, probably a brief pain. But it's necessary. Do I have your permission?"

Nix's voice trembled. "Anything, Doc. Do what you have to."

Cathy had done three or four of these in residency, always under supervision, always with a cardiologist looking over her shoulder. Now she needed an angel over her shoulder. *Please, God, let it work.*

How much? She searched her memory for the right setting. A hundred? No, not enough. She took the paddles from Glenna, slapped them together to spread the conductive gel. "Two hundred joules."

Glenna turned the dial.

Cathy pressed the "Charge" button on the

right paddle. Her voice was strong. "Clear."

Glenna stepped away. Cathy made sure she wasn't touching the table. She put the paddles on Nix's chest, said, "Brace yourself," and pushed the "Discharge" button on the left paddle.

Nix jumped and fell back, limp and sweating.

The complexes slowed, sputtered like a car burning low-test gas, then resumed their race.

"Three hundred joules."

Glenna's voice was full of doubt. "Are you sure?"

Cathy hoped she was. "Yes. Just do it."

Again Glenna adjusted the dial. Cathy went through the routine and applied the current.

This time when Nix relaxed back onto the table, he appeared so lifeless Cathy was afraid she'd killed him. But when she looked up at the monitor, she saw a beautiful sight: normal complexes running across the screen at a rate of seventy-eight per minute.

"What's going on?" Evan Baker stood in the doorway, filling the room with his commanding presence.

Cathy had made reports like this so many times during residency she was a pro at it. "Doctor Baker, Mr. Nix came in with ap-

113

parent digitalis intoxication. His potassium is up, but the digitalis level isn't back. I made a clinical diagnosis and started Digibind. He went into V-tach, unresponsive to Lidocaine. I cardioverted him, and he reverted to normal sinus rhythm after 300 joules."

Baker made no reply. He looked over the chart, asked a few questions, and listened to the patient's heart. Slowly, he folded his stethoscope and jammed it into the pocket of his suit coat before turning to Cathy. "I trust you realize that FP's don't have privileges for cardioversion."

Before Cathy could speak, the ward clerk hurried in waving a lab report slip. Baker snatched it from her, looked at it, and handed it to Cathy. "But I'm glad you were here. The digitalis level is 5.2."

Nix mumbled, "Is that — ?"

"It's a toxic level, almost twice normal," Baker said. "And you're fortunate that Dr. Sewell treated you as she did." His next words made Cathy cringe. "Now, we have to find out how this happened."

Cathy nodded. She appreciated Baker's diplomatic choice of words in the presence of the patient. What he really meant was, "Who committed this act of malpractice?"

Unfortunately, she already knew the answer to that question.

6

Cathy squirmed. Not because the chair across from Marcus Bell's desk was uncomfortable. She'd sat in worse. But she'd never been in a more uncomfortable situation than this.

Marcus picked up Milton Nix's chart that Jane had hand-delivered less than an hour earlier. He opened it and read silently for a moment. "So, how do you think this happened?"

Cathy squared her shoulders and sat up straighter. Time to take her medicine. "Mrs. Nix brought me the pill bottle. The label said, 'Digoxin, 0.25 mg. tabs. Sig: 2 tabs q day.' You can see that's not what I prescribed."

Marcus flipped the pages. "I can see it's not what's on your chart. But what was on the prescription? Is it possible that you got flustered about something, distracted maybe, and wrote it down wrong?"

"Marcus, part of my training included time with one of the best cardiologists in the country." Cathy regretted her tone as soon as the words were out. She took a calming breath. "I've written that prescription at least a hundred times, probably more than that. I wrote that script exactly the way you see it on the chart."

"What did Dr. Baker do?"

"Once he realized I'd made the right diagnosis — and probably saved Nix's life — Dr. Baker acted professionally. He agreed that Nix had a toxic level of digitalis in his system. He didn't imply I'd done anything wrong." *Unlike you,* she thought.

"Did you bring up the dosing error?"

"I told him what I've told you," Cathy said. "Then he phoned Collins Pharmacy. Jacob pulled the prescription and read it back to him. It was exactly what was on the pill bottle."

"So you made a mistake. A big one."

She shook her head. "I couldn't believe it — still don't. I got on the phone and asked Jacob why he didn't call me to question the dosage. That's a lot of digitalis. He said that I underlined the strength and dosage. You know that's what we're supposed to do when we write for something unusual. It tells the pharmacist, 'Yes, I know. But I have a reason.' "

"Which pharmacist filled the prescription?"

"Jacob didn't know. But he said that either of them would probably figure I was giving Nix a high dose to convert a case of atrial fibrillation. So they filled the order just as it was written and that's the way Nix took it."

Marcus rose, turned toward the window behind his desk, and stood with his back to Cathy, his hands in his pockets. "Cathy, you know I like you. I've been in your corner since you decided to come to Dainger to practice. But something like this is serious. The credentials committee may even revisit the status of your privileges. They could require you to practice under supervision for a while. Even suspend your privileges. In the meantime, you need to get Nix into the hands of an internist."

"Already done."

Cathy recalled the scene all too clearly. She and Evan Baker had talked in the hall, then gone back into the treatment room where Gail Nix stood wringing her hands over her husband. The IV bag containing the second vial of Digibind dripped steadily into Nix's vein. Depending on the results of the latest digitalis level, he might need more. The hospital pharmacy had already dispatched a driver to Fort Worth for several additional vials.

Cathy admired and appreciated the way Evan Baker put it. "Mr. and Mrs. Nix, you're fortunate that Dr. Sewell made the correct diagnosis and administered the proper treatment. However, she's told me she thinks that it would be best if a specialist directed your cardiac care for a while. Would you like me to give you the names of the internal medicine specialists in town? Or would you prefer that I stay on the case?"

Cathy realized she'd been sitting there with her eyes closed as she relived that scene. She opened them, took a deep breath, and looked Marcus in the eye. "Of course, they agreed to let him take over the case. I don't blame them. I realize that Dr. Baker could have made an issue with them about the prescription, but he didn't. I hope he'll be sympathetic when — and if — this becomes an issue. Until then, I plan to continue to practice the best way I know how, putting the best interests of my patients foremost."

Marcus stood, but remained behind his desk, the expanse of wood a reminder of the gulf between them right now. "Cathy, I can't sweep this under the rug. For starters, you'll have to present this at the next

Morbidity and Mortality Conference. You know the drill. The staff will discuss why it happened, how it might have been prevented, if the treatment could have been better."

Cathy's face burned. There was no shame in having a patient die or experience a complication if you'd done everything you could to prevent it. But this M&M conference would make her look totally incompetent. Even a third-year medical student knew the proper maintenance dose of digitalis. Who might have tampered with Milton Nix's prescription? How could it have been done? And who could want to hurt her so badly that they risked a man's life to do it? Had the campaign to run her out of Dainger just escalated another notch?

"Mrs. Gladstone, I'm sorry we had to reschedule your appointment." Cathy pulled on gloves, seated herself on the rolling stool, and flipped up the sheet.

"No problem, dear. I understand." Emma Gladstone was the perfect example of maintaining one's dignity while draped in a sheet with both legs held in gynecologic stirrups. "Remember, I've been married to a doctor for almost fifty years."

Cathy carried out the examination the way

she would want hers performed: gently, carefully, with frequent explanations and assurances.

"Jane, I think we're through. I'll step into my office and dictate my findings. Would you help Mrs. Gladstone up? When she's dressed, I'll see her in my office."

Cathy closed her office door, dropped into her chair, and brushed a stray wisp of hair from her eyes. She started to reach for one of the textbooks behind her desk but paused with her hand halfway there. No need. She'd had an excellent rotation through the obstetrics and gynecology department at the medical center. She'd attended a postgraduate conference on gynecologic tumors just a month before moving to Dainger. The biopsies she'd taken would confirm it, but she knew carcinoma of the cervix when she saw it.

Jane ushered Mrs. Gladstone into the office. Before she closed the door, her eyes met Cathy's. The sorrow and compassion there told Cathy that her nurse knew what the exam had revealed. "Do you need me, Dr. Sewell?"

Cathy appreciated the offer, but this was part of her job. She had to do it on her own. "No, thank you."

She motioned Mrs. Gladstone to a chair,

then stared down at the pathology request on her desk. Cathy took a deep breath. This was never easy.

Mrs. Gladstone spoke first. "What kind of tumor is it, Dr. Sewell?"

Cathy's head snapped up. "What makes you say that?"

The patient shook her head and smiled. "You don't live with a doctor as long as I have without picking up bits and pieces of information. When a woman my age begins to have bleeding like that, it's a tumor. You took some biopsies — I'm presuming a four-quadrant biopsy of the cervix. Do you think it's invasive or *in situ?* Any masses in the adnexa? What can you tell me?"

"I think you have early carcinoma of the cervix," Cathy said. "The biopsies will confirm the grade. I don't feel any masses in the ovaries or tubes, but we'll want some imaging studies to confirm that. The treatment, if I'm right, would be either radiation or surgery. Personally, in your situation I'd favor surgery."

"There, that wasn't so hard, was it, dear?"

Harder than you'll ever know, Cathy thought. "We should have the results of the biopsy back in less than a week. Would you like for me to call your husband and give him my preliminary findings?"

"Oh, I'll wait until the results are back. Maybe I'll ask him to come with me on my next appointment. He rather likes you, you know."

This wasn't exactly the way Cathy wanted to make allies, but right now, she welcomed every one of them. "Just be thinking about who you'd like to see for treatment. We can send you to a specialist in Fort Worth or to the medical school in Dallas. I know good people at both places."

"Do you have privileges for this kind of surgery?" Mrs. Gladstone's voice held no trace of irony or guile. Apparently, her husband didn't share all his professional secrets with her.

"No, this is beyond what I normally do. If surgery is required, it would be best for a gynecologist to perform it. Do you want someone here in town?"

"Arthur Harshman is probably the best gyn specialist here. Of course, his manners are terrible, but Ernest says he's extremely capable. What I'd really like, though, is for you to assist him. Maybe we can work on that."

"Mrs. Gladstone, I'm so sorry. If —"

Emma silenced Cathy with an upraised hand and the faintest shake of her head. She reached into her oversized purse and pulled out a small, worn leather volume.

"Please don't worry about me. This matter is in God's hands. There's story after story in here where Jesus tells us that God is in charge; we're all in His hands. I am. You are. So let Him take over. You just do your best."

Cathy sat at her desk, wondering if the air conditioning in the office had failed or the conversation with the pharmacist had triggered the sweat that trickled down her face.

"Lloyd, I really need to see that prescription." She held the phone so tightly that her hand cramped. She switched hands just in time to hear the answer.

"Afraid not, Cath— Dr. Sewell. I don't have the authority to let it out of the store. That would be up to Jacob."

Cathy waited but Lloyd Allen, the other pharmacist at Jacob Collins's pharmacy, didn't offer to help. Same old Lloyd she'd known in high school. If it wasn't to his benefit, forget about asking him.

"Lloyd, I thought you two were partners."

"Nope. Jacob bought the store from my father while I was in Oklahoma. Then he built this new building. Upgraded everything. That was about the time my wife divorced me, so I moved back here and he hired me."

"It must seem strange working for someone else in what was once your dad's place," Cathy said.

"I don't really want to talk about it. And the answer's still the same about the prescription — that's up to Jacob."

"May I speak with him, please?"

There was no answer, just silence, punctuated by mumbling in the background. In a couple of minutes, Cathy heard a series of bumps, probably the receiver hitting the counter as someone dropped it.

She recognized the next voice she heard, even though Cathy had last heard Jacob Collins's distinctive whine in high school. Jacob had been on par with their class academically, but light years behind her and most of her classmates in the social graces. Jacob hadn't fit in with any crowd. He'd asked Cathy out once. It had been all she could do not to laugh. She'd tried to let him down easy, but she had the impression that the hurt lingered for a while.

Whiney or not, Jacob's words were full of conviction. "Dr. Sewell, I can't let you have the prescription. Milton Nix's attorney has already called to warn me about keeping it safe."

Cathy tried to keep her tone steady. So

Nix already had an attorney. "Jacob, how about if I come by and look at the prescription there? Would you do that? This is important."

"Okay, come by today, and I'll let you see it, but you can't touch it." Jacob made it sound as though he were letting her see the Dead Sea Scrolls.

"Can you make a photocopy?" Cathy asked.

"Sorry. I'll let you see the prescription, but that's all."

The conversation had nowhere to go after that, but Cathy decided she'd at least try to be pleasant. It couldn't hurt to have this man on her side. "How's your family?"

There was no spark in Jacob's voice as he replied. "Sherri's fine. You remember Sherri Clawson? She was in your class. We have two kids."

Find something to compliment him on. "I drove to the cemetery recently and passed your house. It's really nice."

"Thanks. It could be nicer if — Never mind. You can come by this afternoon, and I'll pull the prescription out of the file."

As Cathy hung up the phone, some long-buried incident from her days in high school niggled at her. It seemed to her as though it was about Jacob. Or was it Lloyd? Was there something — some grudge from the past — that would lead either of them to manipulate one of her prescriptions just to put her in a bad light, even though it might kill a patient?

She was anxious to see the prescription. After that she wanted to talk with the person who filled it. Jacob had made it plain that, with only a two-man crew, they didn't bother to make that notation on the prescription or the bottle. Cathy knew it was good pharmacy practice to keep those records, but she got the impression that Jacob made the rules for Collins Pharmacy.

Persistent rumors. Economic pressure. Delayed hospital privileges. Now a prescription with a mistake a third-year medical student wouldn't make. Was this part of the ongoing campaign to drive her away? Or had her paranoia progressed to the next stage: out of touch with reality?

She stood up to walk out of her office when another thought hit her and she dropped into her chair. What if she had experienced a dissociative reaction when she wrote that prescription? What if she'd thought one thing and wrote another? That would explain the discrepancy between what she'd charted and what was on the prescription. She was no psychiatrist — she'd have to ask Josh about it to be sure —

but as she recalled, dissociative reactions were common in patients with schizophrenia.

"That's your last patient," Jane said. "For the day and for the week. What are your plans? Will you promise to relax this weekend?"

Cathy handed the file to Jane and shrugged out of her white coat. "Promise. After I stop by the pharmacy, I'm going home and collapsing into a hot bath. Then tomorrow I think I'll take a drive in the country and get away from everything."

"How about Sunday?"

Cathy's initial impulse to dissemble died quickly. By Monday, everyone would know anyway. "I'm going to church with Will."

"Good. Enjoy your weekend."

Cathy retreated to her office and sat there with her eyes closed. The noises of drawers shutting and doors closing finally died away. She heard Jane call, "Night," before silence settled in.

Cathy decided she needed to talk with Josh about her mistake. She wanted him to evaluate her, assure her that her mind wasn't really slipping. Did it merit a phone call now? No, it could wait until her regular session next week.

She opened her eyes and leaned forward, pressing her hands to her temples to still the pounding. She hoped Josh could help her. She started to run down the list of available antipsychotic drugs.

"Stop it," she said out loud. "Stop thinking you can be your own doctor."

Still, the symptoms paraded through her mind like a marching army: A constant sense that someone was out to get her. Actions that were out of character for her. Emotions that went up and down like a roller coaster. Cathy reached for a tissue and dabbed at the tears that rolled down her cheeks. Now she knew what the writer meant when he referred to the "dark night of the soul." A permanent midnight had descended on her heart and soul. She wished she still believed that God heard and answered prayer. Right now, though, all she could do was cry.

Whoever designed Jacob Collins's drugstore had done a bang-up job: wide aisles, bright lighting, and attractive displays. Judging from the number of people lined up at the two cash registers, the merchandising efforts had paid off. Now Cathy could see how Jacob afforded that big house.

The pharmacy department repeated the

modern look of the rest of the store. Despite growing up in a doctor's family, despite being a physician herself, Cathy had never been beyond the mysterious wall of frosted glass and faux marble that blocked out the public. Behind these barriers, men in white or pale blue smocks took prescriptions passed to them by anxious hands and dispensed bottles full of hope in return. Like elves in Santa's toy assembly line, they bustled back and forth, pulling bottles from the hundreds on the shelves and measuring out pills and capsules into little containers before slapping computer-generated labels on them. Now Cathy would step through the looking glass herself.

"Wait for me back here," Jacob Collins said. "I've got to take care of a problem at the front of the store." He punched a four-digit code into the lock and pushed the Dutch door open for Cathy before hurrying off.

She stepped inside and looked around. Large stock bottles of every kind of medication were arranged in alphabetical order on shelf after shelf. One shelf looked different, though. Set at eye level, it featured a display of pharmacy implements from a prior era. She recognized several glass and ceramic mortar and pestle units for grinding substances into a smooth powder. A shiny brass balance scale stood in the center of the shelf, its weights arranged in an orderly row in an open walnut case beside it. At the end of the shelf she spied another small wooden case, open to display a group of metal dies and pegs. She had no idea what that was, but the display was impressive.

"What are you doing back here?"

Cathy looked around to see a stocky woman whose most notable feature was flaming red hair that appeared to owe its distinctive color to Clairol rather than genetics.

"I'm waiting for Jacob. I'm Dr. Cathy Sewell."

"Oh. Sorry, I should have recognized you." The woman's tone softened. She moved a step closer. "Sherri. Sherri Collins." She extended her hand. "I was Sherri Clawson when we were in school."

Cathy took the hand, while her mind conjured up a yearbook picture, and decided that the years had not been kind to her classmate. When she was in high school, Sherri had a figure that turned the heads of all the boys and was the envy of all the girls. Back then, when most of the kids still wore glasses, Sherri had contact lenses — blue contacts that complemented her faultless complexion and long, light brown hair.

The yearbook picture faded. Long-buried memories scrolled through Cathy's mind. Two senior girls vied for Homecoming Queen in a close race. Too close. That changed after a few words whispered in the right ears: "Oh, Sherri would be a great Homecoming Queen. After all, she's on close terms with almost the whole football team — very close."

During halftime at the Homecoming Game, every eye in the stadium followed Cathy as quarterback Will Kennedy escorted her to the center of the field to receive her crown. Runner-up Sherri Clawson trailed behind, escorted by second-string tackle, Jacob Collins.

Cathy forced the images back into hiding and smiled. "Sorry I didn't recognize you. It's been a while. Jacob told me you two were married."

Sherri's eyes narrowed. "As soon as Jacob graduated from high school," she said. "After we married, I got a job in the drugstore. I wanted to go to college, but someone had to make a living." She made a face. "We lived with Jacob's parents to save money, and he commuted to his pre-med classes at TCU."

"I didn't know he'd gone pre-med." Cathy

could have cut out her tongue. Obviously, Jacob hadn't gotten into medical school.

By this time, Sherri looked like she'd chewed and swallowed a lemon. "Medical school didn't work out. So Judge Lawton pulled a few strings, and Jacob got into pharmacy school."

Cathy decided that no good could come from going farther down this road. "He seems to be doing well now."

Just then Jacob hurried in. "Sherri, why don't you go up front and get a Coke out of the machine? Get one for me too. I'll only be a few minutes here."

"Sure," Sherri said. "Nice seeing you, Cathy." She wheeled and hurried away.

Jacob eased onto a high stool at the chest-high work counter. "Let's get this done. I'm in a hurry."

"I appreciate your letting me see the prescription." Cathy pulled up another stool next to the pharmacist, careful not to disturb the pill containers and prescriptions lying on the counter. "It's really important."

"Let me find it." He pulled open the top drawer of one of the half-dozen small filing cabinets arranged under his workspace. He thumbed through the prescriptions in practiced fashion before pulling one out with a flourish usually reserved for rabbits emerging from a magician's hat. "I hope you realize that I can't let it out of my sight. Matter of fact, when you're through, I plan to seal it in an envelope and lock it in my safe. I suspect it will be an important piece of evidence in the near future."

Cathy ignored the jab and focused on the slip of paper in front of her. Little by little, like a child peeking between her fingers at a scary movie, she let her eyes move across the prescription. The top line carried the notation "Milton Nix (DOB 6-29-57)." Cathy's NPI number was handwritten in the space at the bottom right. One refill was authorized. An X appeared in the box for "generic may be dispensed." Her signature at the bottom left no doubt about who had written the prescription: Catherine Sewell, MD.

When she could no longer put it off, Cathy directed her gaze to the body of the prescription. As with all her prescriptions, the information was printed in a bold hand.
DIGOXIN TABS 0.25 mg
DISP: [# 30]
SIG: 2 TABS Q DAY
Two tablets a day of a medication twice as strong as was needed. Milton Nix would be taking four times the normal dose of the heart medication. It looked like her print-

ing. It looked like her signature. But then she realized what was wrong, and she knew this wasn't the prescription she'd written for Milton Nix in her office.

Maybe she wasn't losing her mind. Maybe someone really was out to get her. And they'd almost killed Nix in the process.

7

The church service Sunday morning did little to calm Cathy. True, the handshakes and hugs seemed genuine. The songs brought back memories of happier times, sitting between her parents not far from the pew she and Will occupied today. The sermon spoke of the love of God, and that was where Pastor Kennedy lost her. If God was so loving, why hadn't He protected her parents? Why had she been left orphaned? And where was God's love in all the troubles she had — professional roadblocks and financial pressure and attempts on her life?

As she sat with the Kennedy family at lunch, Cathy let the conversation flow around her like rapids around a rock in a stream. She remained occupied with her own thoughts, and they weren't thoughts of peace and love.

"You seem quiet today." Pastor Kennedy took the bowl of mashed potatoes from his wife and dropped a large spoonful on his plate. "Is there something you'd like to talk about?"

Cathy shook her head. Talking to the pastor about her personal and professional troubles wouldn't help. She was the target for someone — some unknown person who didn't care who got in the way — but what could she do about it?

When Will spoke from across the dining room table, it confirmed the concern she'd read on his face when he'd picked her up that morning. "I don't want to pry, but if you're having problems, this is the place to talk about them. I mean, I'm your lawyer, Dad is your pastor, and we all care about you. You can tell us anything."

"No." The sharp retort came out before Cathy could stop it, but like a genie once out of the bottle, she couldn't get it back. She took a deep breath, put down the fork she'd been using to push food around on her plate without actually eating, and looked around the table. "Will, it may be a legal matter, but I'm not ready to talk about it right now. And Pastor Kennedy, I'm sorry. I don't mean to be disrespectful. But I have to confess — God and I haven't exactly been on speaking terms for the past few years."

"You mean, since your parents were killed?"

"Yes. I guess it was no secret that my mother had —" Cathy couldn't bring herself to say the word. "She had emotional problems. And as a result, she and Dad had some difficulties in their marriage. But he told me she was better. He thought they'd worked things out. My family would be together again. Then God let them get killed!" She squeezed her eyes shut to keep the tears from flowing.

This time it was Dora Kennedy who replied. "Dear, everyone knew about Betty's mental illness. It's nothing to be ashamed of. And even when your mother got so bad, your daddy saw to it that she was cared for."

Pastor Kennedy pushed aside his plate and leaned toward Cathy. "You know, God didn't 'let' your parents get killed, anymore than He 'lets' murders happen or children die in their cribs. Since Adam and Eve, this has been a fallen world. It's not perfect like God intended it to be. But there's a way for folks to —"

"Please," Cathy tried without success to keep her voice level. "I don't want to talk theology. My experience has been that I can't depend on God. Just like I couldn't depend on Rob —" She let the word die unsaid. "Just like I've learned not to depend on any man."

Pastor Kennedy picked up the thread of conversation. "Perhaps not, although I think you're being a bit harsh on the masculine gender." He flashed a smile at his son. "But you can depend on God, you know. You just have to learn to trust Him."

"How can I trust Him?" Cathy said. "I can't even bring myself to pray."

"He already knows your heart. You don't have to say a word. Just listen."

Cathy wished she could let go, take the hand of this kindly man, and tell him everything that was bothering her. But that would involve trust, and right now she couldn't bring herself to trust anyone. Not even God.

Cathy squirmed around in the seat of Will's pickup so she could look at him. "I'm sorry I went off like that."

Will kept his eyes on the road. "No need to apologize. You're under a lot of stress. I want you to feel free to be open with me, and I know my folks feel the same way."

Cathy tried to say thanks, but the words stuck in her throat. She turned toward the window and watched the familiar scenery roll by.

When Will wheeled the vehicle to the curb outside Cathy's apartment, he killed the engine and turned with his right arm over the back of the seat. "You know, when we went off to college I had a dream that I'd come home for Christmas vacation our senior year and propose to you. We'd move to Dallas. I'd go to law school and work nights to support us. You'd go to medical school there. Then we'd come back to Dainger, settle down, raise a family."

The lump in Cathy's throat grew. She stifled a sob.

"What happened to drive us apart?" Will said. "You stopped coming home on vacations. I wrote you letters, but you didn't write back. I called and it was like talking with a cousin. You know, 'I'm fine, how are you?' but no warmth, no feeling. Did I do something to upset you? I need to know."

She kept her gaze forward, looking at his reflection in the windshield. "No one knows this. I didn't even tell my parents. My sophomore year at college, I met someone. A graduate student named Carter Lyles. He was handsome, rich, self-assured, a few years older than me. I guess you could say he swept me off my feet. He promised me we'd be married after he finished his master's degree. But then I discovered he'd

140

made the same promise to two other girls on campus."

Cathy focused on Will's reflected image. "I confronted him. He said it was the way men were. Then he walked away. After that, I'd see him around the campus, but it was as though I didn't exist. He'd look right through me — walk by without a word."

Will took in a deep breath and held it a long time. "So you decided men couldn't be trusted?"

Cathy shook her head. "For a while, I hoped that maybe there was a man out there who was trustworthy. But my fiancé Robert topped them all. That's when I decided that maybe it was a mistake to trust any man." She wiped at her cheeks with her fingers. Will handed her a clean handkerchief, and she blotted the wet tracks. Between sobbing breaths she told him the story of how she and Robert had broken up. "I don't know who I can trust anymore."

Only Cathy's soft weeping and the whoosh of an occasional passing car broke the silence. Will reached out and turned her head with a gentle finger under her chin. "Cathy, I can see where you might think you can't trust anyone again. But, believe me, you can trust me. You can depend on me. After all these years, my feelings for you

141

have never changed."

Could she believe him? She wanted to. Cathy envisioned a scene where she melted into Will's arms, turning loose her fears and worry, preparing to live one of those "happily ever after" stories she used to love in childhood. But the lessons of the past were too strong. Instead, she simply reached over, patted his hand, and said, "Thank you, Will. I hope you'll be patient with me."

"Dr. Gladstone, Mrs. Gladstone, thank you for coming."

Cathy waved the couple to the chairs in front of her desk. She adjusted her white coat before easing into her own chair. Emma Gladstone's chart lay on her desk, the pathology report inside, but there was no need for Cathy to open the folder. She knew what it said. After she'd received it, she'd spent the better part of that evening poring over her textbooks, then online at sites from M. D. Anderson Cancer Institute and the National Institutes of Health.

Cathy made a conscious effort to avoid the mistake she'd seen several times during her training. Ernest Gladstone was a doctor, but his role here was as a husband. It was Emma's health that was the subject of discussion. Cathy would speak to her, not to Dr. Gladstone, and she'd do it in language that was layman-simple.

"Mrs. Gladstone, the biopsies I took confirmed my initial impression of a cancer of your cervix, the neck of your womb. Remember I told you that my examination suggested the cancer hadn't spread, and the imaging studies we did confirmed this. It's what's called a stage zero tumor."

She looked for the first time at Dr. Gladstone. He sat in silence, holding his wife's hand. His jaw was set, his expression grim. He was a man prepared to do battle. Right now, Ernest Gladstone epitomized the downside of being a doctor. He knew too many of the bad things that could happen, and he was powerless to do anything about them.

Cathy looked back at Emma. "There are several treatment options. I'd like to outline them for you and then I'll answer any questions you might have. I'll be glad to assist you in getting an appointment with whomever you choose to treat you."

"Dr. Sewell," Emma said, "this is the diagnosis Ernest and I expected. We're ready to proceed with treatment." She turned to her husband and some unspoken communication passed between them.

"I've been in contact with a couple of my

friends," he said. He mentioned the chairs of the Department of Gynecology at two of the most-respected cancer institutes in the nation. "I'd like the pathologist who read the biopsies to send the slides to both of them for confirmation, but I have no reason to doubt your diagnosis. Both of them have recommended a wide total hysterectomy. Emma and I agree with that, but we see no need to go elsewhere, since Art Harshman is well-trained and quite experienced in the procedure."

Cathy bit back the comment that leaped into her mind. She remembered how hard she'd worked not to embarrass this dear lady during her examination. She could only cringe at the thought of how Harshman would treat Emma. But there was nothing she could do.

"Very well. I'll arrange for the slides to be sent out today," Cathy said. "Jane will have you sign a release form on your way out, and we'll send copies of your records to Dr. Harshman. I presume you don't need us to set up the appointment for you."

"No," Emma said. "But I do have one favor to ask. Ernest tells me that the surgeon will require an assistant for this procedure. I want you to be that assistant. I want you to be scrubbed in and participate."

"I don't think Dr. Harshman will —"

Emma was firm. "I know. You flinched when I said it before, and I imagine you were hoping I'd forget about it by now. And before you start making excuses, I'm aware you and Arthur have butted heads. There's not much that happens in the medical community that I don't hear, usually from one of the doctors' wives. But I'm convinced you're not only well-trained, you care about your patients as persons. Arthur is a machine. A good one, but without an ounce of compassion. I want someone to balance that out while I'm on the operating table." She leaned back and took a deep breath. "Would you do that for me?"

Cathy turned her head a few inches and looked at Ernest Gladstone for a sign, but found none. This was Emma's decision, and he wasn't about to fight her.

"Of course, Mrs. Gladstone," Cathy said. "I'll mention your wishes to Dr. Harshman when I call to tell him about your case." And wouldn't that be fun?

The settlement for her accident had been enough for Cathy to pay off her old car and make a down payment on a small Chevrolet, last year's model that the dealer assured her was absolutely perfect for her needs. In her heart, she wished she'd been able to afford something bigger, sturdier: a Hummer, perhaps, or a Sherman tank. Nowadays, she imagined that every approaching black SUV edged near her car. Today that sense caused her to repeatedly jerk the steering wheel to the right. She figured that if she made it to Fort Worth and back without being pulled over on suspicion of DUI, it would constitute a minor miracle.

Josh called her into his office right on time. She settled into her chair and immediately poured a glass of water from the carafe on the end table. Her mouth may have been dry, but her palms were wet.

"What's the first thing that jumps into your mind today?" As usual, Josh surprised her with his opening remarks. But she didn't have to think long about her answer.

"I don't know if this is good news or bad. I came to you because I was depressed, but I really was worried that I might be showing signs of paranoia, that I might be moving into the schizophrenia that affected my mother. But now I'm pretty sure that I'm not paranoid. I'm convinced there really is someone out there who's out to get me."

If Josh was surprised, he was too experienced to show it. "Tell me."

Cathy took a deep breath and the words

started pouring out. As she spoke, she felt a chill that had nothing to do with the air conditioning. She talked about the black SUV, the rumors around town, the altered prescription.

She paused from time to time, hoping Josh would interrupt or ask a question, anything to break the flow of the story and allow her to relax. Instead, he watched with a perfectly neutral expression. His posture gave her no clue as to whether he thought she was a woman pursued or one going mad.

"I don't know which is worse," Cathy concluded. "Thinking I'm going crazy or finding out that I'm a target for someone who apparently hates me enough to try to kill me, then almost kill one of my patients."

"Let's talk about what brought you here," Josh said. "You were having difficulty concentrating and trouble sleeping. You forgot things. It was hard to do your daily tasks. You had no appetite. You found yourself constantly worrying. Right?"

Cathy nodded.

"You were afraid you were becoming mentally ill. Do you know how common such a fear is among physicians?"

Cathy paused to consider it. "I don't know. I guess it's like so much in medicine. We know too much. Every stomach pain is a perforated ulcer. Every bump is a skin cancer. And mental changes make us think we're going crazy."

"Did you ever think about suicide?"

It was like a slap in the face. Cathy had never told anyone about those feelings, even Josh. "After I ended our engagement, I . . . I actually borrowed sleeping pills from two or three friends so I'd have enough to kill myself." She swallowed hard. "But I couldn't do it."

Josh's face softened. "Cathy, almost four hundred doctors commit suicide each year. And many of those instances are due to depression. Not schizophrenia. Not a psychosis. Just worry, stress, depression. It can be dangerous. But you did the right thing. You sought help."

Cathy started to say something but found that she had no words. She took a sip of water and listened as Josh continued.

"You were afraid that this was the early stage of the same psychosis that your mother had. Do you still think so?"

She ran that through her mind. "No."

"Because you understand what caused your feelings?" Josh said.

"Yes."

"So the depression you were experiencing when you came to see me was probably a reactive depression, not true clinical depression. Right?" Josh leaned forward and rested his hands on his knees. "Cathy, you've had enough psychiatric education to make a pretty good guess at what's behind those feelings. You broke up with your fiancé and cancelled your wedding. Big loss. You turned down a prime faculty appointment at the medical school where you trained in order to get out of the town where Robert had his practice. Big loss. Since you came back home to Dainger, you've rejected advances from two men, one of whom was your high school sweetheart and the other an eligible professional man. You're scared to make a commitment because you're afraid you'll lose again. Another big loss. And it all started with the death of your father and mother. Think that could explain your feelings?"

"I guess."

"Why were you so afraid that what you were experiencing was more than simple depression?"

"My mother was schizophrenic," she blurted out the word that had been in her mind but hadn't passed her lips until now. "And it drove my father away from her. At least, I think it did." As her thoughts cleared, she spoke faster and faster. "And I was afraid that, just like her, I'd driven away the men in my life because I was mentally ill. I truly thought that there'd never be any hope of my having a healthy relationship with a man."

Josh leaned back and tented his fingers. "Let's talk a bit more about your relationships with men."

Cathy looked down and saw that the knuckles of her intertwined hands were white. She made a conscious effort to relax. Finally, she found the courage to speak.

"Dr. Sewell, there's someone in the waiting room to see you. He won't give me his name or state his business. What do you want me to do?" Even though Jane appeared calm, Cathy could read the concern in her nurse's eyes.

"What do you think it's about?"

"He's well-dressed and carrying a little leather portfolio. You know, sort of a mini-briefcase without a handle. He's not loud or insistent. He said he'd sit there until you could see him." Jane ducked her head. "One more thing. He said it would be better if he spoke with you in your office instead of the waiting room."

Cathy had been expecting this. Nevertheless, she could feel her pulse pounding in her ears. She put her hand on the edge of her desk to stand, but sat down quickly when the room went into motion.

"Are you all right? Do you want a glass of water?"

"No, I'm fine. Just feeling a bit weak. I shouldn't have skipped breakfast."

"Let me get you some coffee with cream and a couple of sugars. He can wait." Jane hurried off without waiting for an answer.

While she waited, Cathy stared at the thin manila folder sitting on the corner of her desk, where it had been for the past three weeks. Marcus Bell had wanted to keep Milton Nix's chart, but Cathy insisted on returning it to her office, compromising with Marcus by allowing photocopies to be made for the hospital files.

Jane returned with the coffee and a worried expression. "Why don't I send this guy packing? Or at least make him set up an appointment."

Cathy shook her head. She took her time sipping the coffee, feeling the warmth start to lift the chill that had seeped into the marrow of her bones. Finally, she could not put it off any longer. She buzzed Jane and said, "Please send the gentleman in."

The man closed the door behind him and walked forward until only the desk separated him from Cathy. She didn't stand or extend her hand. No need for pleasantries. She knew what came next.

Cold gray eyes stared into Cathy's. "Dr. Catherine Sewell?"

"Yes."

The man's expression remained perfectly neutral. Cathy thought he might as well have been delivering a deli order or a daily paper. Instead, he produced a thick, folded document from a slightly worn leather portfolio and handed it across the desk. "You've been served." And he left.

Cathy unfolded the sheaf of papers and let her eyes run down the first page of legalese — "In the matter of Milton Vernon Nix" and "Plaintiff" and "Defendant" — Someone else could interpret the exact language for her later, but there was no doubt in her mind about the meaning of the document. Milton Nix was suing her for malpractice.

She fingered the edges of Nix's file, edges that were already frayed. She knew she hadn't committed an act of medical negligence. But now she had to prove it.

8

Cathy could picture Arthur Harshman's face growing redder with every word. He kept his voice low, but even over the phone it was obvious that anger bubbled beneath the surface.

"Doctor, I'm happy to see Mrs. Gladstone as a patient. I thank you for your courtesy in calling to inform me of her problem and in offering to provide copies of her records. I'd appreciate receiving them as soon as possible." He took a breath and exhaled so forcefully that it sounded like a gale blowing across the phone's mouthpiece. "But —" Another breath, another gale. "But I resent being held hostage by a patient's demand that I allow an untrained physician to assist me in doing a Wertheim procedure."

Cathy tried to pour oil on the troubled waters. "Dr. Harshman, I recognize your frustration. I can see your position. Frankly,

I tried to talk Mrs. Gladstone out of her request —"

"You mean *demand,* don't you?"

"I prefer *request,* but yes, she was adamant. If it makes you feel any better, during my residency I scrubbed on three radical hysterectomies as second assistant."

Harshman grunted. "So you've seen three of them. Well, bully for you. But second assistant is another name for observer. The first assistant is a different matter altogether."

Cathy decided to make one more stab at civility. "Dr. Harshman, I can assure you that I'll study like a third-year medical student before the surgery. I'll help you, not hinder you."

"You'd better. My secretary will be in touch when we have the procedure scheduled." He slammed down the phone.

Cathy hung up, swiveled in her chair, and pulled two large books from the shelf behind her. She let them drop with a solid thud onto her desk next to Milton Nix's chart. Her worries seemed to be piling up.

"Charles Ferguson."

The voice on the phone sounded reassuring in Cathy's ear. She leaned forward in her chair and moved Milton Nix's chart into the center of her desk, fingering it like a talisman. "Mr. Ferguson, I'm Dr. Cathy Sewell in Dainger, Texas. I'm insured by your company, and I've just been served with a malpractice action."

"Have you spoken with anyone about this?" Still calm . . . still reassuring.

"After the incident, I spoke with the hospital's chief of staff. It appeared to be a medication error, and I subsequently relinquished care of the patient to one of my colleagues, an internist."

Cathy could hear keys clicking as Ferguson called up her file on his computer. She marveled at how quickly the world had shifted from filing cabinets stuffed with paper to a computer processor small enough to fit into a briefcase, yet with the capacity to hold the information contained in several libraries.

"I have your account here," Ferguson said. "It appears that you are indeed covered by us. Your limits are rather low, though. What is the amount named in the suit?"

Cathy thumbed through the thick document to be certain, although the number was one she was unlikely to forget. "One million dollars plus costs."

"Ummm, that's well above your coverage level. But you practice in Texas and there's

155

a cap on damages. The million is probably a negotiating figure." More clicks. "Tell you what. Please photocopy everything you have and send it to me by express courier. Don't discuss the case with anyone. I'll have our attorneys look it over, and we'll see where we go from here."

"There's one thing you should know. I've seen the original prescription at the pharmacy. It's not the one I wrote. It's been tampered with."

"Can you prove that?"

"Not directly, no. But —"

Ferguson's reply was firm and not nearly so reassuring as his earlier words. "Doctor, we have to base our decisions on things we can prove. And it's not our business to spend our resources investigating shadowy plots against our insured. Frankly, if your case isn't strong and we can negotiate the litigant down to a reasonable sum, it's often prudent to settle these things. We'll simply have to see."

A rush of anger made Cathy's blood boil. "I thought your primary duty was to protect me. That's why I've been paying premiums."

Unlike Cathy, Ferguson didn't raise his voice. She guessed that after he hung up he'd have about a dozen more conversations like this today. Her case wasn't special to

156

him — but it was to her.

"Our primary duty is to stay in business while discharging our obligations. We'll do everything we can to protect you, but that does not involve tilting at windmills, especially if the windmills seem stronger than our lances. Now leave it to us. I'll look forward to receiving your records soon."

"Wait! What if I want my own attorney?"

Ferguson cleared his throat. "You have that right. It would be at your own expense, of course, and we'd expect full cooperation and an open exchange of information with whomever you choose."

"That's fine, so long as it works both ways. I'll send the records."

There was a gentle tap at the door. Cathy hung up the phone and called, "Come in."

Jane stuck her head through the door. "Your first patient is here. Are you ready?"

Cathy took a deep breath. This was something she'd been forced to learn early in her medical training — keeping several balls in the air without dropping one. She couldn't afford any more slipups.

"Be sure his lab reports are on the chart. Put him in a treatment room, get his vital signs, and let him know I'll only be a few minutes." As Jane turned to leave, Cathy added, "Please close the door behind you. I have one more call to make."

Will laid his napkin beside his empty plate, pushed his chair back from the table, and said, "I didn't know you were such a good cook. If I'd known that, I'd have chased you harder and insisted you marry me."

Cathy tried to maintain a poker face while deflecting the compliment. "In medical school, I shared an apartment with two other girls. We took turns cooking, and I learned in self-defense. Otherwise, they'd have thrown me out."

She rose to clear the table, and Will immediately pitched in. They stacked the dishes in the sink, then moved into the living room.

"You have a nice little apartment here," Will said. "Cozy. Decorated in early packing boxes, with accents by Home Depot."

Cathy laughed. "I'm embarrassed. I've been here more than two months, but so far I've only unpacked enough to get me by." She pointed to the coffee table in front of the sofa where they were sitting. "But I did take your advice and dig that out."

Will picked the Bible off the table and opened it to the flyleaf. "Your parents gave you this Bible. It must be a nice reminder of them."

"Not really. My folks went to church as a matter of course, and they took me along, also as a matter of course. But we were never really what you'd call religious."

Will thumbed through the pages. "You know, since I was raised as a preacher's kid, I had no real choice about attending church. When I went off to college, I let church and religion slide. I guess a lot of kids do. But I eventually realized an important part of my life had gone missing. That's when I came back to the church, back to God." He laid the Bible gently on the table. "I hope you can do the same. It would help during the tough times."

Cathy drew a deep breath. "Speaking of tough times . . ."

She took him through the story of Milton Nix's near-death, how she'd been able to save him, only to find that the cause of the problem was an overdose of the medication she'd prescribed. Cathy told him about being served with papers for a malpractice suit and about her conversation with her malpractice carrier. "But I finally got Jacob Collins to let me see the prescription that he has in his files. And it's not the one I wrote!"

"How do you know?"

"The day Milton Nix came in, I couldn't

find my pen, so he gave me a couple with the bank's name on them. I used one to write his prescription, but I tossed them in a drawer right after that and found one of my own pens to use for the rest of the day."

"So?"

"Milton's pen had blue ink in it. I always write with a pen that has black ink. The printing on the prescription in Jacob Collins's pharmacy was black."

Will drummed his fingers on the table. "I think I see where this is going," he said.

She had no trouble following his reasoning. It was the same chain of logic she'd developed.

"Someone got hold of your original prescription. They changed the numbers, made a photocopy of the altered prescription so the changes wouldn't be so obvious, cut out the paper to the original size, and that's what's in the file."

"Exactly."

"So how could they have altered the prescription without it being obvious?" he asked.

"I've thought about that. Let me show you." Cathy pulled a blank sheet of paper toward her, picked up a pen, and printed "DIGOXIN, .125 mg." She held up the pen like a magician calling attention to the next trick, then made a zero that encompassed the decimal point and the number one. After she inserted another period before the two, the prescription called for "DIGOXIN 0.25 mg." Next she wrote "1 TAB Q DAY." It was fairly easy to make a slightly crooked "2" out of the "1." She squeezed a terminal "S" after "TAB" and the job was complete.

Will nodded. "And I guess there's no way to get another look at the prescription in Jacob's files without a subpoena now that litigation has started. Think back to what you saw. Did it look like this?" He pointed to the alterations.

"I think so." She pursed her lips. "Of course, there's no one to confirm that I wrote that prescription with a blue pen except Mr. Nix."

"And, since he's suing you we can't look to him for help." Will crossed his legs and leaned back with his hands behind his head. "Let me be lawyerly, if that's a word. It seems to me that you have a couple of courses of action. You can leave this in the hands of your malpractice carrier, let them settle the suit, which sounds like what they're leaning toward. Or you can take it upon yourself to investigate and gather the information to defend yourself." He bent forward to look directly at her. "Realize that if you choose the latter course, you're not only battling this lawsuit, you're going up against someone who had little enough regard for life that they almost killed one of your patients. Don't you think it might be a little dangerous for a woman to play detective like that?"

"Dangerous for a woman?" Cathy stared back at Will until he blinked. "Why just for a woman?"

"I mean . . ." Will stammered.

"I'm not a frail flower, Will Kennedy. You should know that. I'll fight this all the way."

Will threw his hands up in mock surrender. "Okay, I give. I know you're a fighter. I remember that black eye you gave Billy Dendy back in sixth grade."

"He had it coming. He wouldn't stop pulling my hair." She smiled and it turned into a laugh, probably the first one she'd had in months. "Anyway, can I retain you to help me? I don't know my way around the legal system, and it doesn't appear that my carrier's lawyers are interested in fighting the case."

"Of course, I'll help you. But, for the sake of argument, what would be so bad about settling?"

Thinking back to the hair-pulling in the sixth grade, Cathy slowly twirled a strand of her hair. "It would raise my premium for the next several years, assuming the company would still cover me. It would be a tacit admission of guilt. It would give the credentials committee at the hospital grounds to rescind the privileges I've fought so hard to get. In a town this size, the news would spread like smallpox, and my patient base would drop to zero before the end of the month. And, most importantly, it would give whoever altered that prescription the satisfaction of succeeding at my expense." She dropped the hair and blew to move it away from her mouth. "So, will you take the case?"

"Consider it part of the retainer you've already paid."

"Will, that dollar was just a token. I appreciate the way you helped with the car accident, but this will take a lot more time, I'm afraid. I can't pay much, but I'm sure I can pay you a reasonable fee over time."

Will set both feet on the floor. He reached out and took her hand, and her heart started beating faster. Whoa, this was no time to rekindle old feelings. She tried to compose her features into a perfect poker face.

"Let's barter some more," he said. "Have dinner with me two nights a week, come to church and lunch afterward with me every

163

Sunday, and cover my expenses for phone calls and such. The rest we'll call *pro bono*."

"Tell you what," Cathy countered. "I'll have those dinners with you if you'll let me cook them. And they'll be working dinners. I'll pay all your expenses plus a five hundred dollar initial retainer. I can afford that, I think."

Will nodded. "And church, with Sunday lunch afterward?"

"When it includes your mother's fried chicken? That's a no-brainer. It's a deal."

Cathy stood at the exam room sink drying her hands when she sensed Jane standing behind her. She finished, tossed the paper towels in the waste container, and leaned against the sink. "What's up?"

The nurse's voice was as hushed as an acolyte's in a cathedral. "Dr. Harshman's secretary called."

Cathy supposed that even the mention of Arthur Harshman inspired awe throughout Dainger's medical community. Awe, sometimes mixed with fear. She determined not to let him have that effect on her. "What did she want?"

"Emma Gladstone's surgery is scheduled for next Wednesday morning. First case on the schedule, 7:30 A.M. Dr. Harshman wants you to meet him in the surgeons' lounge at 7:00 A.M. to go over details."

"I'll bet he does." Cathy made no effort to keep the sarcasm out of her voice. "What he wants to do is grill me about the surgery: anatomy and technique and all the details I had to memorize when I was a senior medical student. He's angry that Emma Gladstone insists on having me present during the surgery, and he plans to do his best to make me so miserable that I back out."

Jane apparently decided to let the topic drop. She waited a couple of moments before pulling a second pink message slip from the ones in her hand. "Dr. Bell called. He wants you to call him back this morning."

"Okay. What about the rest of those calls?"

"Same as usual. Insurance companies wanting more information before they'll pay our claims. I've done all I can, but for these you'll have to talk with the medical directors and justify the charges."

Cathy's shoulders sagged. Growing up, she'd seen her father as a hero — a surgeon who saved people's lives, a man admired in the community. There had always been money in the household. For some reason, she had pictured this as the pattern for her practice as well. Apparently, she'd been wrong. Dreadfully wrong. Money was tight. And she certainly wasn't getting much respect, either from her colleagues or from patients like Mr. Phillips. That triggered a memory.

"Did Mr. Phillips ever call back for a follow-up appointment? Or write to have copies of his records sent to another doctor?"

"Nope. I guess he's too busy to take care of himself."

Unfortunately, the old adage held true in medicine. You can lead a horse to water — Cathy shrugged. "I'll be in my office." She took the pink slips and the charts that went with them and headed off to do battle with the insurance companies. On the way, she tossed her soiled lab coat into the hamper and shrugged into a fresh one, nicely pressed and starched. Maybe she'd feel better if she looked professional while she made the calls.

Cathy couldn't believe that Marcus would have anything good to say. She'd talk with the insurance companies first. An hour later, her coat and psyche both a bit wrinkled, she hung up and tossed the last of the charts into her "out" box. She'd received promises to review all the claims and possibly — just possibly — issue supplemental checks for the balances due. Ah, the romance of medicine.

"Let's see what Marcus wants," Cathy murmured. She dialed the number and leaned back, wishing she could put her feet on the desk as she'd seen so many male colleagues do. But she was determined to project a professional image, even when alone in her office.

She endured a full two minutes of music on hold before she heard Marcus say, "Thanks for calling back."

"No problem. What's up?"

"I wanted to give you a heads-up and remind you to be at the Morbidity and Mortality Conference tomorrow at noon."

Warning bells clanged in Cathy's head. "You mean to discuss the Nix case? Can't do it, Marcus. Milton Nix has filed a malpractice suit."

"I'm sorry to hear that, but we still have to review it. That's hospital policy. When the inspectors come around for our accreditation visit, they look at all those records. I don't want them to find that we didn't discuss that one. It would look like we're making an attempt to hide our mistakes."

"Discussing that case in front of the medical staff would guarantee that the details would be all over town by sundown. If the malpractice action goes to trial, there's no way we could get a fair jury pool." Cathy thought for a moment. "Tell you what. You and I and Dr. Baker have talked about it. Why don't you write up a memo and put it in the M&M records with the gist of our discussion and a note that the case is under litigation."

Marcus cleared his throat. "I'm not sure I can do that."

"Look, I really need your help here. I'm not asking you to sweep anything under the rug. Just keep the records sealed until this action is settled. Will you do that for me?"

There was silence for a long moment, and Cathy wondered if Marcus had hung up. Then he said, "Okay, I'll do it." He paused. "I realize you're having a tough time right now. How about having dinner with me tonight? Relax a bit. Cry on my shoulder if you want to."

She needed Marcus's support, and dinner with a colleague would be a nice change. But she hesitated once again. Was it still because she was wary of getting close to a man? Or had Marcus's behavior at the credentials committee meeting tipped her off that he might not always be the ally he purported to be? She wondered if he wasn't

168

really in the camp of the doctors who wanted her gone. And there was also her relationship with Will, though she wasn't sure where that was going.

"Thanks, but I have plans." Of course, those plans were Lean Cuisine in front of the TV, maybe a pint of Cherry Garcia ice cream, and a hot bath, but she figured she didn't owe Marcus a detailed explanation. Let him think what he wanted.

The yellow legal pad was filled with almost undecipherable scrawls. In contrast to the careful printing of her prescriptions, Cathy's notes to herself were hastily scribbled words and symbols, marching helter-skelter in all directions, sometimes connected to other thoughts by lines that gave the whole thing the appearance of a drunken spider's web. She'd eaten her microwaved dinner, at least some of it, although she couldn't recall what it had been. Now she sat cross-legged on the sofa with a pint of ice cream slowly melting on the coffee table in front of her. She couldn't make sense of the who and why and how of the prescription that nearly killed Milton Nix.

Cathy looked up as she heard footsteps climbing the stairs outside, followed by a rapping on the door. She detoured to the mirror to check her appearance. Comfortable old sweats, bare feet, blonde hair pulled back and held by an elastic band, face scrubbed free of all makeup. Unless it was the UPS deliveryman, she was in trouble.

It wasn't the deliveryman. It was Will Kennedy, a bouquet of fresh flowers in one hand, a briefcase in the other.

He stepped through the door. "I take it that this evening is informal."

What a total idiot she was. Of course, this was supposed to be the first of the working dinners for her and Will. A dinner she was responsible for cooking.

"I . . . That is, you have to . . . I'm so sorry. I completely forgot."

Will smiled the same smile that had melted her heart when she was younger — a smile that touched her as she never thought a man could do again. "I sort of figured that. And I'll bet you've eaten." He didn't wait for an answer. "No problem. I'll just order pizza. Shall we set up on the kitchen table?"

An hour later, Will looked at Cathy across the remnants of a pepperoni pizza and said, "I've enjoyed my dinner with you even if Pizza Hut did the catering, but I guess it's time to go to work. First, I need you to sign these forms. I'll send one copy to your malpractice insurer so they'll know I'm on board as your personal attorney. Since the suit's already been filed, I can schedule discovery depositions."

"You'll have to educate me," Cathy said. "Discovery?"

"We have the opportunity to subpoena witnesses and ask them questions under oath. Not just Nix and his wife, but anybody who might have knowledge pertaining to our case. So who should that be?"

"I guess the first people we need to subpoena are the ones who might have had access to the prescription." Cathy flipped several pages and found the chart she'd made. "Here's the list."

Will came around and read aloud over her shoulder. "Milton and Gail Nix. The two pharmacists: Jacob Collins and Lloyd Allen. Anyone else?"

"Not really. And I don't see Mr. Nix playing fast and loose with his own heart medicine."

"We're working on the premise that it was done to hurt you. Who in this group doesn't like you?"

"How about asking if there's anybody in town who does like me?" Cathy heard the self-pity in her voice and hated it. "I thought Milton Nix wanted me to do well enough in my practice to pay off my note at the bank." She gave a sarcastic laugh. "But now he's suing me."

"Any problems with Gail Nix?"

"Not that I know of."

"Lloyd?"

"No."

"Jacob?"

Cathy recalled her last conversation with the pharmacy owner. He'd seemed a bit too pleased when he had said, "I suspect it will be an important piece of evidence in the near future."

The hairs on the back of her neck bristled. "Yes, I think Jacob has to be a suspect."

9

Cathy watched Jane escort the morning's last patient to the front and begin the checkout process. Ten o'clock and she was through for the morning. At this rate, she wondered how much longer she could maintain her practice.

She slumped down behind her desk and brushed her hair out of her eyes. Might as well tackle some more of the paper-work that never seemed to end. Cathy had just added her signature to the last insurance form when Jane tiptoed in with a bulging manila folder.

"Here are the checks for you to sign." Jane's sad eyes conveyed a message that was confirmed when Cathy opened the folder.

She thumbed through the checks: withholding tax, answering service, cell phone, office phone, supplies, rent, Jane's salary. The check on the bottom of the stack was the monthly salary Cathy had allotted herself — not much — just enough to cover her living expenses. Then she looked at the adding machine tape clipped to the front of the folder and compared it with her bank balance. She shoved the last check across the desk. "Here, rewrite this check for half that amount."

Jane shook her head. "This is the second month in a row that you've reduced your salary check."

"I knew going in that it would take some time to get the practice on a good financial footing. Eventually my practice will grow. Someday those insurance claim checks will start coming in. In the meantime, the boss is the last person to get paid. That's simply the way it is."

Cathy picked up her pen and signed the top check in the stack. She looked up when she heard the office door open. "Jane, do we have someone else coming in this morning?"

"Not until after lunch. Let me check."

Cathy couldn't quite hear the mumbled conversation in the waiting room. In a couple of minutes, just as she signed the last check, she heard Jane's voice again.

"Come on in here and lie down. I'll get the doctor."

Cathy was out of her chair in time to meet

Jane in the hall. "What's going on?"

"Mr. Phillips. Severe chest pain, difficulty breathing. Sweating and weak. Probably having that MI we predicted."

"Let's see."

Phillips lay on the examination table, his complexion as pale as the sheet beneath him. Large drops of sweat dotted his forehead. His coat lay rumpled on the floor. He'd loosened his tie and unbuttoned the top buttons of his shirt, but his chest heaved as he struggled for air.

Cathy rolled the portable oxygen tank out of the corner, turned the valve to start the flow, and cinched the plastic mask over Phillips's face. "Jane, give him an aspirin to chew and swallow. Then call 911. We need them here — fast. After that, call the hospital and alert them that we're coming in."

While Jane gave Phillips the aspirin, Cathy slipped a blood pressure cuff on his arm. His pressure was 116 over 70. Down from his previously high pressure, but not in shock — yet. Pulse 84 and a bit thready. Just what she'd expect with a myocardial infarction. She pulled the man's shirt open the rest of the way and applied her stethoscope to his bare chest. She frowned at what she heard: S3, a third heart sound. A classic sign of an early MI.

"Mr. Phillips, I think you're having a heart attack." She applied the leads for an EKG as she talked. "I'll check an electrocardiogram to see how severe it is. We'll transfer you to the hospital as soon as the paramedics get here. Are you with me?"

Phillips nodded weakly but did not speak. The muscles in his temple were knotted, and Cathy could hear his teeth grinding.

Jane bustled in. "EMTs are on their way."

"Give him a nitroglycerine to hold under his tongue." Cathy's eyes never left the EKG tracing. Rhythm stable. Slight ST segment elevation. A few isolated T waves flipped. Still early, probably no damage to the heart muscle yet — if she worked fast.

She hurried to get an IV going before his pressure dropped more and all his veins collapsed. When she had it running, she said, "Mr. Phillips, I'm putting some medicine into your IV."

"Whatever you say, Doc."

"Jane, add a vial of atenolol into a small IV bag, and I'll piggy-back it onto this one."

Phillips's color was better now. What else? Oxygen. Aspirin to slow down clot formation in his coronaries. Nitro for pain relief. Beta-blocker. The next step was an angiogram, but where was the ambulance?

She fixed her eyes on the EKG. No

change. Good.

Sirens screamed in the parking lot, and in less than a minute, two paramedics wheeled a gurney into the treatment room. "What've we got, Doc?"

Cathy recognized the lead EMT as one of the team that responded after her accident. "Acute MI, Mark. Let's get him to the hospital right away. I'll ride with him."

Phillips plucked weakly at her sleeve. "Doc?" His voice was barely audible.

"I'm right here, Mr. Phillips. I'll ride to the hospital with you and turn you over to the specialists there."

"Whatever you say. But I want you around too." He swallowed hard. "And thanks."

Cathy stuffed her white coat into the laundry hamper. "Jane, I'm gone. I'll have my cell phone on if I'm needed."

"How's Mr. Phillips?" Jane called from her desk.

"He's doing well. I saw him this morning on rounds."

Cathy reached into the workroom refrigerator and popped the top on a Diet Coke. After two deep swallows, she held it against her forehead and leaned against the wall.

Jane appeared in the doorway, took one look at her boss, and opened the cabinet

177

above the sink. She pulled down a bottle and held it out to Cathy. "Would you like some Tylenol?"

Cathy shook her head. "Had some earlier. I'll be fine. Stop worrying about me."

"Someone has to. Now tell me about our star patient."

Cathy leaned back against the cabinet. "Dr. Rosenberg did a cardiac cath yesterday. Fifty percent blockage of the left anterior descending coronary artery. He did a balloon angioplasty and put in a stent. Phillips should go home soon."

"Who'll do the follow-up care?"

"Dr. Baker was the internist on call. He saw Mr. Phillips with me in the ER."

Jane snorted. "So he's stealing your patient. You know you're qualified to take care of post-MI patients."

Cathy shook her head. "It's been the practice here that myocardial infarctions are the province of the internists. Family practice docs diagnose them, give the patients acute care, and get them in the hands of the specialist. After Phillips is stable, Evan will send him back to me. Or not." She rolled her eyes. "Maybe I should settle for doing what all the other GPs before me have done." But she knew in her heart that she couldn't be satisfied with that. She'd worked

178

too hard.

In the parking lot, she climbed into the little Chevy and buckled her seat belt. As she backed out of her reserved slot, Cathy pictured her Toyota resting with dozens of other junked cars, consigned to the scrap heap after serving her so faithfully. As she wheeled out onto the road, she looked carefully in all directions. No black SUV in sight.

Will was scheduled to come over tonight for another working dinner. Cathy smiled to herself as she remembered the sight of Will Kennedy, a bouquet in his hand, like a teenager calling on his first date. She might not have been prepared for him on that last visit, but this time she'd be ready. Cathy steered a course for the grocery store, her mind already turning over the choices of what she could prepare.

She was in the frozen food aisle when she saw a familiar face. Might as well try to make nice. "Sherri. Hi. How are you?"

Sherri Collins looked up from her shopping list. "Hello, Cathy. Or I guess I should say, Dr. Sewell."

"Cathy's fine. How are things?"

"Well —" The ring of her cell phone spared Sherri from what was obviously uncomfortable small talk. She gestured an apology to Cathy, answered the call, and moved away.

Cathy hurried through the rest of her shopping, loaded her groceries, and drove off, still wondering if she'd made the right decision in returning to her hometown. She'd thought it might be a safe haven, a welcoming place, after her world had crashed around her. But it appeared that small towns had long memories, including at least one that made Cathy unwelcome. She forced the problem from her mind and concentrated on her driving.

As she approached the next intersection, a black SUV shot out of a side street directly into her path. Cathy stood on the brake pedal. Her car immediately skidded to the right. A lesson from Driver's Ed flashed across her mind: steer into the skid. Still braking as hard as she could, she pulled the wheel to the right. She felt a massive bump and heard a loud bang. The car rocked once before coming to rest, the right front fender tilted like the bow of a sinking ship.

Cathy closed her eyes and rested her head on the steering wheel. She felt the cold sweat that adrenaline brings. Her heart raced a mile a minute. Deep breathing didn't seem to help. How much of this could she take?

When she heard an insistent tapping on her window, Cathy finally raised her head. A man stood outside her door, wearing a worried expression. She pressed the button to lower the driver's side window.

"Ma'am, are you all right?"

She made a tentative inventory of her body parts. Everything seemed to move. No blood anywhere. "I think so. Did you see what happened?"

"Sure did. They pulled out right in front of you. Good thing you swerved." He peered over the hood. "I'll check and see, but it looks to me like you hit the curb hard enough to blow out a tire. Probably bent the wheel too."

Cathy pulled her cell phone from her purse and thought of the calls she needed to make: insurance company, wrecker . . . It seemed like there was something else, but her addled brain refused to cooperate.

Her insurance agent seemed shocked by yet another accident but remained professional enough to assure Cathy that this time she was covered. He asked for details, but she was able to beg off by promising to furnish a full report tomorrow. Right now she wanted to get home.

The service manager at the dealership where she'd bought the car was sympathetic and helpful. He promised to dispatch a wrecker right away. If she'd ride back to the shop with the driver, he'd have a rental car waiting for her.

"How long do you think it will take you to do the repair?" Cathy asked.

"A day, two at the most. That is, if the frame isn't bent. Then it's a whole different ballgame."

Two hours later, Cathy climbed the stairs to her garage apartment, weary and punch-drunk. She dropped her purse and briefcase on the sofa, pulled a soft drink from the refrigerator, and ran a hot bath. She was still soaking in the tub, half asleep, when she heard knocking at her door. She tried to block out the sound, but whoever it was seemed to have more resolve to knock than Cathy had to ignore the noise.

"What now?" she muttered. She eased out of the tub, slipped into a terry-cloth robe, and padded to the door. "Who is it?"

"Will."

Oh, no! Not again. How could she possibly have let this happen? Will would think she was an absolute airhead. She'd fought against the stereotype of dumb blondes all her adult life. Now she seemed to have become a prototype.

Cathy belted her robe tighter before she

opened the door and gestured him in. "Will, I'm really, truly sorry. I was all set to cook for you, really I was, but then I had an accident on the way home. When I finally got here, I just collapsed."

Will dropped his briefcase beside the door and took her by the shoulders. "Are you all right?"

"Just sore and shaken up." Then it struck her. Her groceries were now sitting in the body shop of the Chevrolet dealership. "Give me a few minutes to get dressed, and I'll find something in the freezer that I can cook."

"Never mind dinner," Will said. "Tell me what happened. Are you sure you're not hurt?"

"Will, I'm fine. Really I am."

"Then get dressed, and I'll take you out to eat. Someplace quiet, where you can tell me all about it. You need to relax."

The prospect of having someone else cook sounded wonderful to Cathy. "Okay, but I owe you a dinner. I want you to include the cost of this meal with your expenses for my case."

Will seemed to think that over. She noticed that he still had his hands on her shoulders. He'd made no move to release her, and she hadn't felt inclined to step away. Finally, he said, "I guess that depends on whether the dinner this evening is business or pleasure."

"I thought it was business. What would make it pleasure?"

"This."

She watched him move closer to her, felt his lips on hers. His hands moved to encircle her in an embrace that made the years drop away.

"Cathy, I want us to pick up where we left off," he said. "I've missed you. When I heard you were engaged, it was like someone I loved had died. And now that you're back here and you're free, I don't intend to let you get away from me."

She looked up at him, into those blue eyes that had always seemed able to read her thoughts. Part of her — a big part of her — wanted to stay in those strong arms forever. But she had to be honest.

"Will, I can't make a commitment. Right now my life is a shambles. I'm teetering on a knife-edge, doing my best to maintain my balance. I don't know who to trust. Not even —."

No, she couldn't voice that fear, not to Will. Especially not to Will.

She decided to take a different tack. "I've been through a lot since we broke up. I've put my trust in some men who've let me down." She saw him open his mouth, and she silenced him with a finger to his lips. "No, let me finish. I can't just follow my heart willy-nilly. I've got to convince my head. Can you be patient?"

She watched the sparkle go out of his eyes, but his smile remained. "I'm willing to wait as long as it takes. But promise me you won't go running off this time." He released her and stepped back. "Now put on something special and let's have a nice dinner." He grinned. "On me. I think this one comes under the heading of pleasure."

Being with Will helped Cathy push her problems into the farthest corner of her mind. Over steak for him and fish for her, they talked and talked. Will brought her up to date on local gossip. Cathy was surprised how many of her high school classmates had chosen to stay in Dainger. She related stories from medical school, and Will countered with tales of law school. They lingered over coffee, but eventually — sooner than Cathy wished — they were back at her apartment.

Will parked at the curb and turned to face her, his arm over the seat. "You don't know how much I enjoyed the evening."

"And I had a great time being with you. It was wonderful to relax for a while. Thank you for dinner." Cathy reached for the door handle, but Will stopped her with an upraised hand.

"It's early. Why don't I come in and we can spend an hour or so working on your malpractice case? I promise I'll be a perfect gentleman." He reached back and snagged a worn leather briefcase from the space behind him.

Cathy hesitated. Could she keep this on a professional level? Did she want to? But they did need to start working on "the puzzle of the prescription," as she called it. "Sure. Come on up."

In a few minutes Cathy joined Will at the kitchen table. "I've got coffee going. It'll be ready in a minute."

"Good. Here's where we are." Will spread a number of papers on the table. "Nix has hired Sam Lawton to represent him. I've notified your malpractice carrier that you've engaged me. I talked with the attorney they've assigned, gave him an idea of what we're doing, and he's fine so long as I keep him informed. The case has been set for trial in twelve weeks."

She thought about that. "Can't we move it up? I don't want this hanging over me."

"Believe me, twelve weeks is too quick to suit me. I suspect Lawton's pulled some strings to get the case scheduled this soon. I'd like to have more time. We have a lot of preparation ahead of us." He shoved a paper aside and pulled his legal pad toward him. "Now, I have to get ready to take these depositions we're scheduling. You're sure that someone tampered with that prescription?"

"Absolutely." Cathy frowned. "But I can't prove that what's on that prescription in Jacob Collins's file isn't what I wrote. The only two people in that room were Milton Nix and me. It's his word against mine."

Will scribbled a note. "I want to look at that prescription again now that we think we know how it was altered. I'll make sure that Jacob gets a *subpoena duces tacem*."

"A *what* kind of subpoena?"

"It means 'bring with.' He'll have to produce the original prescription, and we can have a closer look at it. There may be some way to prove it's a photocopy. How about the others on our list? What do they have that we need to see?"

They spent some time discussing Milton Nix, Gail Nix, and Lloyd Allen before deciding to call it a night. Cathy had poured the last of the coffee into their cups when she heard a shuffling noise on the stairs outside. In a moment there was a timid tap on the door.

"I wonder who that could be?"

"One way to find out," Will said. "Shall I get it?"

"No, I'll go." Cathy grinned. "I'm old-fashioned enough to be embarrassed by having a man in my apartment after dark. I may need to explain you away."

Cathy turned on the porch light, looked through the peephole, and saw her landlady standing on the tiny porch with a pie in her hands. "Mrs. Elam?" Cathy swung the door wide. "Come in. What brings you up here?"

"I saw Will's car outside and figured that you two might enjoy some hot apple pie."

Cathy glanced at Will, who seemed quite content to let her handle this conversation. "Why, thank you." Cathy's cheeks grew hot. "We were just working on some legal matters. But I know that pie would go well with this coffee. Would you like to sit down and have some with us?"

"Gracious no, child. If I ate everything I cooked, I'd weigh three hundred pounds. And I was sorry to hear about that malpractice suit that Milton and Gail Nix filed. They should be grateful that you saved his life, instead of suing you for that wrong prescription."

Cathy threw up her hands. "Is there anything in this town that you don't know?"

"Don't worry, hon. I hear it all, but I don't spread it around." Mrs. Elam set the pie down on the table next to Will's page of notes. With no apparent shame, she took a moment to run her eyes down the list. "I see that you've made the connection between Gail Nix and Lloyd Allen."

Cathy frowned. "Not really. What do you mean?"

"Wasn't Lloyd a couple of years ahead of you in high school?"

"Actually, three years," Cathy said. "What about it?"

"So his sister would already have graduated when you started high school."

"That's right. I vaguely remember her. Linda Allen."

Mrs. Elam smiled as though the dull child had finally solved the math problem. "Right. She was Linda Gail Allen then. She didn't start using her middle name until she went off to college. Then she came back to Dainger and married Milton Nix."

Cathy turned to Will and their eyes met. She could see him working through the connection along with her. The situation had either gotten a lot more complicated or a lot simpler. She wasn't sure which.

"This is Dr. Cathy Sewell. Is the sheriff available?" Cathy drummed her fingers on her desk as she suffered through the Summers County version of elevator music when the operator put her on hold. It was a country and western song that brought to mind Cathy's mental image of a Texas lawman: face the color and texture of a walnut, a chaw of tobacco in his cheek, gunbelt cinched below a gut that spilled over the waist of his jeans. She wasn't sure he could help her, but she had to try.

"This is Sheriff J. C. Dunaway. How can I help you?"

She leaned forward as though she could convey her intensity through her posture. "Sheriff, several weeks ago a black SUV ran me off the road, totaling my car and almost killing me. Since then, I've had more than one near-miss encounter with a similar vehicle. Yesterday, it came out of a side street and almost T-boned me. I managed to avoid it, but I crashed into a curb and blew out a tire. I want to know what you're doing to find out who's behind this."

"Hold on for a minute." She heard muffled voices. "My secretary's getting me the files. Meanwhile, can you fill in some of the details for me?"

Cathy ran through each of the episodes, her mood alternating between anger and spine-chilling fear as she realized once more how close she'd come to being injured or killed.

There was a rustle of paper from the other end of the line. "Doctor, I only find one report. That was from your original accident. The deputy who responded reports that he cruised the roads in the vicinity but never saw the suspect vehicle. Did you report your accident yesterday?"

She let her shoulders sag, all the starch suddenly gone from her. "No. I was so upset I didn't even think about it. I knew there was something else I should do, but frankly I was so rattled I hardly knew my own name. I reported it to my insurance agent — and now I remember that I haven't given him the details I promised either. Once the tow truck driver showed up, I just wanted to get away before something else happened to me."

"Let me get more information from you, and I'll ask the deputies to keep an eye out for this vehicle. If you see it in the future, call us immediately."

By the time Cathy finished admitting that she had no idea of the make, model, or year of the SUV in question, she felt utterly stupid. "It was big and black. The windshield was tinted so heavily that I never got a look at the driver. And, no, I don't recall the license number. I think it was a Texas plate, though."

The sheriff's sigh sounded like a gust of wind in her ear. "I'll bet the most common vehicles in this county, aside from white pickups, are black or dark blue SUVs. Why don't I get some pictures of various makes and models of SUVs and drop by your office tomorrow afternoon? Maybe we can pin this down a bit."

Cathy hung up, wondering what the man behind the badge looked like. More importantly, would he be able to help her?

10

"When you finish, Dr. Bell wants you to call him." Jane handed Cathy a pink slip along with the chart of the next patient.

Cathy paused a moment to wonder what Marcus might want. To tell her that the credentials committee members had changed their minds and were granting the extended privileges she'd requested? Not likely. To advise her that they were putting her on supervised probation for going beyond the scope of her privileges? More likely, although she thought she'd done a pretty good job of going right up to the line before turning her patients over to the appropriate specialists. Oh, well, it could wait. She had one more patient to see.

Today, Ella Mae Mercer looked every bit the model of a bank vice president in her tailored navy suit and white blouse, accented by a designer scarf. Cathy bet the scarf alone cost as much as she spent on clothes in a month. The faintly tinted lenses of Ella Mae's glasses — different frames this time — made it hard to read the woman's expression. Cathy wondered if she had several pairs to match her outfits.

"I'll bet you thought I wouldn't be back." The mild sarcasm of the words was tempered by the apparent sincerity on Ella Mae's face.

"I hoped you would," Cathy said. "How are you doing now?"

"Still stressed to death, but handling it better, thanks to the pills you were kind enough to renew. And, since you didn't want to continue the prescription without knowing my medical status, I'm back for all the testing, poking, and prodding you want to carry out, so long as it keeps the medicine coming while I need it."

"Fair enough. If you'll get undressed and put on that gown hanging behind the door, I'll be right back to check you over. Meanwhile, I want to review the new patient checklist you completed on your last visit."

Most of the information on Ella Mae's history form was unremarkable. Cathy found one thing that grabbed her attention, though. The date Ella Mae Mercer listed as the last time she'd consulted a doctor was a week before the car crash that killed Cathy's parents. She hadn't given the doctor's name, but Cathy knew it was her dad from the name on the pill bottles. The reason for the visit was left blank.

Why had her father treated Ella Mae? And why had he prescribed a tranquilizer for the woman? Cathy remembered her dad talking on the phone at home, calls where he frequently said, "I'm a surgeon. You'll have to see your family doctor if you want those. I don't give that kind of medication." One of his favorite expressions had been, "If there's a problem, I cut it out. Then, once the incision's healed, I move on to the next patient. Let the internists and GPs handle all the rest."

For the next half hour, Cathy "poked and probed," as Ella Mae had called it. The woman seemed in excellent physical shape. Finally, Cathy shoved her stethoscope into the pocket of her white coat and stepped away from the exam table. "Jane will draw some blood for routine baseline studies, and I'll let you know if anything turns up there. Right now, I'd say you're pretty healthy."

"Good. How about my medications?"

"The dose of estrogen you're taking could probably be cut back a bit. We're finding that smaller doses carry less risk of breast cancer. The vitamins and supplements are fine. I don't want to discontinue the tranquilizer suddenly, but if you can, I think we should plan for you to eventually get off them."

Ella Mae shook her head no before Cathy finished speaking. "Ordinarily, I'd agree with you. Until I saw you last, I hadn't taken those for several years. But I need them now."

"Why?" Probably not the most diplomatic way to put it, but Cathy felt she had a right to ask for justification before authorizing more of the tranquilizer.

"I'd prefer not to say. Let's just say that I'm dealing with some powerful emotions. I don't drink. I don't do drugs. I need something to take the edge off."

"These emotions. Would you like to share them with me? Perhaps I can help."

Ella Mae shook her head. Then she turned her palms up like a supplicant. "No use talking about them. It's about something that happened years ago. I thought I'd put all that behind me, but it keeps coming back to haunt me."

Cathy's heart hammered in her chest. "And you won't let me try to help you?"

Ella Mae shook her head, and Cathy was struck by the sadness in her eyes. "No, I don't think anyone can help. But thank you for offering."

Ella Mae Mercer stood at Jane's desk, her prescriptions in hand, completing the check-out procedure. Cathy took one last look at the woman whom she suspected had been the cause of her father's near-estrangement from his wife. She hungered for details, but Ella Mae appeared to have no plans to elaborate.

Cathy grabbed a can of diet soda from the workroom refrigerator and took several gulps. She shrugged her shoulders and tried to loosen the muscles in her neck, but the tension wouldn't budge. Probably just stress. She wished she could write herself a prescription for the same tranquilizer Ella Mae took, but all she needed to further complicate her life right now was to start self-prescribing potentially habit-forming drugs.

Cathy made sure that the waiting room was empty before she retreated to her office and closed the door. She collapsed into her chair, leaned back, and put her feet on the desk. Decorum be hanged! She was ex-hausted.

She sat that way for perhaps five or ten minutes. Then her sense of duty overcame her fatigue. She sat up, pulled the phone toward her, and punched in Marcus Bell's number.

"Marcus, this is Cathy. What did you need?" She regretted her tone as soon as the words left her mouth. No need to alienate him. She needed all the allies she could muster. "Sorry, didn't mean to snap at you. Bad day."

"I'll try not to make it any worse. The credentials committee will be meeting again in a couple of weeks. I thought you might like to know that the way you handled Nix's arrhythmia and your care of Mr. Phillips impressed Evan Baker. He seems to be on your side right now. Carl Rosenberg is also coming around. So there's a chance they may reconsider extending your privileges."

Cathy felt her muscles relax a bit. "Great. I was afraid you were about to suspend them, not extend them. I had visions of being on probation as a result of this malpractice suit."

"Actually, they could do that. But I haven't heard any rumbles to that effect. I — Hang on. My secretary's asking me something."

While Cathy waited, she tried to honestly assess where she stood with the credentials committee. And, in case of another tie vote, she wondered if Marcus would come down on her side this time or choose to remain neutral. She wished she could be sure.

She heard more murmurs, then Marcus was back on the line. "Sorry. Administrative problem. Anyway, I thought you should know about this."

"Thanks." She had the phone receiver halfway to the cradle when she heard Marcus say something else.

"Pardon me? I didn't get that last bit."

"I asked if there was any chance of us having that dinner I keep asking you about."

Make a choice, she thought. True, Marcus was handsome and charming. There was no doubt that having him on her side would be important. But she couldn't bring herself to fully trust him. And it would be weird to see Marcus when she hadn't fully decided how she felt about Will. No, she didn't need any more tension in her life.

"Marcus, I appreciate it. But . . . no."

Cathy paused at the water fountain outside Josh's office to wash down a couple of Tylenols. She recalled the advice she'd given so many times to others. If symptoms persist, see your doctor. Well, here she was, about to see a doctor — and probably the one whose services she needed most.

She had hardly settled into her chair when

Josh asked, "How's your love life?"

Cathy looked up, startled. "I beg your pardon?"

"I asked, 'How's your love life?' Surely you recognize the relevance of that question. If you don't, I can remind you of what we've been talking about for the past several weeks."

She squirmed and rearranged her skirt. "All right. As you know, there are two men who seem to be interested in me. One is the surgeon who's Chief of Staff at my hospital. The other is the attorney who's helping me with a malpractice case that's been filed against me."

"Your high school boyfriend."

Didn't the man forget anything? He never took a note. She'd never seen evidence of a tape recorder in the office. She decided on a simple answer. "Yes."

"Do you have feelings for either of them?"

"Actually, I haven't sorted that out. I know I'm fond of at least one of them."

"Fond? That's not the kind of feeling I'm asking about. Does it go deeper than fond?"

"Do you want to talk some more about my not being able to trust men?" Cathy asked. "Because my father died just as I finished medical school, just when I needed him? Because two men I was ready to marry disappointed me?"

Josh shook his head, an unusual display of emotion for him. "No, but think about those three men we've been talking about: your father, Carter, Robert. What did you admire most about them? Until they let you down, that is."

She didn't even have to think. "Strong, competent. I felt safe and secure when I was with them."

"What do you think that says about the way you feel about yourself?"

She reached for the carafe and poured a glass of water.

"Cathy, you know you do that when you want to put off answering."

She put the glass down. "All right. I guess I don't feel secure. I act like it — I have to — but I'm not. I feel like I have to prove myself again and again. Can you imagine how hard it is for a woman to make it in medicine? And then to establish yourself in your hometown, where everyone remembers every mistake you and your family ever made? A place where all the male doctors in their 'old boys club' think you can't hack it in the real world?"

"I recognize those feelings, and they're legitimate," Josh said. "But put them aside and try to analyze your feelings for the men who are currently in your life, the ones you're drawn to."

She took a deep breath. "I need Marcus on my side when I come up against the medical staff. I need Will on my side when my suit comes to trial." She felt the way she always felt when Josh peeled away another layer of the protection she'd built up: vulnerable and shaky.

"And?"

"So I guess I need to be clearer about my feelings for them. Do I value them for what they can do for me or just for themselves."

"That would be a good idea. I'd suggest you begin by considering whether you'd be attracted to them if they had nothing to offer you. Picture them as furniture salesmen, plumbers, perhaps airline pilots. When you do that, you'll know the difference between what you're feeling from your head — even subconsciously — and your heart. And then you can start thinking about love — not need, but love. There's a big difference."

Josh had given her a lot to think about on the drive back to Dainger. A lot.

The morning had been frustrating. Not busy — just frustrating. Three patients cancelled, giving no reason. Several sizable bills arrived in the mail, but no payments came to offset them. Cathy wanted to scream. Instead, she grabbed a cold Diet Coke and retreated to her office. She'd hardly settled into her chair when Jane rapped on the doorframe. "Sheriff Dunaway's here."

"Please send him in." There was movement behind the nurse. Cathy rose and extended her hand. "Sheriff, I'm Dr. Cathy Sewell."

The sheriff strode confidently across the room, and all Cathy's preconceived images fled. The man was in his late fifties or early sixties, muscular but certainly not fat. He wore starched, sharply pressed chinos. His white dress shirt bore a modest-sized shield on its breast pocket. A silver replica of the state of Texas secured his black bolo tie. He carried a snub-nosed revolver high on his right hip. He could have been a detective in Dallas, rather than the sheriff of a moderate-sized Texas county. Certainly, this was no country bumpkin.

"Pleasure to meet you. I'm J. C. Dunaway." He gave her a brief handshake, firm but not aggressive, and settled into the chair across from her. When he crossed his legs, she saw that his black snakeskin boots were shined to a high gloss.

"Thank you for coming here. Do you have

some pictures for me?"

He placed a manila folder on the desk and flipped it open. Inside were a dozen or more sheets of photo stock, each with a large picture of a vehicle. "You know, in the old days I'd have sent a deputy to a bunch of dealerships for pamphlets. Now we go on the Internet, find the picture we want, and print it out. Took less than half an hour to get all these." He tapped a finger on the top picture. "Any of them look like the vehicle that's been giving you trouble?"

Cathy shuffled through them quickly, setting aside two or three, which she studied with care. Finally, she said, "I'm pretty sure it's this one."

He pulled the photo toward him and looked at it, then turned it over and nodded. "Ford Expedition. Are you sure?"

"Not really. You have to admit, they all look pretty much alike, but I think this is it."

"That's a really common vehicle around here, but we'll do some digging. See if someone who owns a black Ford Expedition might have something against you." He scratched his chin. "Or maybe they had a grudge against your family. Know if your daddy had any enemies?"

"Sheriff, he was a physician. The people

he helped loved him. I guess there are always a few folks who hold it against the doctor when he can't cure the incurable, or when the time comes to pay for their care, or when he does something they don't like." Cathy clamped her lips shut. She'd thought of another reason for someone to have a grudge against her father. Had he broken off a relationship a woman thought would end in marriage?

"Dr. Sewell, are you prepared to assist me?" Arthur Harshman's tone implied that he was as likely to get help from a trained baboon as from this upstart family practice doctor.

Cathy forced a smile. "Absolutely. May I go in and say hello to the Gladstones?"

Harshman waved her request away as though he were shooing a particularly pesky fly. "I suppose so, but be quick. I've already spoken with them. I answered her questions, the permit's signed, and Ernest knows that I don't want him in the operating room looking over my shoulder. Don't do anything that might cause problems."

Emma Gladstone lay on a gurney in the pre-op holding area. Her husband stood at her side, holding her hand and occasionally smoothing her hair. They both turned when

Cathy slipped between the curtains that gave them the limited amount of privacy available in that setting.

"Mrs. Gladstone, I just wanted you to know that I'm here. Is there anything I can do for you?"

"Yes, dear. Will you pray with us? I think I'd feel much better if you did." Her reply so nonplussed Cathy that it took her a moment to process it.

To Cathy's surprise, Dr. Gladstone nodded at his wife's request. In Cathy's home, her father's praying had been confined to a rote-memorized grace that he said at mealtimes, primarily, she suspected, to appease her mother. In her residency Cathy had encountered a few doctors who mentioned that they prayed before every operation, but like her colleagues she'd tended to dismiss them as a rather unusual minority in the profession.

"I . . . I suppose so," Cathy stammered.

"Ernest, will you pray first? Then Dr. Sewell can pray." Emma reached out her other hand, careful not to put traction on the IV taped to it, and grasped Cathy's hand.

Dr. Gladstone cleared his throat. "Dear God, I love this woman. She's good and kind and the most caring person ever to walk this earth. Please carry her through this procedure safely. Give her the grace to tolerate whatever comes afterward, and help me be the kind of husband and helper she deserves." There was a moment of silence. Then Gladstone murmured, "And give skill and discernment to Arthur, Cathy, and all those who help them. In your name, Amen."

Cathy was so startled by Dr. Gladstone's use of her first name that it took a gentle squeeze from Emma for her to stammer out her own prayer. "God, please help all of us through this. Help me to do my very best and to be worthy of the trust of these people. Amen."

11

"More traction." Harshman tapped the retractor with the hemostat in his hand. "I need to see right here."

Cathy pulled a bit harder. She'd bent over the operating table opposite the surgeon for over two hours and could hardly bear the pain in her back. Her head throbbed with every movement she made. The air conditioning in the operating room didn't come close to overcoming the heat from the high-intensity lights that glared down on the surgical field, and a constant stream of sweat trickled down her back.

Cathy decided she had to risk the surgeon's wrath. She flexed her shoulders, even though it meant a momentary easing of the pressure she held on the retractor.

"You're doing a nice job," she ventured.

"I should hope so," he grumbled. "I've done dozens of these." He dropped a clamp onto the instrument tray. He straightened,

208

took a deep breath, and used a gauze square to blot blood from the surgical area. "Did a fellowship in gynecologic oncology at M.D. Anderson. Some of us live in Dainger because the pace is slower, and we like the town. Not all of us here are incompetent old coots who couldn't make it in a larger medical center."

Cathy realized she'd made exactly that assumption about Harshman. "I'm sorry. I —"

Harshman tapped on the retractor with his finger, "Take that out now. I think the self-retaining retractor will be enough at this point." Then, like a flashback to her days as a resident, Harshman asked, "What's the most critical part of the operation to this point?"

Cathy gave the answer automatically. "Avoiding damage to the ureter or bladder."

"Have I come close to cutting either one?"

"No. No, you haven't."

"Good. Do you think you could have done this operation?"

Cathy considered that for a moment. She'd known most of the steps, but there were a few points where she wasn't sure where Harshman's next cut would be, while his movements never appeared to be anything less than sure and certain. "No, I don't think so."

"Do you think you deserve privileges to do a modified radical hysterectomy?"

"Dr. Harshman, I never asked for anything like that. I recognize that I'm a family practitioner, and I'm proud of it. But, if you'd read the letters I presented to the committee you'd know that I had a great deal of exposure to obstetrics and gynecology during my FP residency. Actually, I originally planned to go into OB-Gyn, but I changed my mind. What I want now are privileges to perform deliveries. You'll notice that I didn't ask for C-section privileges, even though I've had the training. I recognize that there are competent obstetricians available in town, and they should be doing those cases. I'm not about to steal your patients. I only want to offer more complete care to my patients, especially the women, many of whom would prefer a female physician."

She saw Harshman's mask move as he opened his mouth to respond, but that response never came.

A nurse holding a phone message slip hurried into the room. "Dr. Harshman, your OB patient, Karen Pearson, is in the emergency room. She's cramping and spotting. What do you want to do?"

For a moment, Cathy thought Harshman hadn't heard. He picked a pair of blunt-nosed scissors off the instrument tray beside him and began dissecting in the depths of the operative site.

Just as Cathy was about to speak, Harshman looked up from his work. "I know you've seen her, Dr. Sewell. You know about her case. Now she's at term and she's bleeding. The baby's a breech, so I'd scheduled her for a C-section. What would you do?"

"Is there any sign of fetal distress?"

The nurse didn't seem to know whom to address, so she swiveled her gaze between the two surgeons. "Fetal heart tones were one fifty when she came in. They've dropped to one ten."

Cathy didn't hesitate. "This could be an *abruptio placenta* or a prolapsed cord. Whatever the cause, there's definite fetal distress. She should have a stat C-section."

Harshman nodded once, then turned to the nurse. "I can't leave this patient. Is Dr. Gaines available?"

"He had to drive to the hospital in Bridgeport to handle an emergency there." The nurse didn't throw up her hands, but her voice conveyed the same message.

"Cathy, how many C-sections have you done as surgeon?"

"More than half a dozen — fewer than a dozen. And I've watched and assisted on maybe ten more."

"Contact Dr. Steel," Harshman told the nurse. "Tell him I need him to scrub up and assist me in finishing this case. Then call Dr. Bell. He'll have to scrub with Dr. Sewell. She'll be doing an emergency C-section on Mrs. Pearson."

Cathy bent over the hospital bed, struggling to make her voice comforting and confident at the same time. "Karen, you need an urgent C-section. The baby is in trouble. Dr. Harshman's in surgery and can't drop out. He's asked me to do it. The nurse has told you what it involves, the risks involved. Will you give me permission to do the case?"

Karen Pearson looked up at Cathy. Despite her grimace of pain, there was serenity in her eyes. "Of course. I've been praying that you'd deliver my baby. I didn't really want it to be an emergency, but if that's what it takes, I'm okay."

Cathy nodded to the nurse who stood at the head of Karen's bed. "As soon as the permit's signed, get her up to surgery." She looked down at Karen again. "I'll do my best for you."

"That's all anyone can ever do," Karen

said through clenched teeth. "Remember that."

In the women's dressing room, Cathy exchanged her sweat-sodden scrub suit for a clean one. By the time she strode into the pre-op holding area, the anesthesiologist had wheeled Karen into the operating room. He turned and asked, "Epidural or general?"

Cathy didn't hesitate. "No time for an epidural. General. I want her under the moment I'm gowned and ready."

Marcus Bell hurried up, pulling on a surgical cap. He picked a mask out of the box above the scrub sink. "Fill me in. All I know is that you're doing an emergency C-section on one of Arthur Harshman's patients at his request, and you need me to assist."

Cathy adjusted her own mask and began the scrubbing up process that numerous repetitions had made automatic. She explained the situation to Marcus, who, to his credit, listened without interruption or argument.

"When was the last C-section you did?" he asked, when Cathy had finished her explanation.

"Not quite a year ago."

"That's about five years ahead of me. Do you recall all the details?"

She replied with more assurance than she felt. "I know enough. Between us, we'll get through it. We have to. That woman's baby is struggling — fetal heart tones down to ninety now — and we have to get her delivered."

This was it. Go time. Cathy looked around her. The anesthesiologist stood by at the head of the operating table. Dr. Denny, the pediatrician, sat in a corner, ready to take the baby. Marcus took his place across from Cathy, his eyes conveying no message at all. Karen lay on the operating table, her bulging belly tinted a strange orange-brown by the prep solution and outlined in a surreal square by the green draping sheet.

"Everybody ready?" Cathy paused. "Karen, we'll take good care of you and your baby. I promise." She nodded at the anesthesiologist. "Let's go."

In a few moments, Karen was under. The clock had started to run. Cathy had less than ten minutes to get the baby.

"Fetal heart rate?" she asked.

"Holding at a hundred."

Cathy had a decision to make. Did she have time to make a low "bikini" incision across Karen's abdomen or should she save precious minutes by using the long vertical incision employed years ago? Cosmetic result or safety for the baby? Plastic surgery could minimize scars. If she were on that table, she'd say, "Hurry. Save my baby."

She reached out her hand. The scrub nurse slapped a scalpel into it. "Vertical incision." Cathy fixed Marcus with a look that she hoped carried the authority she didn't feel. "Get a sponge in one hand, cautery in the other, keep up with the bleeding."

"But —"

Cathy's eyes dropped to the operative field. "Marcus, I have a reason for everything I do, but I don't have time to explain. I'm the surgeon. Help me. That's what assistants do."

She plunged the scalpel into the taut flesh of Karen's abdomen. As layer after layer yielded to her dissection, Cathy wondered if her words had offended Marcus. She was surprised to realize that she didn't care. Her priority right now was to do what was best for Karen Pearson and her baby. She'd worry about her relationship with Marcus and all the other doctors on the staff later. If practicing good medicine and putting the patient first got her ridden out of Dainger on a rail, so be it.

"Down to the uterus. Let's get a self-retaining retractor in."

As he had since her initial exchange with him, Marcus complied without comment. To his credit, he'd been an excellent assistant, anticipating her moves and working in smooth tandem with her.

"I'll make a low fundal incision, then extend it with scissors. The presentation's a footling breech. I know how to do the extraction, but I'll need a second set of hands to do it."

She sent a look at Marcus. He nodded once.

"Fetal heart rate has dropped to eighty-five."

"Here we go," Cathy responded.

Cathy let reflexes, muscle memory, and hours of midnight study take over. In seconds, the uterus was open, the amniotic sac incised, and she reached for the baby. "Dr. Denny, are you ready?"

The pediatrician moved closer to the table. "All set."

The information flashed through Cathy's mind like the words on an electric sign. The largest part of a baby is the head. For a C-section, make the incision big enough to deliver the head and there's no problem with the rest. In this case, the baby's legs would come out first, the head last. She'd have to guess at the incision size. Halfway through the extraction, Cathy saw that her incision hadn't been large enough. "Scissors." She held out her hand, palm up, and felt the firm slap of the instrument.

"Do you — ?"

Her eyes never left the operative field. "Marcus, I know what I'm doing."

"Fetal heart rate is eighty."

The words spurred Cathy on. She dropped the scissors and slid her hand down along the baby's head. Words memorized by rote now were turned into action. Hand onto the face, finger in the mouth. Turn a bit. "A little more traction on the legs please."

There! The baby was free. And there it was — a prolapsed umbilical cord, a kink that cut off the blood supply from mother to child. Cathy clamped and cut the cord and handed the baby off to the pediatrician.

As she worked to complete the procedure, her ears waited for that most wonderful of sounds, the cry of a newborn. There was the gurgle of the suction bulb as Dr. Denny cleared the baby's mouth and nose. A moment of silence, then more suctioning. She was aware of murmuring between the pediatrician and the nurse assisting him. As Cathy was about to turn back toward the bassinet, she heard it. Faint at first, then stronger. The insistent cry that signaled a healthy set of lungs.

"Nice work, Doctor. It's a boy."

Cathy stood beside Karen Pearson's recovery room bed and watched the woman's eyelids twitch, then open slowly.

"You and your son are doing fine," Cathy said.

Karen reached out her hand, wincing as tension on the needle in her wrist pricked her. "Thank you, Dr. Sewell. See, God brought us both through it just fine."

"I — Thank you, Karen. Now, you get some rest. I need to go help another doctor."

Cathy shucked out of her surgical gown and hurried to report to Harshman. She paused just inside the door and said, "Mrs. Pearson's doing fine. Footling breech with a cord prolapse. The FHT had dropped to eighty by the time we got the baby out. Healthy little boy."

"Good. We're almost through here. Dr. Steel's done a fine job assisting," Harshman said.

Cathy was thinking that he was too polite to add, "Better than you did."

Instead, Harshman said, "I must admit that I was a bit hesitant to send you off to do that emergency C-section. Glad you got through it."

"Thank you. Would you like me to tell Dr. Gladstone that everything is going well here?"

"Yes, please do. I'll be out in about fifteen minutes to talk with him."

She was halfway through the door when she heard his last words. They stopped her in her tracks.

"Good job, Cathy."

The anesthesiologist had said his good-byes and headed for home. Dr. Denny stopped by long enough to change into his street clothes and offer his congratulations on a successful C-section. Now Cathy and Marcus sat in the deserted surgeons' lounge, side by side on the sagging sofa. Their feet rested on a coffee table littered with the detritus left by previous occupants: discarded surgical masks and caps, pink message slips with cryptic scribbling, and pads of hospital progress notes. Cathy sipped from a cup of vile-tasting coffee. She hadn't wanted it, but Marcus had presented it like a peace offering.

"Thanks for the coffee," Cathy said.

Marcus nodded. "You're welcome."

Marcus was obviously walking on eggshells, so Cathy decided to try easing the tension. "I appreciate your scrubbing with me. I couldn't have done it without you."

"Happy to help, although there wasn't much choice. The case needed to be done stat, and I was probably the most logical candidate to scrub in."

A thought crossed her mind. "Are you angry that Harshman didn't ask you to do it?"

The wait before his answer told Cathy what she needed to know. Marcus blew on his coffee, tasted it, and made a face. "I don't really know. I guess my first thought was that I was more qualified to do it than you are. But, as it turned out, I was wrong."

"You didn't pay any attention to those letters about my qualifications, did you?" She felt the anger boiling up. Maybe it was time to get all this out in the open. "You know, you're just like the other men on the committee. You had your mind made up before that meeting that I would have the same privileges as every GP who's practiced in Dainger since the hospital opened. Never mind that I'm a residency-trained, board-certified family practitioner with undeniable qualifications and excellent recommendations. It was a foregone conclusion that, because I'm a woman, because I grew up here in the shadow of my father — a *real* doctor — there was no way I could ever be as capable as you men." She put the Styrofoam cup onto the table with enough force to slosh coffee onto everything, wishing it were a china mug so she could slam it down.

Marcus tossed his half-full cup into the trash. "No, no. I know you're qualified. It's just that I have to remain neutral in these things. If I take a side, I automatically end up with half the doctors on the staff mad at me."

Cathy rose and bent down until she was almost nose-to-nose with Marcus. "And that's why you didn't want me to speak up at the credentials meeting. And why you didn't vote. You were unwilling to risk making someone on the committee mad. This way, the only person you disappointed was me. And you figured you could make that up by taking me out to dinner. Is that my price? A nice dinner? I'm insulted. Even Judas got more than that!"

Marcus was still talking when Cathy turned and stalked into the women's dressing room. She tried to slam the door behind her, but the automatic closer thwarted her efforts, easing it closed with a soft whoosh. Oh, well. She figured this wouldn't be the last time she had some strong words for Dr.

Marcus Bell. Next time, she'd make her exit a bit more emphatic.

12

"You look different today. New hairstyle?" The remark was so out of character for Josh that it took Cathy by surprise.

"No, same style I've had since I started med school. Low maintenance and plain."

"Maybe it's the makeup. You look different."

Cathy settled more comfortably in the chair. "I guess it's because I feel different. Let me tell you what happened a couple of days ago."

When she'd finished relating her experiences in surgery, Josh leaned back, crossed his legs, and clasped his hands together in front of his knee. "How are you sleeping?"

"I've been so worn out recently that I'm asleep as soon as my head hits the pillow."

"Any more run-ins with that black SUV?"

Cathy shrugged her shoulders. "No. The sheriff's looking into it, and I'm careful."

"Let's review. You came here because you

were depressed — understandably so, given what you'd experienced, although you didn't seem to realize it. Actually, you thought you were on the road to full-blown paranoia. You were afraid you might be showing signs of the same schizophrenia your mother developed. How do you feel now?"

"Better, I guess."

"You're relieved because, instead of being mentally ill, your life is actually in danger?"

"I know. It's crazy." Cathy laughed at her poor choice of words. "You know what I mean. Anyway, this is something I can fight, and I've made up my mind to do just that. And I have some help."

"The boyfriend turned lawyer?" The smile Josh flashed was a rare sight and one Cathy had learned to appreciate.

"Actually, the boyfriend turned lawyer seems to be turning into a boyfriend again. At least, I think so. Right now I want to stand on my own two feet, but it's nice to know someone has my back."

Josh shifted in his chair. "So, do you think we're about done here?"

Cathy shook her head. "I'd like to come back for a few more visits, but maybe we can stretch them out. I've still got some issues I'd like to talk out with you."

"Good enough. Let's do it."

For the rest of the session, Cathy poured out her thoughts as fast as they entered her mind, in a true stream-of-consciousness catharsis. No stopping for a drink of water. No sweat running down between her shoulder blades. No racing of the pulse. Maybe she had gotten a handle on her problems.

Soon, Josh stood and stuck out his hand. "I'll see you in a couple of weeks. Call me earlier if you think it's necessary. But I think you'll be fine."

First a smile, and now this. Quite a red-letter day. She shook the hand Josh offered. "I appreciate all you've done."

Cathy stopped at the secretary's desk to arrange her next appointment. As she was about to leave, she said, "When I shook hands with Dr. Samuels, I couldn't help noticing the calluses on his hands. Unusual for a doctor, isn't it? How did he get those?"

"Oh," the secretary said, "that's from his hobby. He's a carpenter. He spends a lot of time repairing things that are broken — and building new ones."

Cathy envied Will as he sat next to her at the conference table arranging his notes, scribbling an occasional addendum in the margins. No sign of nervousness. Of course, he wouldn't be. This was his office. And he was a lawyer. Depositions were as common for him as cutting hair was for a barber. But she'd never been through one, and she was as nervous as she'd ever been in her life.

The door opened, and the stenographer entered. She took her seat before a strange-looking machine, added a fresh stick of gum to the wad already in her mouth, and stared at the wall with a blank expression.

Will leaned in and whispered in Cathy's ear. "Remember. Pause before you answer. That gives me time to stop you. If you have any questions, you can whisper them to me."

"What if you object to something they ask?"

"My objections will simply be to get them on the record. There's no judge here to rule on them. But anytime I object, you clam up. Okay?"

Cathy nodded. Her mouth felt as dry as the sands of West Texas. She poured a glass of water and sipped from it, but it didn't seem to help much.

"Sorry to keep you waiting." Sam Lawton, Nix's lawyer, ambled into the room. He took a seat at the head of the table, nodded to Will and Cathy, and asked, "Is the court reporter ready?"

"Yes, Judge."

Will responded to Cathy's quizzical look with a whispered explanation. "Even though he was voted out years ago, Lawton's like most judges. He wants that title for life. Don't let it throw you."

Lawton's gray hair spilled over the collar of a wrinkled dress shirt. He wore a blue suit that was five years out of style, accented by a slightly askew red polka-dot tie. Smeared reading glasses perched on the end of his nose. He reminded Cathy of a fine home gone to seed. But Will had warned her that, despite his age and appearance, Lawton's mind was sharp, his legal skills honed by years on the bench.

"Dr. Sewell, let's get started." Lawton's disarming smile was akin to what the snake must have displayed as he approached Eve.

Cathy placed her left hand on the Bible held by the court reporter, raised her right, and was sworn in.

"Now, Dr. Sewell, tell us about your medical training."

Cathy detailed her education, her residency training, and her postgraduate courses.

Lawton nodded in satisfaction, as though he'd just proven something important. She remembered Will's warnings. Don't try to read the man's expression. This was part fact-finding, part mind game.

Lawton led her on through a series of benign questions, and she concentrated on answering truthfully, careful not to volunteer information. Then, out of the blue, the lawyer asked, "And did you deliberately try to poison Milton Nix, or was it an accident?"

Will's voice never rose. "Sam, I'll object to that question and ask my client not to answer." He turned to the stenographer. "Off the record."

The woman took her hands off the keyboard and rubbed them together.

Will shook his head. "Sam, do you take me for a second-year law student?"

Lawton grinned like a fox. "Never hurts to ask, Will. Never hurts to ask."

The questioning seemed to go on and on. Finally, Lawton asked Cathy about her decision to switch Nix from Lanoxin to generic digoxin. She answered without pausing to think. "I thought it would be nice to save him a few dollars."

"Had you been visited by a detail man from one of the pharmaceutical companies that makes this form of digitalis just before you saw Mr. Nix?"

Cathy bristled. "I never let pressure by pharmaceutical companies influence my prescribing. And for your information, generic drugs aren't detailed to doctors like brand name drugs. Maybe that's why they're cheaper."

Will's hand touched her arm and knew she'd violated one of the rules he'd stressed. Answer the question, don't volunteer information, and don't lose your temper.

"Never mind." Lawton pushed his glasses up off the tip of his nose. He reached into a thin manila envelope resting on the table beside him. "This is a photocopy of the prescription you wrote for Milton Nix. Does the dosage appear correct?"

"I didn't —."

"Just answer the question I asked. Is the dosage correct?"

"No."

Cathy looked at Will, expecting him to say something about the prescription being altered. Instead, he turned away and appeared to study the crown molding across the room. For a moment, Cathy flashed back to the credentials committee meeting — men sitting in a room deciding issues that would affect her life, while she sat helpless. Was Will hesitant to go up against Judge Lawton because he didn't want to upset a local power broker? She ground her teeth as she prepared to answer the next question.

After the deposition, Will shook hands with Judge Lawton and said, "Sam, I'll be in touch about deposing your client."

"Just give my secretary a call, Will." Lawton picked up his briefcase. "You know, I was surprised that you're handling this case instead of a lawyer from the insurance company."

"They're willing to let me be the local presence. And I might as well be involved from the start. After all, I'll be filing the countersuit against your client."

To his credit, Lawton showed no surprise except a faint twitch of his bushy eyebrows. "Oh?"

"Sure, for malicious prosecution, tampering with evidence, and a few other violations. We'll be asking for five million." Will butted a stack of papers together and shoved them into his briefcase. "See you, Sam."

"Will, what was — ?"

Will gave his head a single vigorous shake, his meaning clear. They stepped into the elevator and rode in silence to the ground floor. When they finally slid into Will's pickup and shut the doors, he turned to Cathy. "I guess I surprised you."

"You mean the way you let him accuse

me of malpractice without objecting? The way you allowed him to imply that I'm guilty without uttering a word in my defense? Why, yes. You surprised me."

"A deposition isn't necessarily about getting information. It's mainly sparring, seeing if you can get the witness to lose their temper, say something rash so it's on the record under oath. That way, if that information comes up at trial, the witness can't back out of any corner they've painted themselves into without committing perjury. As for what we did today, I doubt that it will affect the trial — if there is one. He might ask you some of those same questions, but if he does, now you're prepared for them."

Cathy thought about that. "So you don't want to argue about anything he brought up?"

Will's eyes never left the road. "Why should I tip our hand? We know what our defense is, but they don't. Let's keep it that way."

"What about the countersuit. We never talked about that."

"Oh, if you want to go to the expense and trouble of filing one, we can do it after we discover who altered that prescription and why, but you'd never win it. Nix surely didn't change the directions so that he'd almost die, so there's no use suing him. He actually filed this suit in good faith. What we can do, after we get to the bottom of this, is see that whoever's responsible is prosecuted for what they did. But we're not about to file any civil suit. I just wanted to throw Sam off balance." He grinned. "He may be old and crafty, but I'm no slouch myself."

She knew he couldn't see her smile, but she hoped her voice showed it. "No, Will. No, you aren't."

"So, next we subpoena our own deponents."

"Pardon?"

"We serve subpoenas to the people we want to depose. Nix, his wife, the two pharmacists. Who else?"

"Let me think." Cathy nibbled on her thumb, a habit she thought she'd broken in her teens. Suddenly, she saw Robert's face in her mind's eye. The rumors? That would be his style. And he wouldn't be above paying someone to run her off the road and frighten her. But arranging the alteration of a prescription — almost killing a patient? Despite his arrogance, Robert was a good doctor. She couldn't believe that of him.

"Well?" Will asked.

"I'm sorry, Will. I'm blank. I can't imagine

232

how anyone else could have altered that prescription. It's got to be one of those people."

Will stopped at a traffic light. He turned to Cathy. "Don't forget to think outside the box."

"Like — ?"

"Someone blackmailing one of the pharmacists. Someone with a key — the cleaning person, a former employee. Someone — ."

"Okay, I get it. Anyone could be behind this."

Will accelerated smoothly into the intersection, then slammed on the brakes.

"Whoa!" Cathy felt the tug of her seatbelt. "What was that?"

"Some idiot driving a black SUV almost hit us."

Emma Gladstone settled carefully into the patient chair. The patent leather purse she held in her lap looked big enough to accommodate supplies for a three-day trip. Cathy wondered how the elderly lady could manage carrying around that load just ten days after major surgery.

Cathy leaned across her desk. "Mrs. Gladstone, can I get you anything? Are you comfortable?"

The woman smiled serenely. "I'm fine, Doctor. I just wanted to come by and tell you how much Ernest and I appreciate everything you've done."

Cathy tried to act as though compliments came her way every day, instead of with the frequency of snow in July. "Think nothing of it. All I did was assist Dr. Harshman. And at that, I had to scrub out before the case was finished."

"Oh, I don't mean just the surgery, although Arthur told Ernest that you were a lot of help. I wanted you to know how much we appreciate your coming by to check on me in the hospital and calling me after I went home."

Harshman actually complimented her? Despite her best efforts to appear cool, Cathy felt her jaw drop when Mrs. Gladstone unloaded this bit of information. Would wonders never cease? "I try to show all my patients how much I care for them."

"And it's appreciated."

"I'm afraid there are some folks who don't share your opinion of me."

Mrs. Gladstone wrinkled her nose. "Oh, that suit Gail Nix had her husband file? I was sorry to hear that."

"Mrs. Nix is behind the suit? Not Mr. Nix?"

"Dear, I have a good idea of pretty much everything that goes on in this town. I heard from a reliable source that Milton was grateful that you saved his life. He didn't care about the prescription error. It was Gail who badgered him into filing the suit. Apparently, she has something against you."

Cathy thought back to the contact she'd had with Gail Nix since returning to Dainger. She'd pegged the banker's wife as a vapid airhead, more interested in her social position than anything else. Why would she have a grudge against Cathy?

After Mrs. Gladstone left, Cathy plunged into her afternoon's appointments and soon was too busy to think further about Gail Nix. With one thing and another, it was late that night before Cathy's thoughts returned to her conversation with Mrs. Gladstone.

During her training Cathy developed the habit of mentally walking the halls of the hospital each night before she dropped off to sleep. She'd review the patients in every room, patients whose lives had been given over to her care. With her switch to private practice, Cathy made only one small adjustment. Now each night she reviewed the patients she'd seen in the office that day. Only when she was satisfied she'd done all she could for each of them was she able to turn over and fall asleep. Not tonight.

Lying in the dark, Cathy wracked her brain to figure out what she'd done to anger Gail Nix. Why had the woman badgered her husband into filing a malpractice suit?

"You've done it now. You're awake." Cathy was surprised to hear that she'd spoken aloud. Maybe she wasn't handling the stress as well as she'd implied to Josh. She slipped out of bed, turned on the bedside lamp, and padded to the medicine cabinet. How about a couple of Tylenol? It might help the headache that had become a frequent companion. Her self-diagnosis was tension headache. Should she go back to Josh and ask him for something to calm her nerves? She'd avoided sleeping pills and tranquilizers all her life, probably because she'd seen her mother take too many of them. That thought cemented her decision. No, she'd gut it out.

She slid back beneath the covers and turned out the light. She was still awake when she heard a commotion outside. What — ?

Quickly, she wrapped her robe around her and groped under the bed for her slippers. She was halfway to the window when she heard someone shouting.

"Cathy! Cathy! Get out. The garage is on fire!"

It took a moment for the words to register. Fire in the garage below her! Cathy snatched the little framed photo of her parents from her bedside table and slid it into the pocket of her robe. At the door, she reached for the knob, then pulled her hand back with a shriek, bringing it to her lips to soothe the burn. Now what? These stairs were the only real way out. Get out a window? Knot bed sheets together and shinny down them? Would they hold? What if she fell and broke an arm or a leg? There seemed to be no other choice.

She pulled the top sheet off her bed, but before she could make use of it, the floor shook beneath her and a thunderous blast assaulted her eardrums. Something hard struck the back of her head, and she descended into silent darkness.

"I think she's coming around."

Cathy had been under general anesthesia only once in her life: a tonsillectomy when she was six years old. She recalled the sensations as she woke up. The strangeness of moving slowly from a dark tunnel into the light. Her confusion as she tried to make sense of the images hitting her retina. She had that same feeling now. Blurred forms hovered over her, their voices reverberating like sound at a rock concert. Only this time, like a velvet curtain, the smell of smoke permeated the air.

"Doctor, can you talk?" She squinted her eyes and made out the face of Joe Elam, concern lining his already wrinkled face. His wife, Bess, stood beside him.

"I —" Cathy shook her head, trying to clear it as she'd seen athletes do after "having their bell rung." The motion set off a pounding in her head like men with hammers holding a convention inside her skull.

"Just lay back." Bess Elam's voice was calm. No panic there. This was a mother and grandmother, used to taking care of bumps, bruises, and any other catastrophe that came along.

Cathy relaxed back onto the grass and tried to remember how she'd gotten here. Then it came to her. A fire. Then an explosion. Her apartment! Everything she'd accumulated in the past ten years was in there. Granted, most of it was still in boxes, but it was precious to her. Insurance couldn't replace the memories some of those boxes held.

"Doc, open your eyes." She forced her lids to respond and looked into the face of

Mark, the emergency medical technician.

"Mark —" She choked and gagged. Someone held a bottle to her lips, and she sipped water. "We've got to stop meeting this way."

"Yeah." His laugh was forced. "Doc, let me check you over. You got knocked on the head pretty good."

"How long was I out?"

"They tell me it was only a few minutes. But I still need to go through the routine."

She lay still as he took her blood pressure and pulse, then shined a light into her eyes. His fingers probed the back of her skull, setting off an encore by the men with hammers.

After he'd finished his examination, she asked, "So, do I get a clean bill of health?"

Mark sat back on his heels. "You ought to go to the ER and let a real doctor check you. Maybe get a CT scan. But best guess? You'll be okay except for a headache."

"Nothing new for me. Thanks, Mark. Can you help me sit up?"

Willing hands helped her to a sitting position. "Now let me try to stand."

Mark and Joe Elam steadied her so that her legs scarcely bore any weight. She swayed for a few seconds, then said, "Okay, let me try it without your support."

"Doc, we really need to take you to the

ER," Mark said.

She knew she was being stubborn — a doctor trying to treat herself — but she asserted her independence anyway. "I promise I'll let Joe drive me there, but I've had enough ambulance rides this month."

She gritted her teeth against the pain that bored into the back of her head when she turned to look around her. A fire engine idled at the curb, its red and white strobes alternately painting the leaves of a nearby live oak. Two firemen coiled and stowed lengths of hose that looked like huge, putty-colored snakes. In addition to the Elams, she recognized several neighbors.

Cathy turned with dread toward the little garage apartment that had been her home the past two months. She expected to see nothing but a mound of rubble and ashes. Instead, although the steps were badly charred and one side of the garage and her apartment above it were covered with smoke and soot, the framework seemed intact. The garage door stood open, and the Elam's car sat in the driveway. Shadows obscured the interior of the garage, but she could make out puddles of water on the floor.

"What happened?" Cathy asked.

Bess Elam answered. "I was in the kitchen for a snack when I saw somebody moving around over here near the foot of the stairs. I knew you were in for the night, so I was suspicious. Then I saw a flicker — like a match or a lighter — and then some flames. I yelled to Joe and he called 911. By the time we got outside, whoever I'd seen was gone and the corner of the garage was on fire."

Cathy rubbed the back of her head. "I remember an explosion. Did your car blow up?"

"We were afraid the car's gas tank would go, so I had Joe run in and back it out. I started uncoiling our garden hose to fight the fire when, I guess, the fire reached some cans of paint we had stored in the garage. Anyway, they exploded. As best we can figure, the force of that blast rocked the floor of your apartment, making you fall back and hit your head. The firemen were here by then. One of them fought his way up the stairs through the flames and carried you down here. End of story."

Cathy knew better. She was pretty sure that this wasn't the end of the story. It was just another chapter. And she hoped it didn't get any worse before she could bring it to an end.

13

Since the Fire Chief pronounced the stairway to her apartment unsafe, Joe Elam used a tall ladder to climb up and pack a suitcase with Cathy's list of things she needed for the next day or so. Cathy stood at the foot of the ruined stairway and wondered what else could possibly happen? If this was an attempt to kill her, how much worse could it get? The obvious answer was that they could succeed.

Cathy spent the rest of the night curled up on the Elam's couch, waking at every sound. The next morning, she stepped out of the front door, thankful that her car had been parked at the curb, safely out of danger. She paused at the end of the sidewalk, her keys in hand, and took stock of her situation. The smell of smoke permeated the blouse, slacks, and jacket she wore. Nothing she could do about that today, but as soon as she could, she needed to have all her clothes cleaned. Would insurance pay for that? She made a mental note to call her agent when she got to the office. More paperwork, more hassles, more problems.

Before Cathy could open the door of her car, Will Kennedy's pickup screeched to a stop behind her and he jumped out. He covered the ground between them in a few quick strides, and the hug he gave her threatened to crack her ribs. "Cathy, are you all right? I just heard this morning about the fire."

"I'm okay, I guess. Just a few bumps and bruises." She went on to explain what had happened. "The Fire Chief agrees with the Elams that the fire was deliberately set. He thinks someone soaked the corner of the garage and the stairs leading to my apartment with gasoline, then lit it and ran. I'm lucky Bess saw him and got help as quickly as she did."

"Do you plan to stay with the Elams for now?"

She'd wrestled with that one all night. "Joe and Bess made that offer, but their house is so small we'd be tripping over each other. Besides, it will be at least a couple of days before my back unkinks from one night on their couch. I don't know if insurance will cover the cost of a hotel."

"I have a better idea. Why don't you move in with my folks? They have a spare bedroom — my old room, matter of fact — and I know they'd love to have you."

The idea of staying with Pastor and Mrs. Kennedy appealed to her. Truthfully, Cathy had been deeply touched by their kindness. It was like having a family again. On the other hand, she wondered if by moving in she'd open herself up to a "hard sell" about coming back to the church.

It was as though Will read her mind. "In case you're wondering, Dad and Mom won't pressure you about where you are with God. They'll pray for you, that's all. Right now we all want you to be comfortable . . . and safe."

Cathy looked at her watch. "Will, I need to talk with you about something I learned yesterday, but right now I have to get to the office. I have patients to see right up to the close of the day, which, considering the shape of my bank account, is a good thing. But having all this to deal with will keep me tied up all day. I hoped we could get together this evening." She looked toward the smoke-stained walls of her little apartment where Joe and two of his friends were already at work building a new stairway. "I can't cook for you, but can we still have dinner?"

"I've got a suggestion. I'll pick you up at your office about — what? Five thirty?"

"Make it six."

"Okay, I'll come by at six. We'll go to my parents' house for dinner. Then we can talk in Dad's study. If you agree to stay with them, I can come back here for your stuff. Deal?"

Cathy wanted so badly to give up control and let someone else take over her complicated life. So far, Will hadn't disappointed her. She hoped that wouldn't change. With more conviction in her voice than in her heart, she said, "Deal."

Cathy opened the back door of her office suite to find Jane waiting for her. "Are you all right?"

"I'm fine, Jane. Mainly I have a little headache, and I smell like the inside of a wood stove. Other than that, nothing that a good night's sleep won't fix."

"Do you want me to cancel some of today's appointments?"

"No need. I'm fine." *And besides that, if my practice grows a bit, maybe I can start drawing a full salary.* "Give me ten minutes in my office. Then I'll be ready to go."

Cathy had been pinching pennies when she moved to Dainger. Now she was glad she'd let her insurance agent talk her into the added expense of renter's insurance. Her call to him took a bit longer than ten minutes, and Cathy sensed that he wondered whether her business was worth all the trouble she had caused him, but when she hung up she'd extracted a promise to have an adjustor contact her within twenty-four hours. The Elam's insurance would cover the damage to their garage and her apartment, but she would be looking to her own insurance for expenses like cleaning, and replacing personal effects. Idly, she wondered about the effect of the heat and smoke on her laptop, her small collection of CDs, her little portable TV.

Cathy emerged from her office and found Jane waiting in the hall. "Mr. Greiner is in treatment room one. He has a wart on his thumb."

There was no doubt in Cathy's mind that Jane's diagnosis would be correct. In all her years as an office nurse, Jane had probably seen ten times as many cases of *verruca vulgaris*, or common wart, as Cathy had treated in her brief exposure to dermatology.

Cathy put down the magnifying glass she'd used to examine the skin lesion. "Mr.

Greiner, I can refer you to a dermatologist who can freeze that with liquid nitrogen. Or, if you want me to, I can use my Hyfrecator. The end result is the same. Your choice."

"What's the difference?"

"A dermatologist would probably use a spray of liquid nitrogen to freeze that wart. You'll get a little blister in the area. When that comes off, the skin underneath it is pink and tender. But pretty soon it will look and feel completely normal."

"Does it hurt?" he asked.

Cathy remembered her own experience when she'd had a wart removed from her finger while in med school. "My treatment felt like a burn, and it took a while for the pain to go away. After that, though, it was fine."

"What about the high-ver-natum or whatever you said?" Greiner asked.

"This is the Hyfrecator." She pointed to a rectangular off-white plastic box sitting on the waist-high treatment cabinet behind her. A thin black cord connected the box to a pencil-like probe with an angled needle on the tip. "It's an electrocautery unit. Probably the most common one in the world."

"So how does it work?"

"I usually inject a little local anesthetic.

Then I put the tip of the needle in contact with the wart and deliver a low-voltage electric current that makes it shrivel up. A scab forms, and when it comes off, the tissue underneath it is all healed. Same end result as freezing."

Greiner seemed to think about the options. "I don't see any need to go somewhere else for this. What you're suggesting sounds fine to me." He shrugged. "Let's do it."

Fifteen minutes later, while Jane made Greiner's follow-up appointment, Cathy thought back to her reasons for going into family practice. One of the main ones was the ability to offer her patients a broad range of services. She had no intention of taking patients away from the specialists. She referred more complex cases to them and was glad to have their expertise to lean on. No, it all boiled down to what she thought of as her "business model." Give the patient the best care with as little inconvenience to them as possible. Now if the credentials committee would give her all the privileges she needed to do that, maybe she could get on with her life.

Cathy looked up from the forms strewn across her desk. Was that a knock at the door? She looked at her watch. Was it after six already? She hurried to the office's front door, unlocked it, and beckoned Will inside before relocking it.

"Sorry I didn't hear you at first. I've been doing paperwork for about three-quarters of an hour, and I guess I got lost in it." She motioned him to the chair across from her desk. "Give me five more minutes and we can leave."

"No problem." He gestured toward the stack of papers. "If you have that many insurance claims to file, business must be picking up."

"I wish. Most of these are claims we have to re-file because the insurance company either paid incorrectly or denied improperly. Sometimes I think they do that to hang on to their money a bit longer. I wonder how many doctors' offices take the denials at face value, bill the patient for the balance, and let it go at that."

Will leaned back and crossed his legs at the ankles. "That's what makes you special, Cathy. You're not 'most doctors.' You take the time to care. The folks in Dainger are lucky to have you practicing here."

She signed the last form and tossed it on top of all the others. "I hope more of them recognize that. Until some of these insurance claim checks come in, it's pretty slim pickings around here."

She emptied the pockets of her white coat before rolling it into a ball. "Be right back. I need to toss this into the laundry hamper." That accomplished, she pulled her purse from her bottom desk drawer and grabbed her jacket from the hanger on the back of the door. "Let's get out of here. I'm starved, and if what your mother serves on a weekday is anything like what she cooks on Sunday, I'm ready for it."

In the parking lot, she pulled her keys out of her purse and pressed the remote to unlock her car. "Shall I follow you?"

"You can, or you can ride with me and I'll come by in the morning to pick you up and take you to work. That way I get to see you even more."

Cathy thought about it for a moment. Why not? She locked her car and allowed Will to open the door of his pickup for her. When they were both belted in, she said, "What makes you so sure I'll end up staying with your folks?"

He backed out of the parking space and steered into the street before he answered. A big grin spread across his face. "Ladies and gentlemen of the jury, I'd like to call your attention to the following points. Dr. Sewell's back is probably still sore from the

Elam's couch. She likes my parents almost as much as I do. And . . ." He paused for emphasis. "My mother's cooking would lure an escaped convict back to prison."

Cathy gave him a playful punch on the arm. "Wait until I'm back in my apartment. I'll cook for you again. But, in the meantime, I'd be happy to enjoy your folks' hospitality — and your mother's cooking."

Cathy opened one of the boxes Will and his father had just carried to the Kennedy's spare room. Because Joe and his impromptu work detail hadn't yet finished the new stairs, and Will adamantly refused to let Cathy climb up the ladder, she'd had to give him a detailed list of what to pack for her. This had proved sort of embarrassing to Cathy, but he assured her that attorneys, like physicians, were hard to shock.

Dora Kennedy stood in the doorway after the Kennedy men withdrew to give Cathy a degree of privacy as she unpacked. "Dear, can I help you?"

Cathy shook her head. "I think I'll be fine. Again, I really appreciate your letting me stay here. I hope it won't be too long."

"Stay as long as you need to. There are clean sheets on the bed and clean towels in your bathroom. And you just make yourself at home anywhere in the house."

"You've really made me feel at home." Cathy thought about what she wanted to say. It sounded terrible, but it was the truth. "You know, Mrs. Kennedy, I'm more comfortable here than the last time I stayed with my parents."

"Cathy, I mean, Dr. Sewell —"

"Please. I've always been Cathy to you and your husband. Let's don't change that."

"Cathy then. I know you may not want to talk about it, but everyone around here knows about your mother's problems. I'm sure you must have been uncomfortable when you were around her after she got to be so difficult. But before she got sick, she was a wonderful person. And your daddy took good care of her."

Cathy shook her head. "Sorry. That's not what I've heard."

Mrs. Kennedy appeared unfazed. "Dear, you can't be a pastor's wife for almost forty years without learning a few things. You've heard rumors that your daddy wasn't faithful to your mother, haven't you?"

"Yes." Cathy started to say more, but decided to leave it at that. After all, most of what she suspected was unproven. But how do you get hard evidence that your father, who'd been dead for over three years, had cheated on your mother?

"I can't give you the details — I know them, but you'll have to hear them from someone else — but I can tell you this for sure." Dora moved from the doorway into the room and picked up the Bible that lay on the bedside table. "With my hand on this Bible, I'll tell you that your daddy was not unfaithful to your mother."

Cathy couldn't believe it. Emotions swirled through her head like a weather vane in a Texas tornado. Relief. Regret. Anguish. Confusion. She slumped onto the bed and buried her face in her hands. "I so want to believe that."

Dora's voice was soft. "Believe it, dear."

Cathy felt tears form. "I feel so guilty. I didn't want to believe my suspicions about Daddy, but I let them taint my memory of him anyway. Daddy, please forgive me." She choked back a sob. "And God forgive me too."

The bed sagged beside Cathy as Dora Kennedy sat down and gently patted her shoulder.

Her voice was like a gentle wind. "Dear, would you like me to pray with you?"

"Please," Cathy choked out. "Yes, please."

Cathy and Will sat across from each other

at the Kennedy dining table. Will made notes on a yellow legal pad while Cathy shared the details of her conversation with Mrs. Gladstone. "I don't know why Gail Nix would have it in for me, but apparently, she's the one who bullied her husband into filing the malpractice suit."

Will leaned back and balanced his chair on the two back legs, keeping himself in position with one hand on the table. "I think maybe I can tell you a bit about that. This all happened about four years ago. You were still in medical school. I'd just come back to Dainger and started practicing law."

Cathy looked at him expectantly.

He brought the chair down, leaned forward, and drained his coffee cup. "This won't be nice for you to hear."

"I've heard a great deal since I've been back here, and most of it has convinced me that everyone knows everything about everybody else in this town, and most of it's bad. Go on."

"Okay. You remember that Gail Nix is Lloyd Allen's big sister, right?"

Cathy nodded.

"She and Lloyd had another sibling, a sister, Mattie. Mattie was the oldest. Got married and was divorced within a year, but kept her married name: Mattie McElroy.

254

She stayed in Dainger — taught grade school." He picked up his cup, found that it was empty, and put it down. "She came to the emergency room one night, throwing up and hurting something fierce. Fever and chills. Really sick. Unfortunately, she'd waited three days before calling Gail to take her to the hospital."

"What happened?"

"Your father diagnosed a ruptured appendix. He did his best to save her. Folks tell me he sat at her bedside for thirty-six hours straight, doing everything he could. But Mattie died."

"Surely Gail's not holding a grudge against my father for that? By the time he saw her she probably had peritonitis. Some people just can't be saved, and especially if you don't see them until they're already half dead."

"True, it doesn't make sense. And neither does it make sense for her to carry that grudge forward to you. But that appears to be the case."

Cathy stood and paced the few steps from the table to the door and back. "Are you sure about this?"

"Sure as I can be. Gail came to me and wanted to file a malpractice claim against your father. In case you're wondering, I'm not really breaching client confidentiality here, because I wouldn't take her as a client. I told her it wasn't malpractice, just a bad result."

"Did she end up getting another lawyer?"

Will shook his head. "Nope, I was the last one in town she went to. She'd already tried everyone else. Nobody would touch the case. So I guess she's stored up all that venom over the years, and now you're the target of her anger."

14

Jane put a cup of coffee and three pink message slips on Cathy's desk. "Will your insurance cover your losses in the apartment fire?"

Cathy picked up the mug and took a grateful sip. Jane's coffee was better than any she'd ever been able to make herself. She'd have to ask the secret. "Apparently so. The Elams have the same insurance company I have, and the adjustor's already been by. Insurance will pay a professional fire restoration company to clean my clothes and linens. My CDs were ruined by the heat, and my TV set appears to have given up the ghost, but the company will issue a check to cover those." She gazed into her coffee cup. "But they can't give me back the photos the smoke and water ruined."

"So how soon can you move back in?"

"Realistically, I'll probably have to live with the Kennedys for at least another month. Maybe more."

Jane turned toward the door. "That shouldn't be too hard."

"Do you mean Dora's cooking? I agree. She's the best."

"That too, I suppose. But what I meant was the chance to see more of Will Kennedy."

Cathy made a shooing gesture. After Jane left, she smiled to herself as she looked at the list of appointments. If this kept up, the practice might actually show a profit soon. That would be good, considering the size of the note she'd signed at the bank when she borrowed the money to set up her practice. Cathy had been thoroughly confused by the legal language, but Mr. Nix had assured her there'd be no problem renewing it after a year. "Just pay the interest," he'd said. Of course, that was then, and this was now. Nix might not be so accommodating anymore.

There was enough variety among the cases she saw to keep Cathy engaged, but every time she had a break, her thoughts turned away from medicine. The witnesses Will wanted to depose had been served with their subpoenas. Today, he would start with the first two on the list: Milton and Gail Nix. The depositions were scheduled, one after the other, in Sam Lawton's office. Cathy wanted to be present, but Will advised against it.

"We'll get together this evening, and I'll fill you in on everything. I don't expect to learn a lot, but you never know."

All day, Cathy wondered whether Gail Nix was behind the wheel of that Ford Expedition. Somehow, that seemed more like something a man would do. Was Gail's brother, Lloyd, the person who was out to get her? He could have driven the car, probably could have set the fire. And it would have been no problem for him to pull Milton Nix's original prescription from the files and replace it with the altered photocopy.

Then again, perhaps this was connected to her father in some way. Doctors might be respected by most patients, but someone could still be carrying a grudge, one they were willing to extend to the next generation.

Did the cause of her problems lie in Dallas? Maybe not just her troubles with Robert. Had anyone suffered from a mistake she made during her residency?

"That was the last patient." Jane took the chart Cathy handed her. "Going home?"

"No, I'll try to finish this paperwork while

259

I wait for Will."

It was almost six thirty when Cathy heard rapping at the outer door. Will stood in the hall, the picture of exhaustion. His tie hung at half-mast, his dress shirt was wilted and sweat-stained. Cathy motioned him in and followed him into her office.

"I take it the deposition didn't go well?" she said.

Will nodded silently before slumping into the chair across the desk from Cathy. He dropped his briefcase and rubbed at his temples.

Cathy gave him a "wait a second" gesture and went to the workroom to get sodas for them both.

Will took his and held it against his forehead for a moment before pulling the tab and gulping half the can. "It was like butting my head against a stone wall. In the law, the term is 'the deponent knoweth not,' meaning that the person giving the deposition denies any knowledge. Maybe they forgot, maybe they can't recall. Whatever it is, it doesn't give the lawyer doing the questioning anything he can sink his teeth into."

"So you didn't find out anything useful?"

"Nix says it was his idea to file the suit. Maintains that, although he discussed it with his wife, he made the final decision. I believe his words were, 'to protect the citizens of Dainger from Dr. Sewell.' Made you sound like a cross between Typhoid Mary and Son of Sam."

Cathy took a sip of her soft drink. "And I suppose they denied altering the prescription?"

Will shook his head. "I didn't bring it up. I asked them how they explained the directions being different from what you had charted, and they both had the same answer: You must have written the prescription wrong, then realized your mistake and tried to cover it up by making the right entry on the chart."

"That's so —"

"Easy." Will held up a hand, palm forward. "Let's don't show our defense just yet. I've still got to depose both pharmacists. I want to get these people alone in a room with a stenographer, under oath, and see if I can rattle them enough that they can't keep their stories straight. Somewhere along the line, maybe I can trip up the person responsible for all this."

Cathy spun around in her chair to look at the books behind her. She didn't know everything that was in each one, but she knew most of it. She was a good doctor —

as good as any other doctor in Dainger, probably better than some of them. Why did she have to go through all this? Who was behind it? Maybe it wasn't one person. Could there be two? Three? Apparently there was no lack of people who had something against her or her family.

"Penny for your thoughts," Will said.

"Just wondering whether we should lump all these incidents together. Is it possible that the person driving the black SUV, the one who almost killed me, is a different person from the one who set the fire? And could a third person be responsible for the altered prescription? Are there two or three people — even more — who are in some sort of a conspiracy to drive me away?"

Everyone else had gone to bed, but Cathy couldn't sleep. She decided to curl up in bed with a book and read. She was about to turn out the light when her cell phone rang. The caller ID showed "Marcus Bell." She didn't really want to talk with him, but she was on call tonight. Maybe she was needed at the hospital.

"Dr. Sewell."

"Cathy, this is Marcus. I hope it's not too late."

Too late for us, she thought. She tried to

put a smile in her voice. "Not at all. How can I help you?"

Marcus cleared his throat. "Actually, I think it's the other way around. As I've told you before, you seem to have impressed the doctors on the credentials committee who voted against giving you extended privileges. Now I think you have the votes you need to get everything you've requested. The committee meets next week. All I need from you is a verbal request for them to revisit the issue."

"And if the vote ends up tied, does the Chief of Staff plan to abstain again?"

"Cathy, you have to understand. I can't take sides. Why don't you just depend on the impression you've made on the committee members to give you a solid majority?"

Her gut instinct told her to hang up on the man. How could she have let herself be attracted to someone this self-centered? Instead, she said, "Yes, please ask the committee to reconsider my privileges. Maybe this time I won't have to depend on your support."

"I can understand how angry you must be."

"Not really, Marcus. You're an honors graduate of a prestigious medical school. You got your surgery training at a top-notch

263

program. You came here with all sorts of recommendations. And, besides that, you're a man. No, you can't possibly understand how angry and frustrated I am to be treated this way." Cathy heard the shrillness creep into her voice. Well, let it. It was time Marcus heard this. "I've heard doctors refer to female colleagues as 'pushy broads' when all they asked for was respect. Well, I've tried not to be a 'pushy broad,' but no more. I intend to stand up for myself — with or without your help."

Marcus started to respond, but she ignored him. He was still talking when she pushed the button to end the call, wishing for an old-fashioned black Bakelite instrument — one she could slam down into its cradle with a satisfying bang.

Jane put a slim number ten envelope on Cathy's desk. "This came for you this morning."

"There's no stamp. How did it get here?"

"Myra Johnson, one of the tellers at the bank, brought it by."

Cathy noticed the return address printed on the envelope: First State Bank of Dainger. Was this about the lawsuit? Why would Nix have a teller hand deliver it? Why not his lawyer? She reached for the envelope, but stopped with her hand hovering in the air. Letter bomb? *Don't be silly. Now* that's *paranoid.*

She slit the envelope with the brass opener that rested inside a mug on her desk, along with a collection of pens and pencils. Inside was a single sheet of bank stationery. The letter, only three paragraphs long, was signed by Milton Nix, President and Chairman of the Board. Although most of it was "legalese," she had no trouble understanding the last paragraph. It began with a sentence that brought her world crashing down around her.

"The Loan Board has reviewed your circumstances and believes that there is an undue element of risk present in the loan as it stands. Therefore, we must ask that you reduce the principal balance of your indebtedness by at least five thousand dollars, as well as paying the interest to date, before we can continue the loan."

Her stomach churned. She swallowed hard to force down the bile and acid she tasted. She hadn't counted on this. The note she'd signed wouldn't mature for another nine months. Several times over the past few months the thought of a seventy thousand dollar debt hanging over her had brought her to the edge of panic. But Nix had assured her: "Simply pay the interest, and we'll renew it for another year." How could the bank do this?

More importantly, how could she pay? Cathy knew, almost to the penny, the balance in her bank accounts. Her personal account was almost nonexistent. The separate account she maintained for the practice had just enough to cover this month's expenses and perhaps a small salary for her. It would be a struggle to come up with the interest payment, but how could she raise an additional five thousand dollars? How long did she have? She read the final paragraph of the letter again and again, each time swiveling her eyes between her desk calendar and the letter. She had less than a week.

Jane still hovered nearby, apparently sensing the letter had delivered bad news. Cathy turned to her.

"Did Ms. Johnson say why she delivered this by hand? And why I'm just getting it? I should have had this at least two weeks ago."

"She said they'd tried to mail it to you twice, but it came back."

"What is it with those people?" Cathy fumed. "First they bounce a check for my insurance premium. Now they can't get my address right. You'd think —"

"What?"

"Nothing. Give me a few minutes before you put the first patient in."

Cathy sat tapping the letter opener on the desk. At first she thought it was far-fetched. The longer she thought about it, the more logical it seemed. Was there someone at the bank who didn't want her to succeed? Was the person so anxious to see Cathy leave town somehow connected with the bank? She ticked off the suspects on her fingers.

Milton Nix? He'd been helpful, gone out on a limb to give her the loan in the first place. Why the change? Cathy could think of one reason — her next suspect.

Gail Nix? She was the one who'd badgered her husband into filing the lawsuit. And wasn't there an SUV in their garage? Was this because of the death of Gail's sister, a death she still blamed on Cathy's father?

Ella Mae Mercer? Cathy hadn't figured her out. Why would she go to the trouble of making sure Cathy received the money to cover her loss after the car crash, and then do this? Or did Will put pressure on the woman so that she had to appear to help. And what had been Ella Mae's relationship to Nolan Sewell? Could that have a connection to this?

Then it struck Cathy. There was one more person with possible access to the digitalis prescription. If Nix went back to his office and left his prescription lying on his desk, what was to stop Ella Mae from snatching it, making the alterations, and returning it before Nix had a chance to get it filled? Cathy couldn't believe the woman would have the knowledge to change the prescription, but then again, with the Internet there was a lot of information out there for the taking. It was a long shot, but it was possible. Or could someone else at the bank have altered the script?

Jane poked her head into the office and waved a chart. "Ready?"

"I suppose so." Cathy pushed herself up out of her chair, feeling as though her spine had turned to mush. "And while I'm with this patient, would you total up our unpaid claims? Then start calling the insurance companies to see if you can speed up those payments."

"Is this about that letter?"

"I'm afraid the letter is only the tip of the iceberg. But right now, that iceberg's about to crash into our ship. I need to raise over five thousand dollars in a hurry if we don't want a repeat of the Titanic."

Cathy waited until Jane left before she swiveled around and pulled a dog-eared directory from the shelf behind her desk.

Please don't let it come to this, she thought. But she had to find out. If everything fell to pieces, did she have a way out? Was there somewhere she could go and start over yet again?

She could only imagine the anguish pursuing this option might cause her. But it looked as though Cathy's chances of staying in Dainger were slim to none. Frying pan or fire? Bad choices, either way.

Before she could lose her resolve, Cathy punched in a series of ten numbers. An electronic voice invited her to enter an extension number or hold for an operator. What was the extension? Once it had been as familiar as her name. Could it have flown from her memory in such a short time?

Think, Cathy. "Please hold for the operator." Was it 2732? Was that it? She punched in the numbers and waited as the call rang through.

"Family Practice."

When she heard the voice, the name of the secretary came to Cathy immediately. "Lisa?"

There was a brief pause. "Yes? Who's calling?"

"This is Cathy Sewell. Is Dr. Gross in?"

"Oh, Dr. Sewell. So good to hear from you. How are you doing?"

Just wonderful — someone wants to kill me, the bank is threatening to foreclose, and I'm sleeping in a guest room in the parsonage after my apartment burned. Couldn't be better.

"Fine," Cathy said. "Just fine. Now is Dr. Gross there?"

"Sure. Let me buzz her."

Cathy was relaxing to the strains of a classical piece when she heard the cheery voice of the department chair, the woman who'd been her mentor during her residency. "Cathy, good to hear from you. How can I help?" That was just like Amy. Right to the point.

"Amy, is that position at the school still available?"

The silence that followed gave Cathy her answer before Amy spoke. "We filled it right after you turned it down. Are there problems with your practice there in Dainger?"

Cathy assured Amy that everything was fine. Oh, there were a few glitches, but nothing unusual. She just wanted to explore her options. Maybe she'd come back for Grand Rounds next month and they could visit. Amy encouraged her to do that, perhaps stay over so they could have dinner together.

As she hung up the phone, Cathy felt her throat tighten, as though someone had just put a noose around her neck and kicked the horse out from under her. Pretty apt, she figured.

That door had slammed shut. There was no way out. No running away from Dainger.

The day seemed to stretch to infinity, but at last Cathy could head home. Well, not really home. Then again, where was home? Did she even have a home? Ugh, enough philosophy.

She had just buckled her seat belt when her cell phone rang. She fished it out of her purse and scanned the display: the hospital. Had there been an order she'd neglected to write? Was she behind on her dictation again? "Dr. Sewell."

"Doctor? This is Glenna in the ER. Isn't Ella Mae Mercer your patient?"

Bells clanged in Cathy's head. "Yes."

"The ambulance just brought her in — comatose. When Ella Mae didn't return from lunch, her secretary got worried and decided to check on her. She found Ella Mae on the couch in her living room, totally unresponsive. The secretary called 911. They brought her here."

Cathy threw the car into reverse and backed out of her parking space. "Is she breathing on her own?"

271

"Shallow. Blood pressure's down, pulse slow. Pupils a little constricted but equal. No signs of trauma."

"Get her on oxygen — mask for now, but we may have to tube her. Start an IV, draw blood for glucose, BUN and creatinine, liver panel, and a tox screen. Get some blood gases cooking. Alert radiology that we may need a head CT. Who's the ER doctor today?"

"Dr. Patel. He thinks she may have had a stroke."

Cathy accelerated, hoping she wouldn't encounter her nemesis, the black SUV. She squealed around the corner. "Tell Dr. Patel not to do anything. I'll be there in two minutes." She took a deep breath. *Be diplomatic, Cathy.* "And thank him for me."

In a few moments, Cathy was at Ella Mae Mercer's bedside. Her examination was swift and focused. No cuts or swelling of the scalp. No stiffness of the neck. Pupils equal in size, maybe a bit constricted, but normal reaction to light. Tendon reflexes diminished generally. No evidence of head injury. A little young for a stroke. "Let's hold off on that brain CT for now."

"Radiology's on standby. I'll keep it that way until you're sure," Glenna said.

"See if one of the ambulance crew that

brought her in is still around." Cathy heard the squeak of rubber-soled running shoes as Glenna hurried out of the room.

The lab work would help, but it would take a while. The physical exam suggested a few things. But if Cathy's suspicions were right, the EMTs should be able to confirm them.

"You wanted to ask me something, Doc?"

Cathy turned and saw a paramedic she didn't recognize standing in the doorway.

"Tell me what you found at Ella Mae's home."

"She was on the living room couch — lying there with her hands crossed over her chest — almost like she'd been . . . laid out."

"Any sign of drugs in the room?"

"Didn't I — ?" He reached into the pocket of his jacket and pulled out a small amber vial. He held it out to her. "I picked this up off the coffee table next to the couch. Thought I'd already given it to Glenna. Sorry. I'm coming off a double shift, and I guess I'm a step slow."

A glance at the label on the bottle confirmed what Cathy already suspected. Now she knew why Ella Mae was in a coma.

15

Cathy put the vial in her pocket. "Besides the pill bottle, did you see any liquor? Beer? Wine?"

"No." The EMT shook his head. "Nothing like that in the room. Just a half-full glass of water on the table next to the pills."

Ella Mae had said she didn't drink. Cathy hoped that was true. If so, it might make the difference between her living and dying. "Thank you. Now please send Glenna back in here."

Cathy turned back to Ella Mae, letting her eyes travel back and forth between the figure lying deathly still on the bed and the monitor displaying her vital functions. Respirations were shallow and slow, oxygen saturation dropping. Blood pressure down, although not at shock levels. Cathy needed to rid the woman's circulation of the tranquilizer as quickly and completely as possible. But before that, she had to make sure

Ella Mae's breathing and circulation were adequate.

"So it's a drug overdose?" Glenna's voice came from behind Cathy, soft yet focused.

"I'm pretty sure it is, and I don't have time to wait half a day for the results of a tox screen. I'm ready to go with that diagnosis."

"What do you — ?"

A sharp electronic screech made Cathy turn toward the monitor. The pulse oximeter showed a dangerous drop in oxygen saturation. When Cathy looked at Ella Mae's chest, she could hardly detect any motion there.

"She's quit breathing. We need to tube her." Cathy snatched up a laryngoscope from the equipment cart in the corner and moved quickly to the head of the gurney. She checked the light at the tip of the scope, then moved the plastic oxygen mask aside and opened Ella Mae's mouth. Cathy slipped the L-shaped instrument in, moving it carefully along the tongue, lifting the epiglottis. Pooled saliva obscured her view of the vocal cords.

"Suction," Cathy said.

The words were hardly out of Cathy's mouth before Glenna slid the tip of a suction tube into Ella Mae's throat and cleared

275

the secretions.

"Endotracheal tube." Glenna slapped a large, curved plastic tube into Cathy's free hand.

Where did the vocal cords go? It had probably been a year since Cathy had done an intubation, but she hoped her instructors had been right when they said it was like riding a bicycle.

"Please, God." She didn't realize she'd spoken the words aloud until she heard Glenna whisper, "Yes, please Lord."

There! She saw the cords, the gateway to the airway she had to enter. Careful now, don't mess this up. Cathy eased the tip of the tube between the cords, and in a matter of seconds a mechanical ventilator pumped oxygen into Ella Mae's lungs at a regular fourteen breaths per minute.

Cathy taped the endotracheal tube in place. "How's her pressure?"

"Still ninety over sixty. Pulse steady at fifty-eight. Want to give her some Levophed?"

"Put some in a bottle of D5W and piggyback it into the Ringer's lactate that's running. We'll try to titrate her pressure back up. And get me some Romazicon. I'll give her a dose IV. That should help."

"Right here," Glenna said. "I drew up 5

276

ml. in the syringe. That way you can give two doses if you need to."

Cathy swabbed the insertion port of Ella Mae's IV tubing with alcohol, inserted the needle, and injected 2 cc of Romazicon.

In a few minutes, Ella Mae's vital signs had stabilized, but she still was unresponsive. Time for the messy part — gastric lavage. Cathy rummaged in the cabinet until she found a nasogastric tube. She lubricated the long, thin tube and passed it through one of Ella Mae's nostrils, advancing it carefully until she was sure it was in the stomach. Then Cathy used a large plastic syringe with a rubber bulb at one end to draw up saline solution. She inserted the tip of the syringe into the tube and gently squeezed the bulb until all the liquid had been delivered. She waited a few seconds before releasing her pressure, letting the bulb expand to create suction that would pull the stomach contents back into the syringe.

The first washing yielded very little. On the second, Cathy hit pay dirt. When she applied suction this time, a number of small, white, oval tablets, still intact, floated into the syringe. She repeated the maneuver a dozen times or more until the return was completely clear. Good. Now to put something into the stomach to inactivate any drug still there.

"Let me have that activated charcoal," she said. "A hundred grams in half a liter of water should do it."

Cathy injected the mixture into Ella Mae's stomach and clamped the end of the tube. She'd leave it in place for a while, just in case.

How were the vital signs doing? She looked at the monitor and saw that Ella Mae's blood pressure had dropped again. Increase the Levophed? If she gave too much, she could give the woman a stroke from bleeding into the brain. If she let the pressure get too low, there could be damage to vital organs from inadequate blood flow. She decided not to let the pressure go any lower. She increased the flow of Levophed into the IV, her eyes glued to the monitor. After five minutes the pressure was at a level that Cathy felt was acceptable.

Cathy closed off the Levophed drip. "Leave that hanging, but I hope she won't need any more."

"So what's next?"

"Now we wait," Cathy said. "Glenna, how long have you been working in the ER?"

"Since they opened this new hospital. I wanted to go to medical school, but my parents couldn't afford it. I went to nursing

278

school on a scholarship, came back here, and this job opened up right about then so I grabbed it. I guess —"

There was a faint hiccup from Ella Mae. She moved her left arm, pulling weakly at the restraint that held it to the side rail of the gurney. Cathy picked up a rubber-headed reflex hammer and tapped at the bend of Ella Mae's elbow, first one and then the other. She thought that maybe the resulting jerk was a bit stronger than before. Or was that wishful thinking on her part?

Cathy put down the hammer. "She may be waking up. I'll hold off on more Romazicon for now."

Gradually, the numbers for blood pressure on the green monitor screen above Ella Mae's head climbed. Her pulse rate sped up slowly. She bucked against the tube in her throat. Cathy watched until she was sure that Ella Mae was breathing more rapidly than the programmed inhalations from the respirator. She flipped a switch and the respirator was silent.

"Let's keep the tube in until I'm sure she's okay. Why don't you call the admitting office and get a room for her? She probably should be in the ICU for the next eight hours or so. And do we have a psychiatrist on call?"

"There's one who comes from Fort Worth twice a week. He's not here today, but he'll drive down for emergencies."

"No," Cathy said. "It's not an emergency. I can handle it for now. But we need to ask him to see her in consultation. Suicide attempts aren't in my area of expertise."

Glenna sniffed and Cathy thought she detected a smile on the woman's face. "From what I've seen, Doctor, there's not much that happens around here that you can't handle. But I'll call and arrange the consultation."

"Thanks, Glenna." Cathy brushed her hair aside. "And if it helps any, I think you're doing a better job of helping your fellow man right here than a lot of the doctors I've run into. So don't feel bad about not going to medical school. You just keep on with your work in the ER."

Cathy settled onto a stool in the corner of the room and wrote an admitting note and orders. She marveled that there was so much talent here in her hometown. Glenna, Will, Jane. She hated to admit it, but she had to include Arthur Harshman. Cathy had thought returning to Dainger constituted an admission of failure, acknowledgement that she wasn't good enough for the big time. Now she wasn't so sure. Maybe the big time was overrated. Maybe coming back home had been a good choice.

Cathy slid her key into the lock and eased open the front door.

"Dear, is everything all right?" Dora Kennedy, her hair in curlers, her flannel robe pulled around her neck, sat in an easy chair in the front room, reading a Bible. "You were so late getting home, we were worried."

"I'm fine. I just had an emergency case that took quite a bit of time. I didn't mean for you to wait up for me."

"You missed supper, but I saved a plate for you. In the old days I would have put it in the oven on low heat to stay warm. Now, I'll just pop it into the microwave."

Cathy followed Dora into the kitchen. She wondered what it would have been like growing up in a home where the kitchen was a center of social life. She could imagine the smells that filled the house as Dora cooked and Pastor Matthew sat at the kitchen table watching her, the two of them sharing thoughts from their day. She envied Will for the chance he'd had to be a part of that experience. In her home, the maid had done the cooking while her mother spent her days sequestered in her room, often taking her meals there as well.

"Can you tell me about your emergency, or is it confidential?" Dora punched a few buttons and waited as the carousel inside the microwave spun and the square box did its electronic magic.

"A patient took an overdose of tranquilizers — pills I'd prescribed, incidentally — and was brought into the emergency room in a coma."

"Were you able to save the patient?" There was concern, not curiosity, in the question.

"Yes. It was a tough fight, but everything turned out okay. The nurses in the intensive care unit will call me on my cell phone if there are any problems through the night."

Cathy looked at the plate Dora set in front of her: lasagna, green beans, a piece of buttered French bread. Dora opened the refrigerator and pulled out a small plate of salad. "Milk or tea?"

"Milk, please. And thank you for saving this for me."

"No thanks necessary." She poured a cup from a Mr. Coffee sitting on the counter, pulled out a chair, and sat opposite Cathy.

Cathy picked up her fork, then saw the expectant look on the older woman's face. She didn't know if she could pray over the food, but tonight she felt as though she should. She bowed her head and said, "God, thank you for this food and for the wonderful woman who prepared it. Thank you for these people who have opened their home and their hearts to me. Amen."

"Is there anything we can do for the woman who tried to commit suicide?" Dora asked.

Cathy paused with a bite halfway to her mouth. Had she said "woman?" She didn't think so. "Do you know about this already?"

Dora nodded. "Yes, we know it was Ella Mae Mercer."

Cathy chewed a mouthful of lasagna and followed it with a swallow of cold milk. Wonderful. "To answer your question, I don't know what any of us can do. I'll ask a psychiatrist to evaluate her. When people try to commit suicide, it's generally a cry for help. Maybe he can find out what triggered this."

"Would it be all right if Matthew and I went by to see her? After you feel she's up to it, of course."

Cathy's answer came out without conscious thought. "Why?"

"Because we care about our neighbors, just like Jesus taught us to. And sometimes praying for them isn't enough. Sometimes it's necessary to put hands and feet to those

283

prayers. Maybe we can do something for her. But we'll never know unless we ask."

Cathy started to speak, then changed her mind and took a bite of bread so she'd have time to think. She'd been content to dump the problem into the lap of a psychiatrist. The Kennedys were willing to get involved themselves.

"Please don't take this the wrong way," Cathy said, "but I have to ask. When you see tragedies, you don't seem to shy away from them. And you don't get angry with God when they happen. I can't understand it."

Dora went to the coffee maker and refilled her cup. She held up the pot with a questioning look and Cathy nodded. She wasn't about to sleep anytime soon.

After handing Cathy a cup, Dora settled back at the table. "We've had our troubles. You were too young to remember, but Will had an older sister. She died when she was a baby. Nowadays they would have called it SIDS or crib death or something. Back then, it was just 'the will of God.' It broke our hearts."

Cathy felt a tug at her own heartstrings. "How terrible."

"Yes, it was. But it wasn't God's fault. And we came through it, with His help." Dora

284

stood and put her cup in the sink. She took Cathy's dishes from her and did the same. Then she looked into Cathy's eyes and said, "God didn't kill your parents. God didn't make Ella Mae try to commit suicide. And God didn't break your heart. He doesn't cause bad things to happen. But, when they do, He's here to comfort us. Learn to lean on Him. Don't give up on God. He hasn't given up on you."

16

Cathy hurried into her office and closed the door behind her.

"Sheriff, I'm sorry to keep you waiting. Busy morning." She leaned across the desk to shake hands with the man, sitting in the patient chair before easing into her own. "What do you have for me?"

J. C. Dunaway waved away Cathy's apology and opened the large manila envelope he held. "There are sixty or so Ford Expeditions in Summers County, and most of them are black. I brought you the list. Take some time to go over it and see if any of these are folks that might be out to do you harm." He handed her two sheets of paper.

"I really appreciate this. I'll have to look at it later, though. Then I'll give you a call."

Dunaway took his Stetson off his knee, where it had been resting. "Glad to help. Now I don't want you to think we'll haul in everyone who owns a black Ford Expedi-

286

tion, put them under a bright light, and try to wring a confession out of them." He gave a wry grin. "Can't do that. But we will keep looking into it. I don't suppose you've had any more run-ins with that vehicle?"

Cathy thought of the near miss in Will's pickup. He'd thought it was probably just a speeding driver caught by a short yellow light. She shook her head. "No, but if I do I'll call your department right away. I drive with my cell phone on the seat right beside me now."

A disturbing thought flashed through Cathy's mind. There'd been no appearances of the mysterious black SUV since Ella Mae was hospitalized. Was hers one of the names on that list of owners? She couldn't help but sneak a peek, then felt a chill when she saw the name at the bottom of the first page: Ella Mae Mercer.

Cathy rose and Dunaway followed suit. She walked him to the door, ignoring the stares of patients in the waiting room, who were obviously curious about what business the Sheriff of Summers County could possibly have with their doctor.

Cathy turned around and started toward the exam room where her next patient waited, but Jane stopped her outside the door. "Will Kennedy wants you to call him when you have a break."

"I'm busy until this afternoon. Did you tell him that?"

"Yep, and he just said, 'Please ask her to call me when she can. It's not urgent, but I need to speak with her before the end of the day.' So I'm telling you."

As it turned out, thanks to a fortunate combination of patients with simple problems and the combined efficiency of doctor and nurse, at ten minutes after twelve, Cathy and Jane looked out on an empty waiting room.

Cathy patted her nurse on the shoulder. "Thanks. That went well."

"I guess we're a pretty good team. Would you like to go with me to the Dairy Queen for a chicken sandwich?"

"No, thanks," Cathy said. "I think I'll have a Power Bar here at my desk while I return some of these phone calls. See you at one."

Cathy shuffled through the half-dozen pink slips, glancing at the names and messages, automatically placing them in what she considered their order of importance. The bottom slip simply had a notation: Call Will Kennedy. That call was probably as important as any of them, but she wanted to be able to take her time with it. She set that one aside.

Twenty minutes later, she had answered the questions of two patients and made office appointments for two more. Then she dialed Will's private number. It was noon and she didn't expect to catch him in, but maybe she could leave a message. Lately, they seemed to play a lot of phone tag.

"Will Kennedy."

His voice brought her out of her reverie. "Will, this is Cathy. What's so important?"

"You are." He laughed. "At least, that's my opinion. I think it's time you and I had a quiet dinner, not an attorney-client meeting, just a social occasion. I propose that you break free from that antiseptic-scented prison of an office at a reasonable time tonight. We can have an early dinner, then see if there are any movies worth seeing."

"But —"

"No buts. I've even spoken with my mother, and she promises not to wait up with the porch light on. That way I can have some privacy when I walk my girl to the door."

Cathy did some quick mental calculations. She should be finished in the office sometime after five. She'd seen Ella Mae this morning, but she decided she'd pop in again this evening to make sure her patient was okay.

"Are you still there?" Will asked.

"Sorry, just thinking. I guess I can get away. Why don't I meet you somewhere at six thirty?"

"RJ's at six thirty it is. Be there —"

"Or be square." Cathy laughed and hung up. It felt as though she were a senior in high school again. And it felt good.

"Nice meal." Cathy dabbed at her lips, then folded her napkin and tucked it under the edge of her plate.

"That's because of the company," Will said. He lifted his cup in a toast, and Cathy responded in kind.

They sipped their coffee in silence, until Cathy turned serious. "I know we promised not to talk business tonight, but you need to know about the letter I received from the bank."

"What letter?"

Cathy explained about the bank's demand.

Will frowned. "You just got this yesterday? Why so little notice?"

"They said they'd tried to mail it but had the address wrong. They can't seem to get anything right there. I'm wondering . . . Oh, never mind." Cathy shook her head. "Will, can they do this? Make me pay early?"

"Unfortunately, they can. I haven't seen the note, but I'm betting there's language that allows them to call it or alter the terms if they think their investment is at risk." Will leaned forward and took her hand in his. "Can you raise the money?"

"I'm trying. I have Jane going through all our receivables, contacting all the insurance companies that owe me money. But, frankly, I don't think I can come anywhere near that figure in less than a week."

Will signaled to the waiter, who refilled their cups and discreetly dropped a black folder onto the table. Will glanced at the bill and covered it with a credit card.

They both took their time getting the cream and sugar just right in their coffee. Finally, Cathy took her coffee cup in both hands and gazed over the rim. "So, I need to decide what to do with my life after Sheriff Dunaway auctions my office furniture and equipment from the courthouse steps." She laughed without mirth.

"Would you allow me to help you? Just a loan to you to tide you over?"

"I couldn't. I've got to stand on my own two feet."

"Then let me give you some advice as a friend. Ask your attorney to talk with the bank president on Monday and see if he can negotiate your way out of this unreasonable demand. How would that be?"

Cathy ran through scenarios in her head. She really wanted to handle this herself. On the other hand, she was pretty sure that Will could negotiate with Nix more successfully than she could at this point. "Tell you what. The payment's due next Tuesday. Give me until Monday evening to see what I can do. I can probably raise at least part of the five thousand dollars. Maybe we can get him to accept that."

"Plus interest," Will said.

She sighed. "Yes, plus interest."

In the car, they considered the movies available and decided that none were worth the effort. Cathy was about to suggest they call it an early evening when Will said, "Why don't we sit on the front porch and just talk? Sort of like the old days?"

The night was mild, a pleasant fall evening. They rocked back and forth in the old porch swing in companionable silence. Finally, Will spoke. "Why did you let a failed college fling come between us? Did you think I wouldn't understand? We all make mistakes."

"Not me." Cathy shivered and pulled her jacket tighter. "I was always the perfect child. That's what my parents expected, or at least, that was my perception. I wasn't ready for anyone to know about my mistake with Carter."

"What about Robert?"

"You remembered his name?"

"Hey, I had his picture pasted to a dart board in my bedroom until you broke off the engagement. But did you consider hooking up with someone who broke your heart some sort of unpardonable sin?"

Cathy shook her head. "I don't know. All I can tell you is that I figured I'd struck out twice with men, and when I came back here I wasn't about to go for the hat trick."

Will laughed. "You're probably the only woman in Dainger who knows what a hat trick is."

"Three goals by the same person in a hockey game. If I wanted to get any attention from my father, I had to learn about sports."

"If you're still interested in sports, maybe you'd like to go to the high school football game with me next Friday night. Everybody in town turns out."

"Thanks, but no. I'd just be thinking that somewhere in that crowd is the person who wants to ruin my life." Cathy looked at her watch. "It's getting late. I know tomorrow's Saturday and you can sleep late, but I have to make rounds in the morning. Then I need to sit down and look at the financial information Jane's gathered for me." She eased out of the swing and turned toward Will. "Thank you for a lovely evening. It was wonderful to just relax and be myself."

"That's all you ever need to be." Will gave her a hug and kissed her lightly. "Just be yourself. There's nothing you can ever do that will make me feel any differently about you."

Cathy thought about those last words as she drifted off to sleep. Will said his feelings wouldn't change. But what were those feelings?

Cathy's starched white coat rustled as she reached to pick up Ella Mae's chart from the rack at the ICU nurses' station. Vital signs looked good. Lab work was fine except for the positive benzodiazepine test on the toxicology screen, confirming what Cathy already knew.

Cathy located the ICU charge nurse sitting at the far end of the counter that served as a workspace for the nurses. "How is Ella Mae this morning?"

The nurse put down her pen and turned to face Cathy. "Physically, I think she's pretty much over the effects of the drug.

Her vital signs are stable. Respirations full and unlabored. Output is fine, so there's probably no kidney damage. But all she does is lie there with her eyes closed."

"Do you know what days the psychiatrist comes to Dainger to see consults?"

"Monday and Thursday, I think."

Shamed by what she'd heard from Dora Kennedy, Cathy decided she couldn't just take care of Ella Mae's physical needs and leave her emotional problems to the consulting psychiatrist. She wondered if she could offer genuine support to a woman who might have tried to harm her, even kill her. Saving Ella Mae's life was one thing. It had been automatic — a duty she felt deeply. This was different. Still, Cathy had to try.

Cathy walked into Ella Mae's glass-walled room and stopped at the foot of the bed. The woman lay perfectly still, her eyes closed, her arms crossed on her chest to the extent that the IV tubing allowed. It was as though she were in a coffin. Cathy remembered the EMT's description of the way he'd found Ella Mae. *As though she were laid out.* There had to be a message in that.

"Ella Mae, are you awake?"

No movement. No response.

Cathy pulled up a chair. She put her hand on top of Ella Mae's and patted it. "You gave us quite a scare Thursday night. I think you'll be fine, but I need to know why you did this. More importantly, I need some reassurance that you won't try it again as soon as I discharge you. Can you tell me about it?"

No answer.

"Would you like something to eat? I think we can let you have a liquid diet, maybe advance to soft foods tomorrow. How would that be?"

The only response was a deep sigh.

Cathy rose and pushed the chair back against the wall. "You know, we can keep you on IVs for a while, but I've got to warn you. You can't lose too many pounds, or we'll never find you among the bedclothes." The attempt at humor fell flat.

At the door, she decided to try one more time. "I'll be by this evening to see you. Maybe transfer you to a regular room. But I still wish you'd talk to me."

Ella Mae's lips hardly moved, and Cathy had to strain to hear the words. "It's all in the note. I'm sorry."

"It's all in the note." What note? It had never occurred to Cathy to ask the paramedic about a note. At the time she'd been more interested in details that might help her save Ella Mae's life. She'd done that, but now she needed to bring her patient back from the depression that still gripped her.

Cathy found a free phone in the corner of the busy nurses' station, thumbed through a dog-eared directory, and dialed.

"Police. How may I help you?"

"This is Dr. Cathy Sewell. I'm caring for a patient who took an overdose in an apparent suicide attempt. I need to speak with the investigating officer."

It took a bit of convincing, but eventually Cathy was put through. The next words made her realize how small Dainger really was. "This is Sergeant Dendy."

"Billy Dendy?"

"Yes, this is Sergeant William Dendy. Who's this?"

"This is Dr. Cathy Sewell. Remember the girl who gave you a black eye in the sixth grade?"

Dendy's tone was warmer than Cathy expected. "How could I forget? I heard you were back in town. It's good to hear from you."

"First of all, I guess I ought to apologize for the black eye."

"Hey, I wouldn't stop pulling your hair. I probably deserved it. How can I help you?"

Cathy explained the reason for her call. "Did you find a note?"

"Nope. No note. Nothing on her computer. The paramedics found an empty prescription bottle, and that was all." Dendy cleared his throat. "The report says this was definitely a suicide attempt. We've closed the books on the case, but if you think somebody tried to poison her we can reopen things."

"No, I'm pretty sure she took an overdose. I just have no idea why she did it. And all she'll say is, 'It's all in the note.' But there's no note."

"Well, if you hear anything we should know, give me a call."

Cathy cradled the phone and tried to ignore the commotion around her. Nurses and doctors crowded into the little nursing station, snatching charts from the rack or shoving them back into their slots. The overhead pager called out sporadically. The business of the hospital went on uninterrupted while she tried to make sense of what she'd just heard.

Why had Ella Mae tried to end her life? And where was the note?

Cathy roused at the sound of the light tap on her door. It seemed as though her head had only touched the pillow a few minutes ago. Was it time to go to work? No, she always set an alarm, and it hadn't gone off. She started to roll out of bed and encountered a wall. Confused, she reached for the bedside lamp, and her fingers found only air.

There was the tap again. "What?" she croaked, her eyes still closed.

"Breakfast is ready. I thought you'd want something before we leave for church."

Cathy's sleep-deprived brain functioned like a lawn-mower engine that sputters until it finally catches hold. Different room. Different house. Dora Kennedy. Then the smell of frying bacon hit her nostrils, followed closely by the scent of coffee, strong and rich.

"I'll be down in a second."

Cathy opened her eyes and found the light switch, squinting as the glare hit her dilated pupils. She padded to the bathroom and splashed cold water on her face. Then she wrapped herself in a robe, shoved her feet into slippers, and shuffled down the stairs. If Sunday breakfast at the parsonage was as good as Sunday lunch, there was no way she would sleep through it.

She found Matthew and Dora Kennedy at either end of the table, with Will sitting next to the place that had been laid for her. This was a far cry from Cathy's usual breakfast of a muffin and coffee. Dora had cooked scrambled eggs, bacon, and biscuits. Two different kinds of jelly, obviously home-made, sat next to a small dish of real butter. A glass of orange juice and a steaming cup of coffee had been placed next to her empty plate.

"Sorry. I overslept," she said.

"Don't worry," Pastor Kennedy said. "Will, would you say grace?"

Cathy longed for several healthy swallows of coffee, hoping it would jumpstart her brain. She silently blessed Will for the brevity of his prayer, joined in the corporate "Amen," and sipped at the wonderful brew in her cup.

"How's Ella Mae," Dora asked, as she passed the bacon.

Cathy wondered how much she could say without breaking patient confidentiality. "Her medical condition is stable." Maybe that would be enough.

"Would it be all right for us to visit her?" Pastor Kennedy asked. "I mean, is it too soon after her suicide attempt?"

Cathy decided that confidentiality was probably a moot point. Besides that, maybe Ella Mae would talk to them. Cathy sure wasn't getting anywhere.

"I believe she's stable enough to have visitors. I'm sure you've been in enough hospital rooms to know when to cut a visit short. I'll leave it to your discretion." Cathy took a bite and revised her previously held opinion that most biscuits had the taste and consistency of hockey pucks. True, Bess Elam's had been better than most, but Dora Kennedy's were like nothing Cathy had ever tasted. They were marvelously light and absolutely delicious. She savored the rich flavor of real butter. Homemade apricot jam was sweet and tart on her tongue. She washed down a bite with coffee before continuing. "I transferred her to a regular room last evening. I don't think you'll have any trouble getting in."

"Where were you all day yesterday?" Will asked.

"Long day, long story. The short version is that after making rounds yesterday morning, I was on my way out through the emergency room when a major trauma case arrived. A minivan collided with an eighteen-wheeler. Driver of the van was DOA. The mother had a ruptured spleen. John Steel was on trauma call and asked me to scrub with him. The two kids in the van were okay except for cuts and bruises. We had to contact a relative to come get them, and I volunteered to sit with them until the family arrived. When I finally got away, I grabbed a burger and ate it in the car on my way home."

"Did the mother survive?" Pastor Kennedy asked.

"She'll be fine, but I pity her and those two children, losing their husband and father."

Cathy expected a response like, "We'll pray for them," or "God will comfort them." Instead, Dora asked, "Are they local? We'll check and see if there's a way to help."

Cathy couldn't understand it. Her perception of the church had always been that it was full of pious people who quoted Scripture but didn't want to have anything to do with the rest of the world. But this family had rolled up its collective sleeves and was ready to help those around them. Had Cathy been wrong? After hearing Dora's story of the death of their baby girl, Cathy's perspective of God's role in the tragedies of the world had changed. Were these folks right when they told her to lean on God for help?

She let the others carry the conversation during breakfast. When she pushed back her chair and started upstairs to get ready for church, she wondered whether she might have been missing out on something.

17

Church was a different experience today. Cathy didn't sing the hymns; she listened to the words. She didn't join in the responsive reading; she let the Scripture speak to her. And when Pastor Kennedy asked the congregation to turn to Exodus 16, Cathy left her Bible closed in her lap, choosing instead to sit with her head bowed, visualizing the scene of God feeding the children of Israel in the wilderness, sending them manna every morning.

She listened as the preacher took this familiar Bible passage and made it real for her. She flashed back to a Sunday school teacher saying something about "He opened the Scriptures to them." That was Jesus, she was pretty sure, but that also seemed to be what Pastor Kennedy was doing today.

"God provides for His children," he said. "We may not like what He provides, though, because we don't see the big picture as God

304

can. I'm sure there were Israelites who prayed for a varied menu. Can't you just hear them now? 'Manna again today?' But there were also those who remained faithful — faithful for forty years as they wandered in the wilderness waiting for the fulfillment of God's promises to them. These were the ones who awoke each morning with a smile, looked out of their tents, and said, 'Oh, look! There's manna again this morning!' "

Pastor Kennedy moved away from the pulpit and lowered his voice, but the microphone clipped to his tie carried his words to every corner of the room. "We don't always like what God sends. We forget that He sees things we can't. God wants to send us blessings, even though we may not recognize them. And when He blesses us, I hope each of us will take the time to thank Him . . . for the manna."

Cathy locked the outer door behind her before she picked up the folder from Jane's desk and took it to her own. She hated to leave the comfort of the Kennedys living room and the company of the family that had taken her into their home and hearts. She longed to relax this Sunday afternoon. But she needed to check her balance sheet. Monday promised to be a busy day.

On her way to the office, she had stopped at the hospital to look in on Ella Mae. There'd been no change. Physically, the woman seemed to be recovering from the effects of her overdose. Mentally, however, it was as though she'd crept into a hard shell to keep out the world. Hopefully, the psychiatrist could help her.

Cathy popped the tab on a Diet Coke and settled into the chair behind her desk. She wondered how long it would be before it was all snatched from her: the desk, the chair, the office furniture. She'd shopped with care, overwhelmed by the cost of computers, fax machines, copiers, a phone system. The seventy thousand dollars that seemed like so much when she signed the note shrank like an ice cube in the sun when she started writing checks on her newly opened practice account.

Right now that seventy thousand dollars loomed like the national debt. And she didn't even want to think of the student loans she'd accumulated during four years of medical school. Thank goodness she wasn't due to start repaying those for a couple of years. Even so, they were part of the load she felt pressing down on her. She guessed that whoever said "Money isn't everything" probably had some.

Before she could do more than glance over the figures Jane had put together, Cathy's cell phone rang. The hospital? She wasn't on call. Ella Mae? She had seemed fine just an hour ago. Cathy glanced at the caller ID. Will.

"Hello?"

"Cathy, this is Will. Are you in your office right now?"

"Yes, I'm looking over my finances to see if there's any way I can come up with five thousand dollars by Wednesday." She sipped her soft drink. "I hated to leave. It was nice spending a quiet Sunday afternoon with you all."

"I enjoyed it too. Don't you think you could use the services of your attorney? I mean, two heads are better than one."

Trusting anyone, even Will, came hard for her. "I don't want to bother you."

"No bother."

She shrugged. Why not? "Okay, come on over."

"Would you open the door then? It's lonely out here."

Cathy hurried to the office door. When she lifted a slat of the Venetian blind, she saw an eye peeping back at her and heard Will's voice in her phone. "I'm sorry, but I don't know the password."

"Funny man."

Will reached into his jacket pocket. "I brought you something. Mom thought you might like one of her special chocolate chip cookies."

"I notice there are two, so I guess you expect me to share. Let me get you something to drink. Diet Coke okay?"

With Will settled beside her at the desk, Cathy ran her finger down the column of figures Jane had prepared. On paper, her practice had started to turn a profit. But it would take at least another month before she received sufficient insurance payments for those paper profits to show up in her bank account.

"It will be a stretch just to come up with the money for the interest on the loan. There's no way I can meet the bank's new terms."

Will popped the last bite of cookie into his mouth and licked his fingers. "See what tomorrow brings. Don't forget what Dad said in his sermon today."

Cathy nodded uneasily. She could agree in principle with leaning on God to supply her needs, but in practice? Not so easy.

"What's that?" Will pointed to two sheets of paper peeking out from under the list of accounts receivable.

"Those are the names of everyone in the county who owns a black Ford Expedition. The sheriff thought I might recognize the name of a person who would want to run me out of town. Or kill me."

"Let me see one sheet; you take the other. Then we'll switch."

Cathy had the top of the alphabet. She put down the remains of her cookie and started down the list. Abernathy. Archer. Bascomb. Bell. Clawson. Conroy.

"Whoa," she said. "Look at this." She handed the list to Will and pointed out a name.

"Marcus Bell," he said. "You think he might be behind this?"

Cathy shook her head. "I don't know. At first, Marcus seemed supportive of me professionally. Then he asked me out a couple of times and I said no. After that, he's been a bit less friendly. But, surely, he wouldn't try to hurt me just because I turned him down for a date." She gnawed at a fingernail. "Besides, the incident with the SUV happened before he ever asked me out."

"Maybe we're looking at it backward," Will said. "Maybe Marcus was out to get you even before he asked you out. Remember how something always stopped you from getting privileges? Marcus was in a perfect position to pull that off."

"I can't believe he'd do that."

"When he saw you in the emergency room after the accident, how long had he been there?"

"I'm not sure," Cathy said. "The nurse said he'd come in to look at a patient with possible appendicitis, but that wouldn't take long. The work-up had been done already. And it was a while between the time of the accident and my arrival at the ER."

Will tapped his fingers against his front teeth. "Could he have been in that SUV on his way to the hospital when he saw you and decided to run you off the road? Or might it have been an accident, and afterward he was afraid to admit it?"

"I don't know." Cathy wanted to scream. "I just want my life back."

Will took Cathy's hand and squeezed it. "Okay. I didn't mean to upset you. Let's finish checking this list so you can talk to Sheriff Dunaway in the morning. In the meantime, be careful around Marcus Bell."

Cathy chewed the last bite of her cookie, but it seemed to turn to dust in her mouth.

"Sheriff, I want to make it clear that I'm not accusing anyone whose name I've marked. These are just people who seem to be the most likely suspects."

Dunaway inclined his head. "I understand, Dr. Sewell. We'll be very discreet in our questions. I'll have one of my deputies make a few calls to see if these folks can verify where they were at the times you encountered that black SUV. Your name won't be mentioned."

Cathy came out from behind her desk and offered her hand. "Thank you. I appreciate everything you're doing."

"Not at all. Not only is it my job, I . . . I don't guess you'd remember. You were only about eight or nine at the time. My son, Jerry, fell out of a tree and hit his head. By the time we got him to the hospital, he had what they called an acute subdural hematoma — bleeding over the outside of the brain. The nearest neurosurgeon was an hour away, and your daddy said that by then Jerry would be dead. He told us he hadn't seen one of these kind of injuries since he was a resident, but he asked our permission to do an emergency operation to relieve the pressure. He called it 'burr holes.' After he did it, he rode in the ambulance to Dallas with Jerry. The neurosurgeon said Dr. Sewell saved our son's life."

Cathy had a faint memory of her father

mentioning the episode, but he never made much of it. "Just another day at the office" was his usual comment.

"Your father was a fine man and a good doctor," Dunaway said. "And he took wonderful care of your mother when she got sick. I think you'll find there are lots of folks around here who still feel grateful to him."

"How is Jerry?" Cathy asked.

"Killed in Afghanistan. Threw himself on a grenade to save his buddies." Dunaway blinked rapidly. "But we were blessed to have him as long as we did, thanks to your daddy's work. God was really good to us."

Cathy found herself touched by the attitude of this man and confused by the picture everyone had painted of her father. Maybe she'd been wrong — about lots of things.

Cathy blew a stray wisp of hair out of her eyes and shrugged her shoulders to ease the tension. It had been a busy morning, and the balance of the day promised to be more of the same. She didn't really have time to make this call, but Jane had said it was important.

"Marcus, Jane said that you called."

"Yes. Thanks for calling back." He hesitated so long Cathy thought she'd lost the connection.

"Marcus, are you there?"

"Cathy, this is hard for me. I know you've been angry with me, perhaps with good reason. I don't know. But I'd still like to invite you out — if not for dinner, then just for coffee. What do you say?"

"I'm sorry I got angry with you for not taking my side," Cathy said. "I realize that perhaps you really do think you should stay neutral in staff matters. And I hope you will believe me when I say that the reason I keep turning your invitations down isn't because I don't like you. I do . . . but as a friend and colleague."

"Just what every man wants to hear. So, things are serious between you and Will Kennedy?"

Were they? Maybe they were. She didn't need to ask how Marcus knew about their relationship. People always knew one another's business in a small town. "I guess they are."

"I'm happy for you. When my wife died, I didn't think I'd ever want to be with anyone else again. Although time dulls the pain, it doesn't take away the loneliness. I guess I thought you might be the answer."

"God has someone out there for you, I'm sure. It just isn't me." Cathy's words shocked her. She had no idea where they had come from. She hadn't said anything like that since God killed her parents.

But now she knew that God hadn't killed them. A senseless combination of speed and a rain-slick road had caused the accident. And maybe God had given her Will to take away her own loneliness.

Late Monday afternoon, Cathy looked over Jane's shoulders and read the numbers on the bank deposit — a few checks from patients, but no large insurance payments. She would need to call Will tonight and give him the bad news: no way could she come up with the five thousand dollars plus more than fourteen hundred dollars in interest that the bank had demanded. She could only hope Nix would change his mind, but that seemed unlikely.

Before sinking into her chair, Cathy shed her white coat and tossed it into the hamper. She tipped her chair forward and reached toward the bottom desk drawer to retrieve her purse when she saw the envelope centered on her blotter — a plain white envelope, no return address, postmarked last Thursday. A Post-it note stuck to the front that read "Elams brought this by" obscured the address. She removed the yellow sticky and noticed the envelope was addressed to her apartment.

The only mail she ever got at that address consisted of circulars, catalogs, and junk pieces addressed to "Occupant." All her bills and important correspondence came to the office.

Quickly, she slit the envelope open and pulled out a computer-generated letter on a single sheet of white paper. Her eyes were drawn immediately to the signature — Ella Mae Mercer. The missing suicide note.

Dear Cathy,

Forgive the familiarity. I know so much about you from my relationship with your father. When you read this I'll be dead. I know that sounds melodramatic, but it happens to be true. I'm guilty of a terrible wrong, and I need to put it right before I die. Then when I stand before my Maker perhaps He won't judge me too harshly.

Cathy looked away, steeling her emotions. *Here it comes — her confession that she had an affair with my father. Ella Mae felt so guilty that he prescribed a tranquilizer for her. Or maybe he broke it off, and she needed the medicine to get through that time.*

Years ago, I forged your father's signature to a check to pay for my mother's burial. The cost of care during her last days took every cent I had. I'd hoped to cover the shortage before your father found out, but I couldn't. He came to the bank to ask about it. It didn't take long before I broke down and confessed, begging him not to press charges. Instead, he pulled his checkbook from his coat pocket, turned to the check register, and wrote in the amount of the check I'd forged. Then he looked at me with nothing but pity in those gray eyes of his. "It's over. Now I'll pray for you."

I know he needed the money himself, because I saw his account records and knew how much he spent every month for your mother's care. But he never said another word about it. That's when he wrote me a prescription to help me through my depression.

My crime has eaten at me all these years. I thought I could ease my conscience by helping you out with the insurance company, but it wasn't enough. That's when I decided I had to make amends before I die.

I hope that, like your father, you'll pray for me.

Ella Mae Mercer

Could it be true that she had misjudged her father so badly? He didn't have an affair with Ella Mae. He'd helped out the poor woman. And he'd probably talked with his pastor and asked him to pray for Ella Mae as he had promised.

What about the difficult times her parents had gone through? Cathy could picture her father and Matthew Kennedy kneeling in the pastor's study, asking God for help in keeping that marriage together. Pastors keep a lot of secrets — so do doctors — but Cathy knew that husbands had no secrets from their wives. That must be the reason Dora could say with such certainty that Nolan Sewell had been faithful to his wife.

"Oh, Daddy, I'm so sorry," she whispered. "I'm sorry I thought those horrible things about you. I'm sorry I let this come between us."

When she folded the letter to replace it in the envelope, her fingers touched something else. She pulled out a stiff piece of paper just small enough to fit into the envelope. A note was clipped to it: "Principal and interest for my loan from your father. Paid in full."

She removed the note and looked at the cashier's check for six thousand, five hundred dollars. She closed her eyes, swallowed hard, and whispered, "And here's the manna!" She could hardly choke out her next words. "Thank you, God."

18

Cathy looked down at the woman lying stock-still in the ICU bed. "How are you feeling this morning?"

Ella Mae's only response was a slight shift of the head, turning her face toward the wall.

"I asked them to offer you a liquid diet. Did you drink anything?"

A nod of yes this time. Good.

"I got the letter . . . and the check."

Now Ella Mae turned her head toward Cathy. Her eyes were empty. There was the faintest movement of her lips, and then she compressed them tightly together.

"I appreciate that you tried to make amends, but I don't think attempting suicide was such a good idea. Not for you. Not for anybody."

"Sorry." The words came out as a croak.

"Did you talk with the psychiatrist when he came by yesterday?" Cathy had read the consultation note, but she wanted to hear Ella Mae's version.

Ella Mae shook her head. "No need. It's all in the letter."

"No, the letter unlocks a lot of mysteries for me, but you've got some work to do to get yourself straightened out." Cathy pulled a chair to the bedside and sat. "If I let you out of the hospital, will you promise not to try to kill yourself again?"

A nod.

"I hope you realize I can't give you any more tranquilizers right now. Can you do without them?"

"I'll try my best," Ella Mae whispered.

"And if I discharge you, what will you do?"

"I guess I'll go back to work."

"Some of the people there probably know about what you did. Can you handle that?"

Ella Mae nodded weakly. "It's no secret I've been under stress. That's what my job is all about. I can handle that." She fluttered a hand on top of the blanket. "But no one knows about the money I took."

"And I won't tell them, either," Cathy said. "But you need some help getting your head together. Will you see a psychiatrist if I refer you to someone? How did you like the doctor who visited with you yesterday?"

Ella Mae pointed to the carafe of water

on her bedside table. Cathy poured a glass and handed it to her. Ella Mae finished the water and handed the glass back. "I didn't like him. He made me feel . . . small. Like, by attempting suicide, I'd forfeited the right to be human."

"Would you drive to Fort Worth to see a psychiatrist? Someone I can recommend from personal experience?"

Cathy could tell she had surprised Ella Mae. Most people thought doctors led a perfect life.

"Would you?" Cathy asked again.

Ella Mae managed a weak smile. "If you give him your personal seal of approval, that's good enough for me."

Despite Will's desire to accompany her to the bank, Cathy insisted on going alone, especially since she no longer needed to negotiate with Milton Nix. She promised Will she'd bring him up to date that evening while they worked on her case.

"I'd like to speak with Mr. Nix, please," Cathy told the teller.

Apparently, the bank employees — along with everyone else in Dainger — knew about the malpractice suit. The woman stammered, "Do you think . . . ? I mean . . . can someone else help you?"

321

"No, this is bank business. I need to talk with Mr. Nix."

Cathy took perverse pleasure in watching the drama unfold. The teller went to the desk of Nix's secretary and held a whispered consultation. Then the two of them looked back at Cathy, quickly turning away when she returned their stare. After a few more words, the secretary scuttled to the door of Nix's office and tapped lightly. In a moment she eased the door open and ducked inside like someone slipping into an air-conditioned room without letting the cool air escape. The teller waited nervously outside the office, obviously unsure whether she should return to her station or stay put. Finally, the door to the inner sanctum opened, and Nix appeared.

Milton Nix was dressed as a bank president should be — or, more likely, as the wife of a bank president thought he should be. The way his three-piece gray pinstripe suit hung on him demonstrated that, no matter how much you spend on the clothes, the final image depends on the person wearing them.

He beckoned to Cathy, who chose to ignore the gesture. Let him come to her. Finally, he ambled over to her. "How can I help you?"

"May we speak in private?"

"Of course." He gestured toward his office.

Once they were seated, Nix said, "I'm not sure of the protocol of the situation, but should we be talking like this? With the suit pending and all? Shouldn't our lawyers be handling all the communication?"

Cathy smiled as she recalled Will's comments to Sam Lawton. "The malpractice suit? Yes, my lawyer is handling that, including preparing the countersuit against you."

Apparently, Sam Lawton hadn't shared this message with his client. Nix's face flushed. He tugged at his collar, and Cathy feared he would go into cardiac arrest again.

"This is about the note I have with this bank. The note, I might add, that you assured me could be handled by paying only the interest when it came up for renewal, giving me a chance to establish my practice." She reached into her purse and pulled out the bank's letter. "May I ask what caused this change of heart?"

"I . . . well, that is . . . the loan committee decided that recent developments called into question your ability to repay the money in a timely fashion. They thought that a five thousand dollar reduction in principal would serve as a good faith mea-

323

sure, allowing us to continue the loan."

"If I pay that amount, will you draft a new note, maturing two years from now?"

"I'm not sure the committee —"

Cathy had a flash of insight. This wasn't about making her close her practice. This was all about Nix saving his own skin.

"You know as well as I do," she said, "that you make these decisions, and the committee rubber-stamps your recommendations. I'll tell you what's going on. You figured the malpractice suit was the last straw for my practice, and you decided to pull the plug on the note to avoid criticism for making it. You could claim you saw how the situation had changed, so you acted to protect the bank's interest. Isn't that right?"

"Well . . . uh," Nix stuttered. "We expect the bank examiners here next month, and we have some notes that aren't well-secured. I was afraid of what they'd say. Requiring you to reduce the principal would show that we were aware of the risk and had acted to lessen it." He pulled the tiny blue silk handkerchief from his suit breast pocket and wiped his brow. "Actually, we've done the same thing with several other notes. It's not just you, Dr. Sewell."

Cathy leaned forward and thought she saw Nix shrink back in his chair. "I'll make you

a deal. You renew the note for two years —
at one point below prime this time — and
I'll pay down the principal by five thousand
dollars."

"Why would I do that?"

She smiled. "Because the other half of the
deal is this. In exchange for a two-year note
at interest one percent below the prime rate,
I'll instruct my attorney not to file that
countersuit against you and your wife."

"Leave my wife out of this."

"Why? As I understand it, and as we'll
prove at trial, she's the reason behind this
whole malpractice suit in the first place. It
will be interesting when Will gets her on the
stand, and it all comes out in open court."

Nix looked as though he'd swallowed a
bad oyster. "What comes out?"

Cathy decided to sink the hook. "Mainly,
how she tried to kill you. Actually, she
would have succeeded if I hadn't saved your
life."

"I don't —"

"She and her brother changed your dosage, then altered the prescription to cover it
up so she could inherit everything you've
got."

"That's not true."

"Maybe not. Or maybe it is. We'll just have
to investigate and see, won't we?"

Nix seemed to collapse inward on himself like a balloon with a slow leak. "I can't do what you're asking, but how about one year at prime plus one percent?"

"Eighteen months at prime," Cathy said.

Nix ran his hand around his collar. "All right. I suppose I could agree to those terms. But you'll still need to reduce the principal by —"

"I know." Cathy brandished the cashier's check. "I believe you'll find that this covers that amount plus current interest, with a few dollars left over. Now I'll wait right here while you have your secretary prepare a receipt and the new note."

"Where did this money come from?"

"Now, Mr. Nix," Cathy said. "You of all people should know better than to ever ask that question. Money is anonymous. All that cash you have in your vault has no history, no scruples, and no identity. Just add this to your little pile, revise my loan, and I'll be on my way."

Cathy thought the day would never end. It was nearly dark when she opened the front door of the Kennedy house. As soon as she stepped inside, she slipped out of her shoes. Holding them in one hand, with her briefcase in the other, she padded into the living room. The shades were drawn, and the lights were off. She reached for the light switch when a voice stopped her in her tracks.

"I remember that about you. Not fond of wearing shoes." Will flipped on the lamp beside the couch where he sat.

Cathy recoiled. "Will, you scared me to death." She took a couple of deep breaths. "Where are your folks?"

He eased off the couch and greeted her with a hug and kiss.

"Mom and Dad have already left for a meeting at church. They've eaten, but they left some supper in the oven. Join me?"

When they were settled at the kitchen table, Cathy said, "I went by the bank today. I used the check from Ella Mae to pay what they demanded."

"So you're square with the bank? You renewed the note?" Will helped himself to another of his mother's biscuits. "What did Nix say?"

"Not much, after I brought up the possibility of a countersuit and a trial where his wife's history would come out."

Will almost choked. "You know when I mentioned that to Sam I wasn't serious."

Cathy smiled. "I'm not a lawyer, so I guess I can be excused for not understanding that.

Anyway, Nix agreed to give me a new note at prime, renewable in eighteen months by paying the interest only."

"What happened to the woman who wanted my help because she didn't know where to turn?"

"You know, I think she's learning that she's pretty capable. That doesn't mean she can't use some help from time to time, like a white knight riding by in his pickup to rescue her when her trusty steed crashes."

"I was thinking more in terms of legal help," Will said. "But I'm glad you look at me that way. I'd like to make the arrangement more permanent. Have you thought about it?"

"Not . . . really." Cathy's heart pounded, and she took a moment to calm down. "We were awfully close a few years ago, and I'll admit that I had a vision that we'd eventually marry. But that was then. A lot has changed."

Will shook his head. "Nothing could have happened that would make me stop loving you. There, I've said it. I love you."

"Nothing will change the way I feel" had been ambiguous. But this was "Nothing would make me stop loving you." How Cathy had longed to hear those words. More than that, she longed to say them back to Will. She wanted to, but somehow she couldn't. How could she explain this to him? And how could he possibly understand?

"Two men have already told me they loved me. They said they wanted to marry me. I thought I loved them. I told them so. Then they let me down. I'm still working on healing those wounds."

"And — ?"

"And I promised myself that the next time I told a man I loved him, I would be one hundred percent sure."

"You're not sure about me?"

"At this moment I am. But I don't want to make another mistake. It would only hurt both of us. I'm almost there — maybe even ninety percent. Can you be patient with me a little longer?"

Will pushed back his plate. "Would it help if I withdrew as your lawyer? Honestly, it would be hard for me to do, because I want to help you, but I'd do it."

"No, I need your legal help. More than that, I trust you." The words just came out, but as she heard them, Cathy knew she really meant them.

"Okay, I'll try to be patient."

Cathy could see Will make a visible effort to shift into professional mode. "If I'm still your lawyer, we need to talk about our defense of this malpractice action. As I see it, it hinges on showing that someone tampered with that prescription and that you weren't responsible for Nix's overdose. And, of course, in the end you were the one who saved his life."

"That's all well and good," Cathy said, "but we have no proof, just suspicions."

"Maybe if I file for a continuance — ask for more time."

"No!" Cathy slammed her hand down on the table, and the silverware rattled. "I'm tired of having this hanging over my head. I've been thinking about it all day, and I believe I know how to smoke out the person responsible."

"How?"

She shook her head. "No, it's a one-person job, and the less you know about it, the better."

Jane tapped on the open door of Cathy's office. "Want me to bring you back a sandwich?"

"No thanks," Cathy said. "I brought yogurt and an apple. I'll eat at my desk. I've got some stuff to do."

Cathy waited until she heard the outer door close and lock. Then she opened Mi-

330

crosoft Word on her computer and began typing. It took her several tries to achieve the right blend of threat and greed.

How many copies would she need? That depended. Who could have changed the prescription? Who had means, motive, and opportunity? She opened a new document and made her list.

The two pharmacists, Jacob Collins and Lloyd Allen, were the most logical suspects. They had ample opportunity. They had the knowledge. She wasn't sure what the motive might be, but maybe that would come out later. For now, she needed to be sure they got the bait.

Sherri Collins, Jacob's wife, also had access to the pharmacy area. She could certainly have done it, but would she know how to alter the prescription? Motive? No problem there. It seemed that everyone in town had something against Cathy, and Sherri was no exception. Then Cathy realized she couldn't send a note to both Jacob and Sherri, or it would be obvious to them that she was on a fishing expedition. No, it had to be Jacob. Leave Sherri off the list.

How about Gail Nix? Cathy had been bluffing when she told Milton his wife had tried to kill him, but it was certainly possible. She'd have needed the assistance of her brother, Lloyd. If Gail and Lloyd talked, would a letter to each make them think Cathy knew they had collaborated? Would it make them more certain that their plot had been discovered? She decided to add Gail's name to the list.

She couldn't bring herself to believe that Milton Nix had altered his own prescription, but had he left it on his desk at the bank before getting it filled? If he had, who could have gotten hold of it long enough to make the change? Only his secretary and Ella Mae had easy access. Motive aside, Cathy couldn't believe that either of them possessed the medical knowledge to make the alterations. No, leave them off the list.

Any others? Her mind kept coming back to Marcus Bell. He had a black Ford Expedition. His attitude toward Cathy had been ambivalent, to say the least. A doctor would know how to change the digitalis dosage. How could he have gotten the prescription? It wouldn't be hard for a physician to visit the pharmacy department and use some pretext to gain access behind the counter. Maybe Marcus sent the pharmacist looking in the shelves for some weird drug, taking the opportunity to palm the prescription as it lay on the counter. A little work in his office, then another trip back. Maybe even hand the altered script to the pharmacist and say he'd picked it up by mistake. Much as she hated the thought, Marcus's name went on the list.

Was there someone else? Yes, there was — a person with medical knowledge and a definite grudge against Cathy. She didn't see how he could have carried it out, though. It was far-fetched. Or was it? With a sigh, she wrote down Robert's name on the list and transcribed a Dallas address beneath it.

She'd carefully avoided adding one name to her list, stepping around it as gingerly as she would have avoided a landmine. There was one person who had intimate knowl-edge of all her actions since the first day the black SUV had made that near-suicide run at her. A person who had a right to hold a grudge, however much he might deny it. Of course, he didn't drive a black SUV. He drove a pickup. What if he had two vehicles? She'd never seen inside his two-car garage. Maybe the other half wasn't filled with tools and Christmas decorations.

She sighed and chided herself. His name wasn't on the list of Expedition owners. And he said he loved her. However much her head told her not to blindly trust a man, she knew — knew for certain — that she

could trust Will. No, she couldn't —
wouldn't — suspect he was capable of such
duplicity.

Cathy computer addressed five plain white
envelopes, adding the notation "PER-
SONAL." She stuffed copies of her letter into
the envelopes, added stamps, and dropped
the small bundle into her purse. She'd mail
them on the way home. They should arrive
tomorrow — Friday. Then came the hard
part — waiting to see who would respond.

She hoped her simple message would be
enough to flush out the person whose actions almost killed Milton Nix and threatened to destroy her professional career:

I KNOW HOW YOU MANAGED TO
ALTER THAT DIGOXIN PRESCRIP-
TION. HOW MUCH ARE YOU PRE-
PARED TO PAY FOR MY SILENCE?
IF IT'S ENOUGH, I'LL LET MY
INSURANCE COMPANY SETTLE
THE SUIT. I'LL LEAVE TOWN AND
NO ONE WILL KNOW WHAT YOU
DID. COME ALONE TO MY OFFICE
AT 9:00 SATURDAY NIGHT.
— Cathy Sewell, M.D.

19

Mercury vapor lamps bathed the barren asphalt of the professional building's parking lot in blue light when Cathy pulled into her reserved space on Saturday night. Her throat tightened when she saw that the security light nearest the door had burned out, creating a tunnel of darkness she'd have to negotiate. She locked her car and hurried toward the building, shivering despite the mild breeze. The tingle between her shoulder blades made her tighten the muscles, as though that action could protect her from a bullet or a knife.

Once inside, Cathy hurried down the dark corridor to her office. She fumbled with her keys and slid inside, slamming and locking the door behind her. She stood for a moment with her back against it, breathing deeply and trying not to hyperventilate.

Quickly, she threw a switch and bathed the outer office in light. Despite her fear of an attacker, she eased past the reception desk and raced from room to room, turning on lights to reassure herself that no one lurked behind a closed door.

In her office, she slipped into her white coat and finished her preparations. She looked at her watch. Eight o'clock. Soon she'd know the truth. But, the more she thought about it, the crazier her scheme seemed. And if it did, could she handle the person who showed up, whoever it might be? She breathed a silent prayer, surprised that it seemed as automatic as though she hadn't stopped praying more than three years ago.

The ring of her cell phone interrupted her thoughts. She picked her purse off the desk and pulled out the cell. "Anonymous caller," read the ID. Was it one of her suspects? Only two of them had her cell phone number: Marcus and Robert.

She took a deep breath, held it, and blew it out in a sigh before she answered. "Dr. Sewell, this is J. C. Dunaway. I got your cell number from Will Kennedy. I hope I'm not calling too late?"

Cathy realized her hand cramped from gripping the phone so tightly. She switched the instrument to her right hand and flexed the fingers of her left. "No, no. You just startled me."

"I wanted to bring you up to date on our search for the driver of your black Ford Expedition — let you know we're still on it."

"Do you have a suspect?" she asked.

"Afraid not. As of this afternoon, we thought it was Kenny Johnson."

"Who's Kenny Johnson? And what would he have against me?"

"Nothing," Dunaway said. "Kenny's just a teenager who got hold of the spare key to his dad's SUV and decided it would be cool to ditch school and go joyriding with a buddy from time to time. One of my deputies stopped the pair this afternoon for reckless driving. He recognized the vehicle as the type we were interested in. He asked a few questions, and the boys acted so guilty the deputy decided to bring them in and let me talk to them." Dunaway chuckled. "Didn't need the bright lights and rubber hose to get the truth out of them. I put them in two separate rooms, and Kenny's buddy ratted him out in about five minutes."

"But you said he wasn't the one who's been hounding me."

"Nope. Unfortunately, they weren't out by Big Sandy or on the road to the cemetery when you had your run-ins. Already confirmed they were in school both those times. No doubt about it."

Cathy cleared her throat. "So you're no closer to finding out who's trying to kill me?"

"We've eliminated a bunch of folks, and we're still working on it. Thought you'd like to know."

Why didn't that make her feel better? The sheriff could still be "working on it" during her funeral. Maybe it was truly up to her to put an end to this thing.

Cathy thanked the sheriff and hung up. Someone in a black SUV tried to kill her. Someone — maybe that same mysterious stranger — set fire to her apartment. And someone altered one of her prescriptions and caused an incident that involved her in a malpractice suit while adding fuel to the derogatory rumors circulating about her in town.

"I'm not paranoid," she whispered like a mantra. "Someone really *is* out to get me."

Cathy settled down to wait. She was half asleep in her chair when the buzzing of the office phone awoke her. She wasn't on call this weekend. When the answering service didn't pick up, she noticed that the call was on her private line. She lifted the receiver and punched the lighted button.

"Dr. Sewell."

"Cathy?" At the sound of the voice, Cathy had to fight the urge to hyperventilate. She'd never appreciated how accurate the expression "Her blood ran cold" was until that moment.

"Robert? How did you get this number?"

"I have connections. What's this about my altering a prescription? I know your mother was psychotic, but I never saw any indication of it in you until this. Are you all right?"

Cathy took several calming breaths. "Robert, it's a long story. The short answer is that I'm not paranoid. Someone really is out to get me."

His familiar laugh made Cathy's heart clench. "Just like we said in medical school, huh?"

"It's not funny to me. But I do appreciate your calling. I'll write you and explain it after it's all over."

"Anyway, I'm glad you haven't gone around the bend." Robert cleared his throat. "And I'm sorry about sending you that clipping and note. I did it without thinking, and now I realize it was a terrible thing to do. Can you forgive me?"

Cathy's first impulse was to simply hang up. But then she recalled something she'd heard in church recently — forgiving others the way we want God to forgive us. "Robert, I forgive you . . . for everything. And I wish you and your wife happiness."

She hung up and sat with her head in her hands for a long time. Then she pulled her list toward her and drew a line through Robert's name. One down, four to go.

Cathy leaned forward, her elbows on the desk, trying without success to concentrate on an article in one of her medical journals. A faint tap on the glass of the outer office door caught her attention. She tiptoed to the waiting room and edged up to the Venetian blind that covered the door. She separated two slats far enough to identify Marcus Bell standing in the hall outside, shifting from one foot to the other, his eyes darting back and forth down the hall.

Marcus? Had she been right? Was he the one behind all this? She tried to swallow a softball-sized lump in her throat, but it wouldn't budge. Her hands shook as she unlocked the door.

Marcus rushed in as though he were being chased. "Cathy, what's the meaning of this note?" He pulled a wrinkled piece of paper from his shirt pocket and thrust it at her. "You know I didn't change that prescription." He squinted at her, as though seeing her for the first time. "Are you — ? Do you think someone's out to get you?"

Cathy stifled a wry laugh. Poor Marcus. He thought she'd gone off the deep end. "No, Marcus. I don't think that. I know they are. I'm not paranoid. I'm not delusional. But I do know that someone changed Milton Nix's prescription to guarantee that he'd wind up with digitalis intoxication. I still don't know if what they did was aimed at me or at him, but whatever the motive, we both suffered the consequences."

"And you think I did it?" Marcus said with righteous indignation.

Cathy decided to bluff. After all, he was here. Maybe he was the guilty party. "It's possible. You could easily have altered that prescription."

Marcus shook his head. "I don't know what you're talking about. Cathy, I'm sorry to say this, but when the credentials committee meets on Monday, I'll recommend that your hospital privileges be suspended until you undergo psychiatric evaluation." Abruptly, he turned and stormed out the door, closing it firmly behind him.

She drew a line through another name. Two down, three to go. Who would it be? Cathy turned off the lights in her office and moved back into the waiting room, settling into a dark corner to watch for her nightmare to walk through the door.

She didn't have to wait long. A tentative tap sounded on the door. She eased over and peeped through the blinds. What she saw allowed her to eliminate two of her three remaining suspects. The figure standing in the shadowed hall was a woman. She had her back turned to the door, looking nervously around, but Cathy had no doubt who it was. It had to be Gail Nix.

So Gail had been in league with her brother, Lloyd. He must have altered the prescription. Cathy guessed that the two of them planned to split the money Gail inherited if Nix died. And Cathy would get all the blame. Death by medical misadventure.

She took a deep breath and opened the door.

20

"Sherri!" Cathy staggered backward as Sherri Collins forced her way past her and slammed the door.

"Lock it," Sherri said. When Cathy didn't move, the woman pulled a snub-nosed revolver from the purse slung over her shoulder. "Lock it, I said. Then move back to your office."

Cathy did as she was told. Where did Sherri fit into the picture? Was she here on Jacob's behalf? Had Jacob reacted to Cathy's letter by doing something rash? Suicide, perhaps? Was that why Sherri was so angry?

Cathy started to sit behind her desk, but Sherri waved her to one of the patient chairs, then stood over her, the gun steady in her hand.

"Why are you here?" Cathy asked.

"If you were married, you'd know that marking a letter 'private' won't keep a spouse from opening it. I intercepted your little blackmail letter to Jacob." Sherri pulled the other patient chair out and sat, careful to stay out of Cathy's reach. "I'm not here to pay you a dime. I'm here to kill you. And I have lots of reasons."

"I don't understand."

"You should. I've hated you since high school." Sherri's eyes narrowed. "Didn't you think I'd find out about the rumors you spread just so you could be Homecoming Queen? Without that I would have won fair and square. And my boyfriend wouldn't have dumped me. The only boy who would date me after that was Jacob."

"But I —"

Sherri brandished the gun. "I would have done anything to get out of this hick town. Jacob told me he planned to apply to medical school. I thought I'd spend the rest of my life as a doctor's wife with no worries."

"But Jacob's a successful pharmacist. Surely, you have a good life."

"I wish," Sherri said. "Our house is mortgaged to the hilt. The same goes for this professional building Jacob built. I know that he hated to lease the space to you, but he's so deeply in debt he needed the money. Of course, if your father hadn't refused to help him get into medical school, he'd be a doctor, making lots of money, and I

344

wouldn't have to scrimp to get by and keep up appearances."

Cathy wasn't sure she could reason with this woman, but she had to try. "Sherri, my father wouldn't write a letter of recommendation for Jacob because his grades weren't good enough for medical school. His MCAT score was borderline at best. He never would have made it beyond the first interview."

"Don't blame it on Jacob's Medical College Admissions Test. He told me how he figured that test was rigged. Your father probably had some of his cronies falsify Jacob's grades because he didn't want too many doctors coming back to Dainger. There might not be room for his precious daughter to practice here."

"Are you the one who tried to kill me with a black SUV?" Cathy recalled the closed doors of the three-car garage at the Collins house.

Sherri cackled. "Thought I had you a couple of times."

"But there's no black SUV registered in your name."

"Of course not. It belonged to my father, Frank Clawson. He died six months ago, and the registration's still in his name."

Cathy couldn't believe this. "Did you

change that prescription so I'd get sued for malpractice? Did you want me to fail — want me to leave Dainger?"

Sherri laughed again, just like the patients Cathy had heard on the psychiatric ward during her training. "What I wanted to do was get Milton Nix out of the way. Then your prescription gave me the opportunity to throw suspicion on you at the same time. I mean, you ruined my life. Why shouldn't I ruin yours? If he died, you might be charged with manslaughter."

"How did you make the change?"

"Good timing and good luck," Sherri said. "I saw the prescription on the counter, waiting to be filled. I laid my purse down next to it, and when I picked up my purse, I had the prescription too. A little work with the copier in the office, put the new prescription back, and no one was the wiser."

"How did you know how to change it?"

"You don't think Jacob got through pharmacy school on his own, did you? I helped him study. Every night. Every subject. I could pass every test before he could. It was easy."

Cathy tried to make sense of it all, but the pieces wouldn't fall into place. "But why would you want to harm Milton Nix?"

"Nix's bank holds the mortgages on our

house and the professional building. Three weeks ago, Nix called both the notes. He insisted we pay down the indebtedness before he'd renew them. Jacob showed me the letters. If we didn't comply, the bank would foreclose. We'd lose everything. I knew we couldn't meet the deadline, but I figured if Nix were sick or dead, the bank would back off in all the chaos. I hoped it would buy us the time we needed to get the money together." She looked at the gun in her hand. "Funny. I couldn't bring myself to shoot Nix, but I don't think I'll have any trouble shooting you."

"Wait. I've got to know. Did you set fire to my apartment?"

"Of course. Apparently, I didn't do a great job with the fire, though. Otherwise, you wouldn't be here."

"And is Jacob in on this? Does he know you changed the prescription?"

Sherri shook her head. "No, he wouldn't have the guts. If it weren't for me, he'd just whine about the past. I'm the one who has the courage to strike back at you and your father."

"Why are you so bent on revenge? My father's dead. Isn't that enough?"

"Oh, I had some revenge on your father even before he died. Remember those old

347

tools displayed on the shelf in the pharmacy? The mortar and pestle, the scales, the pill press?"

An idea formed in Cathy's mind. Could anyone be so cruel? "Yes."

"They're not just for decoration. Your mother's gynecologist put her on hormones. I volunteered to be a good neighbor and drop off the prescription on my way home. The first month, I gave her the medication just as Jacob had poured it out from the stock bottle. But after that, each month I discarded about half the pills and substituted some I made myself. So she wasn't getting estrogen and progesterone every day. Half the time it was my own little gift to her."

Cathy wanted to ask questions — lots of questions — but she stood there dumbstruck.

Sherri smiled, obviously enjoying herself. "I used some connections I made when Jacob was in pharmacy school to get the raw material, and I turned out some professional-looking pills, I must say. Your mother asked why some of the tablets didn't have a company logo on them, but I told her we were using generics from two different companies."

Cathy dreaded the answer, but she had to

ask. "What did you give her?"

"Every time she took one of my little homemade pills, your mother got five hundred milligrams of mescaline."

"No!" Cathy immediately made the connection. Mescaline was a strong hallucinogen, like LSD and peyote. But, instead of giving people pleasant multicolored visions, mescaline had a different psychological effect, a much more dramatic one. The person turned paranoid and lost contact with reality. It was the perfect way to mimic schizophrenia. Cathy balled her hands into fists. She could only imagine the horrors her mother had faced in the grip of that terrible drug — and the torture it had inflicted on her father.

"I see you've figured it out," Sherri said. "No, your mother wasn't psychotic. And your father had to live with a wife with mental illness until the day they both died."

It was almost too much for Cathy to grasp. Her mother wasn't psychotic. There was no history of mental illness in the family. She could think about marriage, about her own family, without the fear of passing on that illness to her children. She didn't have to worry about her future husband having to deal with a psychotic wife.

If Sherri weren't holding a gun on her,

349

she'd probably breathe a sigh of relief. As it was, Cathy could only marvel at the pure evil of this woman's action. "How could you do that? How could you put my parents through such torture?"

Sherri shrugged. "Just imagine. If Jacob had gone to medical school instead of becoming a pharmacist, I'd never have learned how to do it. Talk about poetic justice."

Cathy wanted to jump out of her chair and charge this monster who had ruined so many lives. But first she needed to get control of the gun. She put her arms on the chair and started to push up.

"Don't even think about it," Sherri said.

Could she reason with this madwoman? Doubtful, but she had to try. "Other people know what I've found out. How do you expect to shoot me and get away with it?"

"Cathy? Cathy!" She recognized Will's voice over the loud knocks at the door.

"Let him in, won't you?" It was an order, not a request, and was accompanied by a sharp gesture with the gun.

Cathy eased the door open and started to speak, but before she could say a word the pressure of the gun in her back silenced her. She backed up and Will rushed inside. When he saw Sherri, he stopped dead still.

"Come in and close the door," Sherri said, as casually as she'd invite someone into her home for coffee and cookies.

"What — ?"

Sherri moved the gun back and forth between them. "Just go on into the back and I'll explain to both of you." She herded them into the back treatment room and gestured for them to stand together against the far wall.

Sherri closed the door and leaned against it. "Here's what happened, Cathy — I won't call you Dr. Sewell. It's stuck in my throat every time I've said it for three months. I phoned Will and pretended to be the 911 operator. I told him we'd had a call from you. You were in your office getting something from a high shelf when you fell off the ladder and broke your ankle. I told him you'd asked us to call him, and he said he'd meet us here." She grinned without mirth. "Isn't that sweet?"

Cathy looked at Will. "Sherri's the one who altered the prescription. She —"

"That's enough," Sherri snapped. She leveled the gun at Cathy's chest. "Now here's the way it's going down. First, I'll shoot you in the heart." She turned toward Will. "Then I'll shoot you in the temple. I'll put the gun in your dead hand and fire another

351

shot into Cathy so there'll be powder residue on your hand. I'll arrange the bodies to make it look like a murder-suicide. True love gone bad."

Cathy stepped back, stopping when she bumped into the treatment cabinet. The instruments and equipment it held rattled.

Sherri looked at Cathy, but then swung her gaze and the gun back toward Will. Cathy put her left hand in front of her as though shielding herself, hoping the movement would serve as a distraction while her right hand brushed lightly over the shelf behind her. *Where is it? Please, God, let me find it.*

"Sherri," Will said, "you know you can't get away with this. Give up. Turn yourself in. I'll help you get a good defense lawyer."

"No sale, you shyster. It will be a pleasure shooting you too. Lawyers are parasites. Matter of fact, I may shoot you first."

Sherri took a step toward Will. Cathy turned her body to follow the action. Sherri spun and waved the gun at her. "Don't try to be brave."

"Please, please don't do this." Cathy's foot touched the control pedal. Now if she could only — there it was. Her right hand found what she sought. She grasped it like a pencil — no, like a scalpel. She'd have one chance.

"I think I'm about to faint." She swayed slightly.

"Oh, don't pass out. I wanted you to see this coming. I guess I'll have to put a bullet in you first." Sherri shuffled forward until she stood face to face with Cathy.

"Don't," Will said.

Sherri brought the gun up, but before she could level it, Cathy jabbed the needle tip of the Hyfrecator into the woman's arm and stepped on the pedal. A loud buzz and the smell of burning flesh filled the air. Sherri screamed, dropped the gun, and grasped her right arm with her left hand.

"Why, you —"

Will scooped up the gun and jammed it into Sherri's ribs. "Watch your mouth. You're lucky she just went for your arm."

Cathy took a deep breath and let the Hyfrecator tip fall from her hand. "Look at it this way, Sherri. If you had any warts on that arm, they're gone now."

21

Cathy unbuckled her seatbelt and climbed slowly out of Will's pickup. "What time is it?"

Will checked his watch. "One A.M. Are you as tired as I am?"

"I thought we'd never get out of the police station."

"Be glad you're not Sherri Collins. She'll spend the night in a cell."

Will used his key to open the front door. Inside, Dora and Matthew Kennedy dozed side by side on the living room couch. As soon as the door closed, they awoke and rushed to envelop Cathy and Will in hugs.

"You children come into the kitchen. I'll fix some coffee," Dora said.

After everyone settled around the kitchen table, Pastor Kennedy said, "We gathered from your phone call that you were in some sort of mix-up with Sherri Collins. What happened?"

It took half an hour to explain the events of the evening. Finally, Cathy yawned broadly. "Sorry, but I'm totally wasted. I need some sleep."

"You get some rest, child," Dora said. Then she added, "Do you want to go to church with us in the morning? I mean, this morning?"

Cathy's first impulse was to beg off, but then she realized that church might be a great place to spend time after all that had happened to her. "Yes, please. See you in a few hours."

Cathy awakened to the tantalizing aroma of coffee and frying bacon. She looked out her window at a fiery red sunrise. The streets of Dainger were empty this early on Sunday, but soon they would be filled with families on their way to church. Families. And the Kennedys were her family now.

She missed her mom and dad — she guessed she always would — but there was comfort in what she'd learned. Her mother hadn't been schizophrenic. Her father had been a faithful and loving husband as well as a dedicated physician. For the first time in years, Cathy felt hope for her future. Her life wasn't back to normal yet — that would take a while — but it was moving in the right direction.

Downstairs in the Kennedy dining room, she sat by Will as Dora placed plates and bowls on the table. Matthew said, "Son, would you ask the blessing this morning?"

Will's hand touched hers. She grasped it and squeezed. She reached out with her other hand and took Dora's, completing the circle.

"Father, we're so thankful for all our blessings. We're thankful for this food, for this Lord's Day that you've given us, and especially for helping Cathy and me through our experience last night. As you have taught us, we pray for our enemies, that they might find you and turn away from evil. And we pray for guidance in our lives that we may always mirror you to those around us. In Jesus' name. Amen."

"So, why didn't you tell me about this crazy scheme of yours?" Will asked.

"Because you'd have wanted to be there, and I thought I could handle it myself," Cathy said. "After all, it was my problem."

"One that almost got you killed."

"I should have asked for help."

"I have to admit, though, it did get us to the bottom of the matter." Will wiped egg from the corner of his mouth. "Of course, what Sherri said to you before I came in won't help us defend that malpractice suit.

It's your word against hers. The police can only hold her for assault and possession of an unlicensed firearm."

"What if we had a recording of everything she said?" Cathy countered. "If one of the parties agrees to being recorded, isn't the conversation admissible in court?"

"Yes," Will said. "But how did you pull that off?"

Cathy tried not to look too smug. "On Friday, I went to Radio Shack and bought a miniature voice-activated recorder. It was in the pocket of my white coat the whole time, and I turned it on before I opened the door for her. It's upstairs in my purse."

Will lifted his coffee cup in a toast. "Here's to Cathy Sewell: amateur sleuth, exceptional doctor, and a beautiful woman."

Cathy watched Will maneuver his pickup into a slot in the church's parking lot. It was a larger vehicle than her compact car, but he handled it with grace. She had to admit, he looked good behind the wheel.

Will turned off the motor but made no move to exit the vehicle. "We've got a little time before church starts. Would you like to sit here and talk?"

"Sure. You know, I've been wondering, ever since that day you rescued me after my wreck, why do you drive a pickup?"

Will turned so that his right arm was over the top of the seat behind her. "I guess it's sort of my way of saying to the folks in town, 'I'm not better than you are just because I'm a lawyer.' A lot of people resent professionals like you and me. I make a good living, but I never flaunt it. I don't wear a suit unless I'm in court —"

"Or church."

Will laughed. "Or church. I live in a nice home, but it's not as ostentatious as some in town."

Cathy turned that over in her mind. "I guess there's a lot of jealous people out there. I mean, when you live in somebody's garage apartment or a spare room in the parsonage, when you drive a compact Chevrolet, and if you worry about meeting expenses every month, you don't figure that people are jealous of you just because you're a doctor."

"But you found out differently, didn't you?"

"Yes, I did. I found out that jealousy and envy can turn a whole town upside down." Cathy shook her head. "No matter what the reality was, Sherri's perception was that my father kept Jacob out of medical school. So she coveted everything my parents had, and then everything she thought I had. All that hate and envy destroyed my parents' lives and almost caused Milton Nix to lose his."

"Not to mention your career," Will said.

"That, too." Cathy looked down at the Bible in her lap. "What will happen to Sherri now?"

"The District Attorney has his choice of charges: attempted murder, arson, forgery, manslaughter, all the way down to malicious mischief. Unfortunately, what you recorded her saying won't help in a criminal proceeding, because she hadn't been read her Miranda rights. On the other hand, once the police start digging, I'll bet they can come up with more evidence."

"What about Jacob?" Cathy asked.

"I don't think there's any way he was involved in this."

Cathy thought about what lay ahead for Sherri and Jacob. "You know, I recognize that Jacob's constant venting of his anger and frustration at not getting into medical school may have triggered Sherri's actions, but I have a hard time not feeling sorry for him. Sherri has ruined their lives."

Will started to reach for the door handle, but Cathy stopped him with a hand on his arm. "I haven't asked you yet. Can you get the malpractice action dismissed?"

"I guarantee you that when I tell Sam Lawton how this scenario played out, he'll drop the suit like a hot potato. I think you can consider your need for a lawyer at an end."

"Oh, no!"

"What? Just because you don't need me professionally doesn't mean we can't see each other again."

Cathy dug into her purse for a piece of scratch paper. "No, no, that's not it." She pulled out a ballpoint pen and scribbled a note, which she tucked into the front of her Bible. "I just remembered. I've got to call Marcus Bell today. I sent him one of those letters I used to smoke out the culprit. He showed up last night thinking I'd lost my mind. He's probably calling a meeting of the credentials committee right now."

Will laughed. "If he gives you any trouble, let me handle it. I was kidding about not being your lawyer any more."

Cathy flinched when a black SUV pulled up beside Will's pickup. It took her a moment to realize that she had nothing to fear from such a vehicle anymore. Then the door opened and Ella Mae Mercer climbed out, conservatively dressed in a simple black dress accented by a single strand of pearls.

Cathy rolled down her window. "Ella Mae.

How are you?"

Ella Mae nodded to both Cathy and Will. "A bit shaky, but better. I have an appointment with Dr. Samuels next week."

"That should help," Cathy said.

"So will what I'm about to do."

"What's that?"

Ella Mae reached into her purse and pulled out a small Bible. "Pastor Kennedy and his wife came to see me in the hospital. They prayed with me, and we talked a lot about how I couldn't forgive myself for what I'd done when I stole that money from your father. They convinced me that before I could get rid of that guilt I needed to take advantage of God's forgiveness. I'm here to follow up on that." Ella Mae took a deep breath. "I hope I can sleep tonight without the burden I've been carrying all these years."

"I'll pray for you," Cathy said. The words came out so naturally that she might have been saying them every day for years. She had changed so much since moving to Dainger.

They watched Ella Mae walk through the doors of the church. "I'm glad she's been talking with Dad," Will said. "I hope she'll be able to turn things around and make some changes in her life."

"I'm due for some changes in my life too," Cathy said.

Will gave her a questioning look. "Such as?"

"I always thought that if I had just seen Mom and Dad that night — the night of my graduation — I could have helped them put things right between them. Now I know that I couldn't. It's not my fault they were pulled apart. And I guess it's not my fault — or God's — that they died that night." Cathy brushed a tear away from the corner of her eye. "And I've always felt stigmatized because of my mother's mental illness. I was so afraid I might develop schizophrenia too. I couldn't bear to think of burdening any man with the responsibility for taking care of me the way my father took care of my mother. But now I know the truth."

"And that changes everything," Will said.

"Yes." Cathy's smile trembled. "I need to change the way I look at life. Staying with your parents has shown me the kind of family I really want — not perfect, just loving and forgiving."

"That's the best kind."

"And I realize that I have another kind of family right here." She looked at the church building. "A family of faith. I haven't exactly been on great terms with God, and I'd like to remedy that today."

Will sat silent, and Cathy feared she'd said too much. She reached for the door handle, but Will stopped her with a hand on her shoulder. "Do you think you might be open to considering a family of your own now?"

The smile that spread across Cathy's face seemed to well up from deep within her heart. "I'd need to consult my lawyer before I respond. But I think the answer is yes."

DISCUSSION QUESTIONS

1. Dainger seems to be a typical small town. What is your impression of the "character" of such small towns? Do they present any unique challenges or opportunities for Christians trying to live out their faith? Have you had personal experiences of such a situation?

2. The first scene has significant symbolism: the black SUV, the accident that leaves Cathy helpless, her rescue by a "white knight." Is there a biblical parallel to the story told? What other symbolism did you note throughout the book? What about similarities of some people in Dainger to characters in the Bible?

3. Cathy Sewell is troubled on many fronts. Her initial reaction to her first reversal was to "run away home." Was this an appropriate reaction? She's also running away from God. When do you think this began? What started her reversal? What

factors altered her reaction to adversity?

4. Will Kennedy waited patiently for Cathy, even though she had hurt him. Why do you think he was so long-suffering? How do you think you would have responded? Would your attitude change after Cathy's response to their first encounter?

5. Cathy obviously feels guilt at the role she imagines she played in her parents' death. Are there factors that amplified that guilt? Which characters contributed most to her recovery from those feelings? Which might have worsened it? How would you have counseled her?

6. Can you find a positive attribute in Mr. Nix? Mr. Phillips? With which of Cathy's patients do you most identify? Why? How well does Cathy succeed in putting her personal feelings aside when rendering treatment? Why is this so?

7. What is your opinion of the way Pastor Matthew and Dora Kennedy try to reach Cathy? Is her response realistic? Have you ever dealt with someone who was estranged from God? How did you approach it? What worked and what didn't?

8. Can you reconcile Dr. Marcus Bell's treatment of Cathy in his role of hospital chief of staff and as an eligible male toward a single female? Were there clues

in his behavior that suggested where his loyalty lay? Is sexism the only reason Cathy was initially denied the privileges she requested?

9. What words would you use to describe your initial impression of Ella Mae Mercer? Did that impression change as the story unfolded? What factors were responsible for the way she behaved? With her checkered past, do her actions in the last chapter of the book redeem her? If not, what would be necessary to do so?

10. What do you think were the best and worst characteristics of Jane (Cathy's nurse), Dr. Josh Samuels, Dr. Ernest Gladstone, Glenna Dunn (ER nurse), Emma Gladstone, and Dr. Arthur Harshman? Do you share any of these characteristics with them? How would you change to correct any of the bad ones?

11. A number of people in Dainger seemed to have a reason to hurt Cathy. In which of these cases did the fault lie with Cathy? Did the fault lie with the people in some instances? Putting yourself in the same situation, what steps might you have taken to defuse the situation?

12. As the novel starts, Cathy is a frightened, unsure, lonely woman. By the end, she is confident, secure, and ready to accept the

love being offered to her. What steps brought about this change? What do you think was the most important factor or person in this transformation? Did you learn anything from Cathy's journey? Will it make a difference in your life?

ABOUT THE AUTHOR

Richard L. Mabry, M.D., is a retired physician and medical school professor who achieved worldwide recognition as a writer, speaker, and teacher before turning his talents to nonmedical writing after his retirement. He is the author of one nonfiction book, and his inspirational pieces have appeared in numerous periodicals. He and his wife, Kay, live in North Texas. Visit his website: www.rmabry.com.